MUSE

MUSE

BRITTANY CAVALLARO

KATHERINE TEGEN BOOKS
An Imprint of HarperCollins *Publishers*

Katherine Tegen Books is an imprint of HarperCollins Publishers.

Muse
Copyright © 2021 by Brittany Cavallaro
All rights reserved. Printed in the United States of America.
No part of this book may be used or reproduced in any manner whatsoever without
written permission except in the case of brief quotations embodied in critical articles
and reviews. For information address HarperCollins Children's Books, a division of
HarperCollins Publishers, 195 Broadway, New York, NY 10007.
www.epicreads.com

Library of Congress Control Number: 2020948242
ISBN 978-0-06-284025-7

Typography by David Curtis
Map by Daniel Hasenbos
20 21 22 23 24   PC/LSCH   10 9 8 7 6 5 4 3 2 1

First Edition

For Emily Henry and Chloe Benjamin, for believing

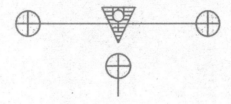

In the dusk of the evening as I stroked Macak's back, I
saw a miracle which made me speechless with amazement.
Macak's back was a sheet of light, and my hand produced
a shower of crackling sparks loud enough to be heard all
over the house. . . . My mother seemed charmed. "Stop
playing with the cat," she said. "He might start a fire."
But I was thinking abstractly. Is Nature a gigantic cat?
If so, who strokes its back? . . . I cannot exaggerate the
effect of this marvelous night on my childish imagination.
Day after day I have asked myself, what is electricity . . . ?

—Nikola Tesla

. . . you who have existed
to resist me as I made you up.

—Stephen Dunn, "Loves"

PREAMBLE
MAY 1782

He had heard the rumors for weeks before the letter reached Mount Vernon, but when it finally arrived, he found himself unprepared to answer.

The envelope sat on his desk where he'd left it, leaning against a tallow candle. It was before dawn, perhaps four or five in the morning, and he'd passed an uneasy night considering the implications. He was so seldom home in Virginia, and at first he allowed himself to think that was the reason for his restlessness. At the presidential mansion in Philadelphia, he was often woken up by little sputterings of noise: a carriage rattling down the brick road, a tomcat howling at the night sky. At Mount Vernon, all was quiet, like a heavy blanket over the mouth.

And now he was awake.

He made his customary rounds, lighting the fire, quickly bathing, buttoning his shirt as daylight stole in. The letter slept on his desk.

Before he turned to face it, he took a breath, and considered the fields outside his window. He had left this place when the country had been founded; he had hired workers to tend his fields while he went north to tend to his country instead. But he was here now, overseeing the last of spring planting—well, looking in on the planting, at least. Virginia didn't need him anymore.

He didn't miss it, Virginia, not in the way he thought he should. Instead it stole over him in strange moments: midnight, ink-stained, reworking a letter with Monroe's notes in mind, and suddenly he was fourteen again, copying out *The Rules of Civility and Decent Behavior*, his quill nib leaking all over his palms. Mount Vernon's spring breathing in through the window.

A cockerel crowed outside, and he knew he must open the envelope.

He had to do it now, before his household was awake. But first he let himself do the thing he'd been avoiding.

He let himself imagine what it might say.

One thing he knew for certain: the American army was afraid. They had just won a decisive battle against the British and the French, and they were justifiably proud, and now they were afraid, because soldiers who were paid only through the goodwill of individual states—and not through, say, taxes imposed by Congress—were soldiers who didn't rightly know where their next meal came from.

They were soldiers who didn't believe in their Congress. In any Congress at all.

And say that, rather than passing laws to pay the army, Congress refused. Say that, perhaps, those generals who were tired of waiting met one night under cover of darkness. That they each swore an oath to secrecy before beginning to speak. Together, they would write their president a letter. They would remind him how their country loved him, how a benevolent monarchy had ruled Britain well and for years. Why shouldn't America improve on their idea? Why, they could even imagine a country without something as inconvenient as a Parliament or, say, a Congress.

What was the purpose of elected officials? None that they could see. Only partisanship. Infighting. Disunity.

He was reading the letter now, he had it in his shaking hands, and though he wanted to throw it in the fire—this letter that asked him to destroy all he'd built—he told himself to stop first, and think. To consider, fully, the question.

He trusted his own judgment. He knew those who among his men would make good leaders. James Monroe, perhaps, and Thomas Jefferson. (Had Benjamin Franklin not been struck by lightning, he'd have been an excellent choice as well.) If they were not forced to cater to the whims of the public, if they did not need to seek reelection in Congress— why, they could certainly accomplish the work that was important to them. Give them each a territory, the way the British did with their colonial Governors. Let them rule it as he saw fit.

And his grandson, George, was only a year old, but he and Martha had the raising of the child, and he knew that he'd instill in him the values he'd grown up with. The ones he'd so painstakingly copied out when he himself was a boy.

Little George would make a good king someday, he was certain.

When you considered the idea—*considered* it, mind you, not yet acting on that consideration—it made a certain kind of sense.

Oh, it was absurd. He would answer the letter quickly and put on his workman's boots and ride Nelson out through the morning fog until he forgot this notion altogether.

George Washington set himself down at his desk. He took up a piece of good British paper and shrugged up his cuffs and dipped his quill.

Dear Sirs, he wrote, and then he stopped, his nib dribbling onto the page.

It was, he had to admit, a hell of an idea.

PROLOGUE

When George Washington is crowned sovereign of the First American Kingdom, he decrees that his country be separated into provinces, each led by a Governor selected from his most trusted lieutenants. As new territories are claimed for the Kingdom throughout the nineteenth century, King Washington—and his heirs, the King Washingtons that follow—draw new borders and appoint new white men to lead.

To the west, Alta California and Willamette; to the south, Nuevo México and the tiny duchies of West and East Florida. Livingston-Monroe, named for the men who purchase the territory from France, make up the country's heartland. St. Cloud stretches down the Mississippi River, while the seat of the King, New Columbia, extends along the eastern seaboard.

Once Washington is declared King, elections cease altogether.

In the years that follow, Governors pass on their territories to their sons, who become Governors in turn. Hungry men, these new Governors: eager for glory, eager for progress and for action.

These Governors are skeptical of what they call "foreigners."

These Governors are determined to keep power however they can.

All except for Remy Duchamp, the youngest Governor in the American Kingdom. He is interested in intellect, invention, innovation; he is less interested in maintaining the armed borders of his province, St. Cloud. Now, in 1893, he looks to put on a great Fair the likes of which the world has never seen.

But the great Fair is months late, and St. Cloud has grown restless. There are rumors of trouble on the western border. Rumors of war.

And in St. Cloud's largest city, Monticello-by-the-Lake, a girl holds the nation's future in her hands.

ONE
APRIL 1893

It was death to stop at the corner of Augustine and Dearborn in the city of Monticello-by-the-Lake at the end of a working day.

Claire Emerson knew that, standing beside her best friend, Beatrix, in the crowded road. Even now, as she stood on her toes to look up at the posters pasted onto the brick wall of the Campbells' building, she had her elbows drawn in to her sides. Not to clear a path for the horse-drawn carriages; not to make way for the electric trolley squealing up the street, its cables throwing off indifferent sparks; not as a courtesy for the people streaming past—the working girls off to the dressmakers', the men with their hats and coats and grim, sun-scrubbed faces, the newsboys waving their rags, the scientists smelling like ambition and smoke, the soldiers like last night's liquor. Not to make way even for the lumber cart rattling along down the road, its long, bristling logs threatening to break free and roll like the thunder of God himself straight down Augustine Street to the glistening lake beyond, flattening every last thing in their way. It had happened last week, killing two horses, three steelworkers, and a seven-year-old orphan. It would happen again whether or not Claire cleared a path.

She was folded up onto herself on this street corner because, while she wanted to see the new posters pasted to the Campbells' building brick, she didn't want anyone to steal the package in her arms. She didn't have a lot of control over her own life, but she *could* control whether tonight her father slapped her full across the face again.

"But then," she said to Beatrix beside her, "if he notices that I'm missing one of the socket wrenches he paid for, he might do it anyway."

"Hush. He won't notice, you know he won't even look through the bag until the morning. And besides, you know I'm good for it." Beatrix craned her neck, trying to get a better look at the poster. "I'm never going to get this engine working if I have to rely on my own coin for the materials. Let's consider it a donation."

Claire smiled, despite herself. "Is it a donation if you've forced me to do it?"

"I'm not forcing *you*. I'm forcing Jeremiah Emerson. And we hate him." She said it like it was fact.

Claire supposed it was. She shifted the knobby bundle to

her other arm. "I still can't see what it says. We can come back tonight, after the day's died down."

"Your father won't be home yet, you don't need to rush. And anyway, it'll be about the Fair."

"Of course it's about the Fair. It always is. It'll still be about the Fair when we come back. And besides, I'll be gone by week's end, does it really matter if—"

"Everyone will *know* already," Beatrix said, and as if the thought spurred her on, she propelled herself forward. Though she was tiny, her wild blond bouffant made her easy to follow. It had survived both her work at the stockyard and her long, hot walk home in a boater hat. Now her hair survived the crowd, sure and steady as a halo above her pale face.

She was back in moments, face grim, and she took Claire by the arm to pull her away—careful, as always, to make sure she didn't touch Claire's skin with her bare hand.

"What did it say?" Claire asked, but Beatrix was two steps ahead and affected not to hear. Down Augustine Street, past the orphans from the Home for the Friendless marching in their long gray lines, their lunch pails hanging from their grubby hands. The little girl who had died had been one of them, Claire knew. She dropped a coin into one of their buckets.

Through it all, Beatrix moved like a dancer, and Claire her poorly practiced partner. *You'd never think she was the one who was half blind,* Claire thought, but she supposed it made a certain kind of sense. One only had to look at the cloth-of-gold eye patch her best friend wore to know that Beatrix had to watch her steps. The watchfulness made her graceful, and that grace carried them through the congested streets.

Beatrix stopped at the foot of the stairs up to the El railway station, at the end of a very long line of men. She adjusted her skirts, and then, discreetly, her corset.

Claire gave her a sympathetic look. She was struggling, too, to catch her breath under her laces.

"It's going up tomorrow," she said. "The Fair. That's what the poster said. It's going on, as scheduled."

"You were expecting another delay," Claire said.

Beatrix hesitated. "I was hoping for one. For you. We've had so many, and so close to the scheduled start—I was just hoping that if you'd have some good news for him tonight—"

Claire hardly heard her. She wasn't sure why it was such a surprise, that the Fair would go on. But then, when it had been delayed for so long, who could blame her?

"I can tell your father for you," Beatrix was offering.

At that, she snorted. "That would make it worse, and you know it. Sunday just needs to come and go without him suspecting anything."

The two of them climbed the metal stairs, slowly, as the crowd boarded the train. It waited, sleepy as a cat, painted as always in the governor's midnight-blue livery.

"He wants to be paid for his work."

"I understand, but if he won't get paid until after his Barrage, you'd think he'd want it to happen sooner—"

Claire lowered her voice. "There's still a problem with the Barrage."

"I'm sorry?" Beatrix laughed, shook her head. "No. But you said—"

The unexpected April heat, the awkward weight of the package she carried, the long black curl plastered to her temple. The dread of seeing her father not twenty minutes from now. "He swears it will work," Claire said, fiercely enough that her best friend blanched. "And we'd all better hope it will, because if our creditors come by again, they will break his *hands*, Beatrix, and God only knows what Duchamp will say—" The woman behind them coughed delicately. "*Governor* Duchamp will say. Much less the General. We have a permanent pavilion waiting. It has our name on it. Our name—and if the Barrage isn't a success, if my father fails, and if Sunday comes and he's in one of his rages, I won't be able to—"

"All aboard!" The conductor's voice was a trumpet. "This is a Monticello train, calling at Lordview, Woodlawn, Delaware, and Almondale!"

The crowd surged forward, taking the two girls along with it, and as she clutched her package to her chest, Claire seethed. She had never seen anything like this in her seventeen years. So many *bodies*. People from all over the First

American Kingdom, there to gawk at the city Claire lived her life in, like it was an amusement or an oddity. They were there in that train car with her, people from her own province, Monticellans and St. Clouders and the backwoods farmers who tithed corn and soybeans to their Governor; Livmonians, those settlers from the province of Livingston-Monroe, weathered in their muslin shirts; wasp-waisted girls from New Columbia with their parasols, their clutching children; folk from every corner of their country and from Britain and Persia and Japan besides. All of them here for the Governor's Exhibition and Fair.

They had been here for a month now, clogging up Monticello's dusty roads, lunching by Monticello's glimmering lake, making Claire's life louder and harder and just all-around worse, and tomorrow the Fair they waited on would actually open. The axe would finally fall.

"All aboard!" the conductor shouted again, and Beatrix yanked her skirts away from the closing doors, and all at once the train fell silent as it rattled away from the station.

"I'm sorry I was cross," Claire said. She was horribly aware of the man next to her, of the two inches of skin between her gloves and the long sleeves of her dress. How close he was to touching her.

"I know," Beatrix replied. They had said it to each other before. They would say it again.

"Come by at eight tonight? One last hurrah."

"Eight," Beatrix murmured back. "Don't forget my tails."

* * *

The train had emptied out before pulling into the station at Lordview. The neighborhood had originally been called Lakeview, for its sweeping view of Lake Michigan, until one of Governor Duchamp's courtiers had been granted the bluff overlooking the bathing beach to build his own mansion. Now, instead of the lake, the neighborhood gazed upon the high walls that surrounded Lord Anderson's gardens. Some wag had started calling it Lordview, and that was that.

As Claire walked down her neighborhood's dusty streets, she brooded over the package in her arms.

The Fair.

The Fair, a grand show of American ingenuity, of wonders the public had never even dreamed of. A fair that St. Cloud had won the rights to host against every other province in the First American Kingdom. A fair that had stood half completed, its great Ferris wheel still just bones and timber when the Governor was laid to rest in the mausoleum overlooking the Jefferson River, when his young son took the reins.

It would be years late, and the bane of Claire's existence.

She mulled all this over as she walked the road back to her house, her lumpy package clutched to her chest. The sky was fading from its milky yellow to the milkier red of sunset, and all along Belmont Avenue, the streetlights were turning on. The suburb stretched out in all directions, a plan more than a place. So much of it was still just mud and churned-up dirt. It had been built to grow into. Here and there, a house stood like a tooth in an empty mouth.

If she walked more slowly than she usually did, if she let her mind wander, it was because she knew what waited for her at home. Her father in their too-expensive house, sequestered in his study. Their young maid slaving over the wood-burning stove, trying to turn out a dinner that would make Jeremiah Emerson smile. Nothing made him smile, and the maid resented it, resented that she alone was left to deal with the household while Claire was sent off on special errands. Genius girl, she called her, because when Claire returned home, she was ushered into her father's study, and there she often stayed until dark.

The house came into view through the ever-present smog. It was pretty, she supposed, gabled and painted blue, though as she approached, she saw that the glass in their sitting-room window was cracked. She stopped for a moment to stare.

Who had done such a thing? A creditor, surely. Still, it had been expensive to buy a pane of glass so large, and it would be expensive too to replace it. She walked through the wooden door and right through the kitchen, where the maid, hair hidden under a kerchief, was frying up rashers of bacon.

"Have a good day?" Margarete asked. It wasn't a friendly question.

"No," Claire said, shortly, because she hadn't, and though the other girl would never believe her, she would have traded their places in an instant. It wouldn't be a problem if Jeremiah

Emerson didn't heap the work of three servants on his house-keeper's small shoulders. "Any callers?"

Margarete correctly heard "callers" as "creditor thugs."

"Only the one," she said, her accent lingering at the edges of her words. "We hid. He went away. It wasn't so bad."

"After breaking the window to send a message."

"As you saw." Margarete turned back to the stove. For a girl fourteen years old, she had a surprising gravity to her manner. "He's in his study, talking to someone from the Governor. Waiting for his genius girl, I'm sure."

"Of course," Claire said, staring up at the staircase, and then heard what she'd just said. "Margarete, you know that I'm not—you know that it's a punishment, don't you?"

"A punishment?" Slowly she held up her ash-blackened hands, her skin white beneath. "Let's talk about punishments, then, the next time I'm to do the laundry. Maybe you can haul the water or work the press."

Few maids would have spoken that way to their employer's daughter. But few maids were girls adopted as a sister and then treated as a servant.

Claire set her jaw. It was fair for Margarete to say it, but that didn't mean it didn't hurt. "I'll be in his study."

"Tell him I'll have supper in thirty minutes!" Margarete called as Claire climbed the stairs.

Though their house was lavish looking from the outside, on the inside it was spare. The walls were unpainted, the floors unpolished. The Emerson house was one meant to be tended by an army of servants and decorated with an expert's touch, but there wasn't any gilt on the trim or paintings on the walls. It looked like what it was. A house purchased with the promise of wealth, left bare when that wealth never arrived.

Jeremiah Emerson wouldn't be paid again for his Barrage until it exploded its terrifying fireworks across the Monticello sky.

Claire lingered in the empty hallway, outside her father's study door. He would have spent his day down at Jefferson Park, in the pavilion that had been built to house his inventions. When Governor Duchamp had first ordered the pavilions built, they had been little more than wood painted to look like marble. Then the Fair was delayed again, and again, and eventually it was clear that the pavilions needed to be reinforced if they were to survive the harsh Monticellan winters. They became, in fact, the things they had been only meant to reference. Buildings of gleaming white marble, speckled and veined like something out of ancient Rome.

Jeremiah Emerson would have arrived with the dawn at the building that wore his name. He would have spent the day inside with his workmen, tearing down and rebuilding his mighty gun, the gun that only fired for its inventor on those days that his daughter had blessed him.

And on the days it failed, Emerson would come home and take those failures out on his daughter.

At least today she had a moment to compose herself out here on the landing. The housekeeper hadn't said who was in with her father, but she knew who it was.

The General. He had a name, but no one ever used it. Why would they need to?

"—we can't countenance another delay. We need a show, and an impressive one. That boy may very well think that this Fair is about our kingdom's ingenuity. I suppose leaders need to have ideals." His tone was acid when he spoke of his young Governor. "What I need is an assurance that our borders aren't invaded while we're congratulating ourselves on our smarts. The Livmonians need to be afraid of us. Properly afraid."

"Then give me another day to get it right," her father said. "Let the Barrage go on the second day, or the third. Or next month! If the Fair's to run until fall, we can build anticipation—"

The General snorted. "You've had enough time. There were German firms that were offered your contract, as you well know. But all I heard from that boy was of your gargantuan gun. Well, your gargantuan gun still doesn't damn well work. And you know the real reason for this show. Our neighbors to the west need to see some real *might*. They want to get a taste of us, take our lands? We'd blow them to smithereens. So much for that." A thud, like he'd swung his boots down to the ground. Had he been sitting on her father's desk? Claire felt a wash of annoyance and admiration.

"So much for *my* genius, you mean." Her father's voice was sour.

"As you said. I'll expect you in the morning." Claire scuttled back from the doorway as she heard him approach. "Tell your pretty daughter hello for me."

A shot, expertly aimed. "Of course," Jeremiah Emerson said, and Claire was almost proud at how he hid his despair.

She waited with her hands clasped at the top of the stairs for the General to leave. What she saw first was what she always did, what she was meant to see. His uniform. The fitted jacket, midnight blue, and the softer blue of the pants below, the half cape with its ermine trim, and everywhere, gold scrollwork, like an endless poem made of thread. That thought would be lost on the General, a man whose neat dark mustache looked like it was trimmed against a ruler.

"Miss Emerson," he said, reaching out to take her hand in a way he surely thought was charming. He was a handsome man, but it was an afterthought. His uniform was fit to swallow any beauty he had.

"A pleasure." Claire kept her hands where they were, and after a moment, he dropped his.

"Your father"—he said this conspiratorially, as though Jeremiah Emerson weren't still five feet away—"will be the death of us, you know."

"I thought that was why you hired him." When he raised

his eyebrows, Claire said, "Death."

"Yes." The General smiled. "Of course. He'll do it well, when all's said and done. And tell me—"

"If you'll excuse me," she said. "I've been holding this bag of wrenches for three hours now." With her foot, she shut the door behind her.

Claire knew she should be more careful with him. The General could fabricate some offense, have her thrown in jail. He could withdraw her father's contract. He could finally make the marriage proposal he'd been threatening for months; he could make it, take her to bed, then withdraw the offer immediately. He could wreck her life in any of a dozen ways for mouthing off to him, but Claire was Claire, and she'd never met a bad decision she didn't like.

Sunday, she thought. *Sunday. All I need is to make it till this Sunday.*

"Your wrenches," she said, dumping the bag on her father's desk.

Jeremiah Emerson scowled. He was a beefy man, with thick, corded arms and a thatch of dark hair. He strutted around in shirtsleeves, looped his fingers through his suspenders, left his jacket crumpled in a ball on the floor. Claire often thought that he had cultivated his idiosyncrasies in the same way as his inventions—deliberately, with great care.

"You're late," he said.

"What did the General want?"

"Don't pretend you didn't hear."

Claire kept the desk between them. It was safest that way. "What do you need me to do?"

He studied her. "Open the bag," he said. "No. With bare hands. Come on, girl, you know better than that."

She drew her head up high. Gently, she pulled off one glove, then the other, and laid them before her.

"On with it."

Claire untied the grosgrain ribbon and tugged open the mouth of the bag. The wrenches inside gleamed dully. The study wasn't bright enough to allow for intellectual pursuits or professional exploits; the electric lamps that were everywhere else in the city were missing here. This room was still lit by gaslight, another money-saving measure. Any real work Jeremiah Emerson did was at his pavilion in Jefferson Park.

This room was for conversations with the Governor, and the Governor's staff. It was for organizing his notes for the next day.

For tormenting his daughter.

"The wrenches."

Claire wanted to take up the lot of them and pitch them into her father's face. Black his eyes. Knock out his teeth. Rattle the brain that wasn't smart enough to get them out of the mess he had created, that relied on this insane superstition instead. She'd gone far enough to lift a pair of torque wrenches when her father clucked his tongue.

"One at a time," he said, his eyes bright with anticipation.

He didn't have to give her instructions. She knew what she was expected to do. In one open palm, she cradled the tool. With the other, she drew her fingers together over it, like a priest would sprinkle water on a child.

"I bless this tool," her father said.

"I bless this tool," Claire said, low.

His chin went up sharply. "Did you mean it?"

"I meant it."

His hands seized, and in a galvanic motion, he lunged forward to pull it from her hands.

"You have to mean it, girl," he breathed, the wrench bright in his fingers. "You have to mean it, or else I'll be in the same place I was this morning. Do you know how they looked at me when I walked in? All those porters, those immigrant whoresons I found down in the stockyard—I gave them better *lives*, I offered them clean work, to lift and carry and mind my work, and after my failures, those same men had the audacity to look at their employer and pity him today! I will not have that! I will not be *threatened* by foreigners who were not born to this great American Kingdom, these—these Germans who want my contract, and *moreover*, I will not have sedition in my own house! You know that you are blessed—"

Claire took a shuddering step back, hands clutching her skirts.

"—you know that you are blessed and that it is required

of you to share those blessings with me. I am your *father*. You have been standing each night in this house I have raised over your head and you think that you can fool me? That you can withhold what is mine by right because of your feminine whims and caprices? No." He was whispering still, harsh and forced, his hands convulsing around the wrench. "No. I say no to that. I say you will not bring down this dishonor upon my home."

Some small, screaming part of Claire thought, *He'll beat me with that wrench.* She thought, *He should have been a preacher.* She thought, *No one will ever believe just how powerless I really am.*

"I bless this tool," he growled.

Claire swallowed. "I bless this tool," she said, and the words were crackling and strange in her mouth.

With a clang, he dropped the wrench onto the pile. He held his hands out, like she was a child again and needed help climbing up to her feet after a fall.

She placed her hands in her father's. By now, she knew what he wanted.

"I bless this man," he said, and waited.

Claire looked into his horrible, eager eyes. "I bless this man," she said, and what she thought was, *I hope you die in your sleep*, and though every night she wished it, every morning she woke to him still there, still breathing.

"Bless my work in this exhibition. Bless it, and *mean it*,

goddammit, or it's your head on the platter too."

"I bless his work," she whispered.

If that was the case, if she had so little control, how much power could a girl like her possibly have?

Jeremiah Emerson waited, head cocked, as though some angel was going to whisper in his ear. "Let me get my clothes for the exposition," he said finally. "You'll bless those. You'll bless my notes. It shouldn't take more than a few hours. You won't need to know a thing about them, of course. I wouldn't expect you to." He sighed. "I only wish that I could take you to the pavilion tonight. But I can't risk it. Not until tomorrow. A man shouldn't show his weakness that way."

"In what way?" she asked into the waiting silence.

"No one should take his heart out with him in public. No one," he said, and swept off to his bedroom, leaving Claire to stare disbelievingly after him.

TWO

Jeremiah Emerson's madness, as his daughter understood it, had begun after her mother's death. More precisely, it had started in the weeks before.

Her brother was already training furiously for his escape; he intended to play baseball for the royal touring team. Her father had been working at a munitions firm, developing a project he called a "grenade," and when he came home at night to their little tenement apartment, his face and neck were dusted with the black powder that was the mark of his trade. The talk was all of explosives, of their potential in combat. He tinkered and tinkered, but he could make nothing explode.

Claire had been eight years old. Her father was her own private king. The last Governor Duchamp—Leonard, the current Governor's father—hadn't ever put too much stock in women, and though reformers put on men's trousers and stomped through the streets howling for work and respect and autonomy, they were eventually rounded up and put into asylums, where they could get the help they needed. One had to appreciate one's place in society.

Everyone knew that women were the angels in the house. They inspired men to do good works out in the evil world; they made their homes a place of comfort for those men to return to.

Claire's father might have been her king, but her mother only paid lip service to his rule. Every morning, Susannah Emerson kissed her husband at the door, and when it shut she took Claire into the kitchen, pulled food from the larder, and began quizzing her on mathematics as she mixed up the dough for her buttermilk biscuits. While the two of them pressed the clothes they'd spent hours scouring, Susannah taught her daughter Milton and Donne. She sewed their clothes while teaching her geography and the history of the American Kingdom, and Claire threaded her mother's needles while she listened. Sometimes the little neighbor girl with the eyepatch would come by with apples or new-made cheese or a cloth of her own to sew, and Susannah would set her a place for her to listen, too.

But Beatrix wasn't there on the day that Claire remembered best. That day, while making a dress for her daughter—a gray poplin with billowing sleeves, the last of her mother's dresses Claire would ever wear—she asked what Claire thought of their young Governor.

Claire shrugged. "He's French. I don't like him much."

Susannah Emerson had pursed her lips as she laid a half-finished sleeve out on the table. "Do you know the story?" she began. This was how all her mother's history lessons began. A story. She smiled down at the length of poplin before her. "The Duchamps have been woven into the fabric of St. Cloud for nearly a hundred years."

The original Governor, Montague Duchamp, had been a Frenchman who had helped the young American Kingdom win the War of 1812. He'd been a spymaster; his agents embedded themselves into the British units up in frigid Canada, fed them lies about their American enemy. Fifteen cannons became twelve. Five hundred troops became fifty. The British underestimated their enemy's resources, and because of it, their American enemy won.

In thanks, King George Washington carved out a province for Duchamp. The long stretch of land that swaddled the Mississippi was given into his keeping; at that time, it was the farthest west the American Kingdom stretched.

Duchamp, in an attempt to maintain the peace, named his new province St. Cloud after the town in Île-de-France where he had lived as a boy. And if by chance his new subjects found their ruler unpatriotic, they would be appeased by his ruling seat—Monticello-by-the-Lake, a city perched on Lake Michigan, a city named for Thomas Jefferson's estate that he'd so admired on his visit to the country's capital to meet the King.

By all accounts Duchamp ruled his own province fairly and well.

His grandson Leonard hadn't. When the neighboring province Livingston-Monroe began to nibble away at their western border, establishing military outposts on the Mississippi's western banks, Leonard Duchamp shrugged at them. Let them have what they would; his focus turned ever back to Monticello.

This Duchamp patronized artists, built skyscrapers, paved the roads. Had his guard ignore the brothels and the dance halls if they looked respectable enough from the street. All the lines between "looks nice" and "is nice" began to blur. When the first European prince deigned to visit the city, he disdained a soiree at the Governor's Mansion for a night in the city's sordid Levee district, where, in a gilded pool hall, he played roulette with thieves and sipped his champagne from a courtesan's shoe. The city grew ever wilder, ever lusher, ever hungrier to rage out beyond its borders.

And when Leonard Duchamp died suddenly a year before his Great Exposition was to be staged, his young son, Remy, was thrust into his role and told to make the marvel happen.

"It's a complicated place, our city," her mother had said, holding her piecework up to the light. Claire had abandoned her work to listen, her chin resting on her hands. "But I don't think it's a bad place to live."

"Father thinks it's evil," Claire said.

"Not evil. Alive."

She shook her head. "Father doesn't want me to go out into it alone. Not without someone to keep watch over me."

At that, her mother paused, then set the unfinished sleeve onto the table. "Never be afraid of being alone, Claire. I've taught you well enough, and why? For you to be your own best company. You can mind yourself."

It was the closest her mother ever came, in words, to defying her father, and when the typhus swept through their tenement two weeks later like a wave and took her beautiful mother with it, down and out the front door in a pinewood box, Claire held on to that one moment of rebellion.

Her brother left only two months later. Though Ambrose had always been a fine athlete, he had been so anxious the morning of his tryout for the King's baseball team that he'd snuck out to vomit in a flower bed. Ambrose had always told her she could be whatever she wanted, a queen or a mathematician, and so she took both her brother's hands in hers and told him he was the best shortstop in the world. When he didn't seem to believe her, she took his baseball bat and blessed him, touching each of his shoulders the way a queen might, and he went off into the morning and came back with the news he'd made it through to the next round.

She didn't bless him then. It felt silly, childish, and anyway she didn't think he needed it, talented as he was. But Ambrose couldn't catch a thing the next day at tryouts. Couldn't hit the ball. The coach told him, bemused, that he'd give him one more shot. That final morning her big brother hauled her out, his "good-luck charm," to bless him again. He even went down on one knee like he was her knight, and rode off to his tryouts with Claire's handkerchief in his pocket.

Suffused with confidence, Ambrose made the team. Claire told her father the whole story at dinner, after Ambrose had waved goodbye to them from the window of the King's train, but Jeremiah Emerson only paid her half attention.

For the rest of her years, she would think back on that innocent story told over cold pigeon pie and wonder. Was that the moment where the train derailed?

Because her father's work grew wilder and stranger, and he grew stranger with it. After Susannah's death, after Ambrose's departure, Jeremiah left his young daughter in the house alone. Often after work he would stay out for hours, carousing in the Levee district he so disdained. When he returned home, stinking drunk, he'd wander into his daughter's room to cry. "I can't live in this sinful city," he'd sob, kneeling by her bed. "I can't live in this house. This is a land of death." And then he'd leave his daughter in the dark, to her ever-worsening dreams.

Jeremiah Emerson didn't touch his daughter, much less hug her goodnight. He couldn't even look at her straight, this girl with her mother's face. He arranged for the necessities, and let her grow.

He had a horror of their tenement home that he claimed was tainted by sickness. But he didn't air the place out or move his family. He didn't do anything; he didn't seem to mind if that sickness he so feared took his daughter.

He waited. For what, Claire didn't know.

In the meantime, she played by herself, dirty and unkempt, her own best company. She snuck out to eat meals with Beatrix's family, and though the Lovells had so little to share, they welcomed her to their table. When their tenements felt too small, Beatrix and Claire ran wild through the Monticello streets, and Jeremiah Emerson never knew the least of it. When he came home in the evenings, he seared his meat on the stove and cut her off bits with his knife, as though she were a dog. Most nights he left it at that, left the dishes to molder on the kitchen sideboard and his daughter to put herself to bed.

Claire prayed every night for her brother to come home to help, to fix things, but their mother's death didn't seem to affect Ambrose at all. At the very least, it didn't bring him back to Monticello-by-the-Lake. Instead he sent Claire letters and money, when all she wanted was for him to come and take her up in his arms and carry her away from this place.

Two years passed. Then her father brought a girl home. A German orphan from the Home of the Friendless, meant to cook for them and do their chores. She would treat Miss Claire like a lady, Jeremiah said, and in return she would have a place to sleep. Margarete scowled from underneath her new bonnet and said she would.

While the urchin rolled up her sleeves and got to cleaning their kitchen, Jeremiah Emerson took his daughter by the hand and sat her next to him by the fire. He expressed surprise at her height, as though she'd been doing all this growing in purposeful secret.

"Things are going to be different, girl," he said.

He was making progress on his work. He was developing a new kind of gun. Something that could make *big explosions*, ones he indicated with his hands, as though explaining to a dog the size of a promised bone.

Claire wanted to bristle at the implication. Her mother had taught her calculus, but she had taught her too to love her father. She settled on nodding, as though she were amazed.

A promotion would be coming soon. Did she understand what that was? And when Claire nodded again, so happy to see her father's joy, he looked down at their clasped hands and said, "Do you know? I feel like maybe we should all have ourselves a treat. Lemon ices!"

She nodded again, bewildered. There hadn't ever been money for treats, or so she'd thought.

"Lemon ices and—no. I'll send the girl out for ices. I have an idea for—an idea. I won't say what. Here," he said, and dug a handful of coins from his pocket to put on the table. "Go. I'll be in the other room."

Margarete looked up from the kettle she was heating

over the stove. "That's enough coin to feed this family for a week," she said, bitterly, and Claire realized, despite her lessons, how little she knew about the world.

The promotion came the next day, as her father had promised. He would oversee the team building the gun he had spoken about; from now on, he would come home with his face clean. Again he sat with his daughter in front of the fire and took her hands. "Let me tell you about my day's work," he said, and the next day, "Let me tell you about my successes," and the next he told her of his triumphs, and then his quick rise to the top, the house that he had bought them in Lordview, the servants that they would have, his giant hands clutching her small ones until she thought that she had lost them entirely, that he would take her hands from her altogether.

He touched her, his only constant, and he claimed that her touch brought on miracles. As though that half-heard story she'd told him about blessing her brother had rooted in him somewhere, grown wild in the absence of the sun.

She had her mother's spirit, he said; it was in her, animating this magic, spurring his successes. She was blessed, and she would never leave him, and if someday he would grow to despise her for the very things he now worshipped, if she dreamed of him choking to death on his black powder in the night—well, it was no matter. A good daughter would never disobey her father.

THREE

Back in her room, Claire rang for Margarete.

It wasn't something she was in the habit of doing. She didn't like to treat the girl like a servant, and so when Margarete rapped on the door, Claire answered it with bills in her hand.

"Three dollars," Claire said, "if you go downstairs, count to one hundred, then loosen the screws on the pot rack."

It was an outrageous sum. Still, Margarete's eyes narrowed. "I can't do this again."

Two months ago, when they had last pulled this trick and the pots fell all at once in an explosion of sound, Emerson had thundered through the house, shaking with anger at the builders who had so poorly installed his kitchen. But he hadn't shouted at Margarete or brought in a man to reinforce the ceiling. He'd just screwed the rack back in and hung the pots back up. For Claire's father, that was remarkable restraint.

And for the time it'd bought her, she thought it a good bargain.

"Four dollars," Claire said, "and another dollar Saturday night. My final offer."

They looked at each other.

"Fine," Margarete said, and snatched the bills.

"Count to one hundred!" Claire hissed after her. She shut the door as quietly as she could, then rushed over to her massive four-poster bed, counting in her head.

One hundred: silence. One hundred twelve: noise. A riot of noise. And Claire *pushed*.

Her bed moved a full foot. The sound was excruciating, and still it was buried under the sound. Through the wall, Claire heard her father curse and shove back his chair. "Margarete!" he yelled.

Claire was already pulling up the loose floorboard under her bed. She had about ten minutes until her father asked why her door was closed.

Closed to him, he would say. He liked to have his daughter where he could see her at all times.

Under the floorboards was everything of value Claire owned. Two full suits of male clothes, with gloves and top hats to match, the name *Ambrose Emerson* embroidered inside the jackets. Twenty-two dollars in cash (well, seventeen, after she paid Margarete), a full year's savings. A photograph of her mother, an infant Claire on her lap, both of them staring hard at the camera. A train ticket, from Monticello-by-the-Lake to the city of Orleans in Livingston-Monroe; an immigrant identification card under the name Mary Wallace. A cardboard box. And a stack of letters tied with blue ribbon.

Claire reached down into her corset and slowly, carefully, pulled out a leather sheath. Inside was a hunting knife, which she added to her cache.

She'd purchased it on her father's credit that afternoon. Despite everything, some small part of her had flinched at the thought of adding to his financial misery—but she would be long gone by the time that bird came home to roost.

It had only been a minute. Her father was still storming around downstairs. Her hands moved, as though of their own accord, to the bundle. *I just need to remind myself it's real—*

Still kneeling on the floor, she shook out the most recent letter and read.

Dearest penguin,

I spent the morning straightening up what is to be your room. My teammates had a good laugh at my expense, doing women's work, but I aim to take every precaution. Housekeepers can be bribed, and Father knows the name of our hotel. When you arrive, I want everyone to believe you're Cousin Mary just over from Ireland. I have your papers for you, enclosed. Don't ask from where—it's best you don't know.

I want you to cease all protestation that you will be "mucking up my life." You won't be. I worry that you still believe I don't care about you. I promise that Father was burning your letters rather than mailing them; I never received a one. I would have come for you instantly had I known his madness had progressed.

Besides, I have no life to muck up. I practice all day with the team; I go to banquets on the weekend; I shake hands with children; I sleep. And since I don't have a mistress, I have plenty of room in my suite. Being the King's shortshop comes with some perks. We can even get you a cat, if you'd like, though of course you'll want to run that by your future husband. Both Rory and Thomas are eager to meet you. I told them both it would be your choice. Rory thinks he has the best of Thomas since he's Irish, like you. Little does he know. I hope you like a man with a brogue.

All joking aside, I want to remind you that time is of the essence. We see a fair amount of soldiers at our games, and at the hotel restaurant after, and all anyone can talk about is the tension between Livingston-Monroe and St. Cloud. St. Cloud is small, weak, ripe for the taking. Those border skirmishes we saw earlier this year? That was nothing.

I hear word of a coup, a bloody one. I hear rumors that the Governor himself is in danger.

I hear word that the Livmonians plan to invade.

Word has it that we'll be called up to play a game for Duchamp's Fair, but neither Rory or Thomas are first-string players. After you make your choice, I am certain your new husband can get a dispensation to stay in Orleans for a honeymoon so you won't have to return.

This is our only chance to get you out, penguin—while Father's distracted and before the border becomes too dangerous to cross. Don't lose heart now. I know you can do this.

I will meet you at the Orleans station with flowers in hand.

Burn this.

Your loving brother,
Ambrose

Hands shaking, Claire folded it up and returned it to the pile. She knew it wasn't safe to keep it, or any of her brother's letters, but she couldn't bear to destroy the only proof of her impending escape.

Otherwise, she might begin to believe she'd imagined it.

She had taken too long. Quickly she took out the two men's suits and stuffed them under the quilt on her bed, threw the top hats into her armoire, snatched up the shoebox and set it beside her. She was replacing the floorboard just as her father came up the stairs.

"Open this door, Claire!"

She opened the shoebox and let its contents fall to the floor, then shrieked.

"For crying out loud—" Her father burst into the room. "Another mouse?"

She nodded, hugging herself. "I heard it scrabbling and I pushed the bed to see and oh, it's too horrible—"

"It's dead. You scared it to death." Grunting, her father bent to pick the mouse up by the tail. Claire opened the little box, and he dropped it in.

"I'll dispose of this," he said. "Margarete is crying downstairs. The ceiling fell in."

Then it matches the broken window, Claire thought but did not say.

Her father shoved her bed back into place. It screeched, a horrible sound. "This house can go to the devil," he said, and left.

It was the last of her fake mice. It had better be worth it.

Sunday, she thought fiercely. *In two days, I will have a new life.*

At two minutes past eight that night, Beatrix was waiting at her gate in shirtsleeves, a top hat, and a pair of men's trousers.

"Tails," she said, turning on her heel and spreading her arms like an acrobat.

Claire rolled her eyes as she lifted her brother's old frock coat onto Beatrix's shoulders, careful not to graze the exposed skin at Beatrix's neck. "Your Majesty," she said, but she was smiling.

Beatrix knew of Jeremiah Emerson's particular madness, his theories about his daughter's powers. She agreed with Claire that they were rot. She agreed with Claire too that it was best not to test the matter by touching each other too freely. ("What if he's right, and then you're responsible for my smashing success, and I need to cut you a share of my aeronautical discoveries?" Claire had laughed and replied, "I've snuck you enough supplies, you should give me a share anyway.")

"Hush." Beatrix turned with an unnecessary flourish. "You look swell, as always. I think I've pinpointed it. It's the nose. The straight nose and how it looks under the hat. Very dashing."

Claire laughed. It was an unusual point of pride for them, that Beatrix was the prettier girl but Claire the better-looking man. When the two of them ventured out at night, it was always in male disguise. Claire's father's position at the Fair meant that he knew people in every corner of the city, and he sent his daughter on errands often enough that her face was known to them, too. If Claire's midnight excursions were reported back to him, he'd lock her up for a month.

Beatrix had been the one to suggest the suits. With her eyepatch and her particular world-eating stride, they didn't do much to disguise her, but Claire thought she rather liked the feeling of control that settled over her when they walked about as boys. No dropping your eyes demurely. No blushing behind a hand. None of that punishing awareness of everyone else and what they wanted from you. You could pretend, for a moment, that the world was interested in what *you* wanted.

"He's sleeping, then," Beatrix said, meaning Jeremiah Emerson.

"He's tinkering. He'll tinker till dawn."

"And then wake up to find his daughter missing."

"I aim to be back by then," Claire said, "unless your plans for tonight end in my death by my father's very moral hands."

"No last meal, then?" Beatrix's face, for once, was serious. "You know if it doesn't go as planned, he'll find a way to blame you."

Claire was pointedly not thinking about tomorrow, about the Barrage, about Sunday, about her father's hands on her wrists. She couldn't. If she wanted to keep her heart in her throat, she would install it there herself.

"This is the last time," she said. "I wanted to go out one last time with you. Whether or not he kills me tomorrow, whether I manage to leave on Sunday—"

Beatrix shifted. "I want you to be safe," she confessed. "I don't want you to go. Why can't I have both?"

"I know," Claire said.

They clasped hands for a long minute.

"Well. How many offers d'you think you'll get tonight?" Claire asked, blinking against her tears.

Beatrix knew a change of subject when she heard one. "At least three." She tossed her cane and caught it, then slipped her free hand into the crook of Claire's elbow. "Offers aren't the point of tonight, though. *Revolution* is."

They took off down the road, a pair of jaunty gentleman with the world at their feet.

"I maintain that 'revolution' is a strange word for what you all are doing," Claire said. This was a well-worn topic for the two of them, and Beatrix tended to take Claire's criticism the way she took everything else—with a salty smile and a shake of her head.

Not tonight. Beatrix's shoulders stiffened under her jacket. "*I* maintain," she said slowly, "that you would better understand our project if you deigned to attend any of our meetings instead of guzzling champagne at the bar."

"I support you in all your endeavors," Claire said. She hadn't meant to upset her friend. "But my support isn't the same as my participation. You know that. And besides, what does it matter? I'm leaving."

Beatrix tipped her head to the side. Her cloth-of-gold eyepatch glinted, caught the light. It had been a gift from a fellow she'd met a few months back, a speculator who'd replaced her black eyepatch with an accessory as golden as her hair. "You don't fit in this world any better than I do,

Claire Emerson, and making pure little wishes with your pure little heart won't do anything to change that. Sometimes compromise is necessary. No matter *where* in the American Kingdom you live."

At that, Claire whistled. "A shot across the bow."

"That was rather too harsh," Beatrix reflected.

"Were you practicing for the next man you need to cut down to size?"

"Only if I'm using your sword." Beatrix's fingers tightened on Claire's arm. Skin on cloth. This was allowed. "Fine, then. Don't come to our meeting. Go find yourself a forward-thinking man in Perpetua's mews instead. It's a fine night for a short romance, don't you think?"

They took the train back from Lordview to the Loop, and a hansom cab from there to the Levee. As their carriage clattered down Dearborn Street, Beatrix rolled up the curtain so the two of them could see out. This close to the stockyards, you could still smell the butchered meat, and though Claire knew it would mark her as an outsider to the neighborhood, she covered her nose anyway. Two girls in violet gowns, arms trailing with ribbons, ran past down the gravel road into Freddy's Fast Feet on the corner, and as the girl in front wrenched the door open, the sound from Freddy's flea-bitten orchestra came spilling out into the street like blood.

One of the girls screamed. Claire shuddered.

"She's only meeting her beau," Beatrix said. She hadn't

covered her nose the way Claire had. "Not being murdered."

"She's screaming as though she's being murdered."

Beatrix shrugged, and Claire could tell her nonchalance was as affected as her two-tone brogues. "Maybe that comes later." It was the Levee, after all.

Their hansom shuddered to a halt in front of the Perpetua Club.

The doorman looked at Claire and Beatrix, dapper in their tuxedos, and gave them a small smile. Claire pressed two dimes into his palm: their admission fee. With one white-gloved hand, he pushed the door open. The music that thundered out was a storm of brass. A trumpet keening.

"Ladies," he said, because at the Perpetua Club, everyone knew about the long hair hidden under their toppers.

Claire was shaking hers out, but Beatrix, as usual, had kept hers on. It depended on her mood, whether she took off her disguise. "It depends whether I want to be in control or not, really," she'd said.

"You're always in control," Claire had countered.

"Well, yes," Beatrix had said, surprised, "but it depends if I want that known or not."

The butler took Claire's hat; he winked at Beatrix, and only took her cane. It was hard to see him in the dim light, to hear his hellos over the crash and echo of the orchestra. Already more men were piling in behind him, more girls in fluorescent gowns. Some were far more expensive than their garish colors would have suggested. On the daytime streets of Monticello-by-the-Lake, social class was easy to suss out, but the girls behind Claire could be either dignitaries or washerwomen.

The one thing they weren't were prostitutes. Once, the Perpetua Club had been called something else, had served a visiting prince his wine out of a courtesan's shoe, but the club didn't run girls anymore. Not since Perpetua (no last name, thank you very much) had taken charge. As usual, she was pouring drinks, her white hair beautifully, architecturally piled up onto her head. In its tilt and scope, it echoed the tower of champagne flutes she had built before her on the bar.

"Beatrix," she said, holding a smoking bottle of bubbly like a gun she'd just fired. "Here for a meeting?"

"The Daughters of the American Crown don't convene for another half hour," Beatrix said, flopping down onto a stool. "I do hope the sandwiches we ordered will be appropriately quaint and delicious."

Perpetua raised an eyebrow. She knew the true nature of the DAC; they met in her club, after all. "Well, then. How goes the flying machine business?"

"Wretched." Beatrix tucked her delicate hands up under her chin. "Make a girl feel better and pour that champagne, will you?"

"This isn't for you, dear, it's for the Guard and their guests." Perpetua nodded her head toward the tables at the edge of the dance floor. Claire could see the sea of the St. Cloud men's midnight-blue uniforms and—shockingly—the red of the Livmonian soldiers among them. The men were laughing and elbowing one another like they'd never been at odds. Like their provinces were allies, not in an uneasy stalemate.

A coup, Ambrose had written. Something was coming.

"Strange bedfellows," Claire said quietly, under the din.

Perpetua must have been reading her lips. It was a skill that served her well, running the city's loudest—and most notorious—dance hall. "You've got sharp eyes, girl," she said. "But a common cause can build bridges."

"What's tonight's cause, then?"

"Besides promoting the well-being of our beloved monarchy? Booze," Beatrix said, and Perpetua threw her head back and laughed.

"Let's not talk about the Fair or the crown. Let's talk flying machines," Claire said, settling in next to Beatrix. "Let's talk about my genius friend. How *did* the rest of your day go?"

"Wretched," Beatrix said again. As always, her friend was distracted, peering out toward the dance floor like she was looking for someone particular in that garish sweep and sway. It made it hard to hear her. "I adjust the angle of one wing, the glider banks. I adjust the other? The glider banks. I want the glider to bank? It crashes. In full view of the men at the stockyard. Sometimes, I swear to you, they see me as their entertainment. I'm not looking to be a one-woman carnival."

Claire was sure that *was* what the stockyard men had thought when they'd first clamped eyes on Beatrix: a bit of fun, some sad little girl with one eye and a hammer she surely didn't know how to use. Even with the protection of her brother's presence, she was a laughingstock. Claire loathed being underestimated. It made her push the world further and further away. But Beatrix took double the punishment her best friend did, and it made her draw danger, make it dance.

The fourth time her warehouse was robbed, Beatrix had turned up on Claire's doorstep drunk. "I hate them so much," she'd said, "that I want to celebrate it."

"Who are you looking for? You're going to crane your neck right off," Claire said, watching Beatrix scout the dance floor. "If it isn't already broken from the last time you took your glider out to play."

"Say that, and I won't invite you out the next time I do."

Claire knew that Beatrix was joking, but it twisted her heart anyway. Saturdays on the beach with Beatrix—the wind, the postcard light, her best friend in her ridiculous goggles—were the only times Claire knew that she was happy. She even loved the magnificent blunder of her crashes, so long as Beatrix didn't almost drown, or break her leg, or fracture her collarbone.

Again.

"You're looking for Bertie and Olivetta, aren't you," Claire said. She'd seen that bird-dog look on Beatrix before. "Are they even here?"

Frowning, Beatrix accepted a glass flute from Perpetua, who always capitulated when it came to the champagne. "This business with the Fair has attracted a lot of flies."

"Flies?" Claire coughed. "The Wright sisters are flies now?"

"Flies. Thieving mayflies." And Beatrix threw back the champagne as though she were a sailor and it were very good rum. "Excuse me."

Claire watched her friend weave through the crowd in her ill-fitting suit. The electric lights found her gold eyepatch, lit it like a star. Her meeting was due to start in ten minutes, but in the meantime, Beatrix appeared to have another agenda.

"I think she might be off to start a fight," Perpetua observed.

"More likely than not."

"You won't go stop her?"

"Of course not." Claire stood, champagne flute in hand. It was their last night together, after all. "I'm off to join her."

The orchestra had struck up a tremulous waltz. Claire sidestepped a box-stepping soldier, then another, her drink cradled to her chest. The room was hot, the lights low, the music loud. She craned her neck to see Beatrix slip off the dance floor and past a table of dicing men to a doorway beyond. With a glance over her shoulder, Beatrix slipped inside.

"Whoa there, fancy man," a red-coated soldier said, grabbing Claire's arm. She could hardly hear him over the noise. "A lady dressed as a gent?"

If she were Beatrix, she'd have a snappy rejoinder. She wasn't. Claire settled for shaking off his hand. "Excuse me," she said, but the man cursed and followed her.

"It ain't right," he bellowed, reaching for her again. "You ladies shouldn't be in a den of sin in the first place, much less masquerading as your betters."

Claire sped up—past the dice table, the men screaming for sevens; past the waiter with his tray full of empty glasses; into the small hallway that led, she knew, to Beatrix's meeting, and safety.

"Slow *down*," the man huffed, like a child.

Past the tall leafy plants, the statuary and the elegant vases, the portraits of Perpetua all in a line (Perpetua as the English Queen; Perpetua as Demeter, bow hunting in a glade), Claire could see the shapes of women slipping into a doorway, her friend with her hand on the knob.

"You're coming?" Beatrix called. "I didn't think you were coming!"

"One moment," Claire said, and turned neatly on her heel. The soldier behind her had slowed, blinking. He was, she noticed, very drunk.

"This is not a place for you," she said, enunciating in the quiet of the hall. "Do you understand?"

"The powder room?" He looked down again at her trousers. "But you aren't in skirts—"

"Every other place," Claire said, pulling off a glove with her teeth, "in this god-awful world might be for you, and you alone. But this one isn't." She drained her champagne, then thrust the flute into his hands, making sure to brush her fingers against his. "Get me another, will you?"

But no matter how she wanted it to be true, Claire didn't grant her own wishes.

Claire perhaps didn't grant any wishes at all.

The man fetched her no champagne. He stood and stared, and Claire stared back, right into his eyes, and who knows what would have happened if Beatrix had not returned to drag her through the doors of the Daughters of the American Crown headquarters.

FOUR

It was, in fact, a powder room. The man had been right about that.

Perpetua's boasted quite a nice one: tufted, overstuffed divans, sinks with golden swan-necked spouts. Mirrors everywhere for her clients to admire themselves in. The toilets were in the room beyond, an afterthought. This was first and foremost a lush little sanctuary, funded in no small part by the Daughters of the American Crown.

Claire didn't know how many members there were altogether, but the opening of the Fair at long last had brought in Daughters from all over the country. A good twenty of them were here already. Draped over chaise lounges, adjusting a stocking by the cosmetics table, checking their faces in the mirror. They were all in skirts, all immaculately turned out. All of them but Claire and Beatrix.

"What on earth were you doing out there?" Beatrix asked

as they perched on a pair of gilt chairs.

"Testing a theory." She would have said more, but a thin, angular woman in a green-striped dress leaned over her as though she were a piece of furniture.

Claire knew her face. She braced herself for impact.

"Beatrix," the woman said, pleasantly. "You look absurd. What ridiculous point are you trying to make, wearing trousers like that?"

"Hello, you old weasel," Beatrix said. "Still flying your glider in a hoop skirt? Tell me . . . what *does* that do to your aerodynamics? Have you ever caught a stray gust and gone airborne yourself? Become a rather unbecoming balloon?"

"Please," Olivetta Wright said. "I'm the brains. *Bertie* does the flying."

"Ah." Beatrix smiled. "I wouldn't dare fly one of your gliders either."

"You mannerless child!"

Claire rolled her eyes. This was clearly the most fun either of them had had in ages. They kept on bickering merrily as the final members trickled through the door.

"I should go," Claire said in Beatrix's ear, and stood. "I imagine that lurker is gone by now, and if he isn't, I'll just leave through the window."

Beatrix tugged her back down. "Sit. Learn something. What are you going to do out there, anyway? Brood into a glass of bubbles at the bar?"

Claire had, in fact, planned on doing exactly that.

"Stay," Beatrix said, then grinned wickedly. "If you hate it, you can always excuse yourself to the powder room."

"Beatrix."

A matronly woman had arranged herself in front of the only exit. Her hair was piled high, nearly as high as Perpetua's, but her face was solemn as the Bible.

Claire was trapped. She might as well listen.

"Ladies," she said. "It's so good to see you all here. A warm welcome to our sisters from our scion organizations in the east, west, and south who have traveled all this way. We give thanks for the Fair. We will rarely have this good a cover for a national meeting again."

The woman next to Claire chuckled to herself. "My husband thinks I came all the way from Carolina to ride the Ferris wheel," she murmured. "Like I would set foot on that thousand-foot death trap."

"As some of you know, my name is Rosa Morgenstern." The woman at the front clasped her hands before her. "I have the honor of leading this chapter of the Daughters of the American Crown. Let's begin with news from our scion organizations. Ladies, if you'll join me?"

They stood.

Claire had never seen people from every corner of their kingdom before, not all in one place. The rain-lush valleys of Willamette. Alta California and its cliffs, its palm trees, its fruit hanging heavy on the branch. The mountains of Livingston-Monroe that gave way to plains that tumbled sweet and low and hot into the waters of the gulf. Nuevo México, its deserts, its horses; the tiny hostile duchies of West and East Florida, ruled by a pair of Washington cousins in perpetual war; and New Columbia, the grande dame of them all, the seat of their King. Claire had heard that its residents still spoke an English that had the pricked-up consonants of their British forebears. St. Cloud was the last, the smallest save for the Floridas.

It was the only province of all of them that Claire had ever seen.

These eight provinces made up the Great American Kingdom, a land that was wider, tip to tip, than the great continent of Europe. King Washington oversaw it all from his jewel-box estate in Mount Vernon, the estate where his rule had been breathed into being, and their country was a glorious beacon of hope. This is what Claire had been taught, what she had read. But the women she listened to now told a different story.

The representative from Willamette told of their Governor, who took advantage of his duchy's isolation to take what he wanted from his women. "You'll go to the grocer, or take a walk with a friend, and one of his men will see you. They're always out 'shopping' for their man. If you're chosen, that night a knock will come at your door. The soldier will tell you to pack your things. For a trip, he says. A trip . . . when the Governor's finished with you—a few days later, maybe a week—he returns you, gives your husband some money for his trouble." Her eyes went cold, unfocused. Finally she said, "Mine spent it on drink."

In Alta California, there was news of a woman mayor, the first of her kind. "Don't cheer yet," the representative said; she had been appointed by their Governor for "special services to the Crown." Some said she was his former mistress, with a cache of exquisite blackmail. Others, that she had been a clerk in his offices and helped him skim off a pretty sum from his province's coppers. She was doing the same now to the town, levying taxes that left her citizens high and dry. Her detractors were legion, and all said the same thing: "This is what happens when you put a woman in charge."

The Floridas had erected a wall between them that needed papers and visas to be crossed. Nuevo México was in the midst of a succession war between its Governor's twin sons, making the governing of the province a faraway thought. New Columbia alone was flourishing under the hands of King Washington's many advisers. What of the King himself? "He spends all his time in France," the representative said, "at the gambling houses in Marseilles, and his advisers want to keep him there. The kingdom is far easier to rule without the King."

Finally a little red-haired woman stepped forward. She toed the carpet with an embroidered slipper. "I have little to say of Livingston-Monroe," she began, "as it is a blank slate. We have land, resources, few towns, few expectations. Few for women, fewer for men. In my town, as far as I can tell, men treat their wives with some respect."

Olivetta Wright raised her eyebrows. Beatrix hooted; she wasn't the only one.

Claire found herself looking around, her arms curling up and around herself. This is it? she wondered. This is the bar they have set? That wives are occasionally listened to as though they were people?

The red-haired woman continued. "Jobs can be hard to come by, due to . . . the porous border with St. Cloud. What we *do* have is a sizable standing army, built up these past years for the reason many of you have suspected. Our leaders line their borders with outposts, men, engines of war."

"St. Cloud is the reason why," someone muttered. "A plum ripe for the picking." And the muttering spread fast across the room.

Claire felt a flush of contradictory feeling: hope for her idyllic-sounding new home, fear for the home she was leaving.

"Thank you, representatives." Rosa Morgenstern climbed back to her feet, arranging her skirts. "Yes, the report from St. Cloud is much as you have heard. We have a French whelp for a Governor, locked away in his mansion, playing with his toys. He has spent untold time and money crafting this Fair, meant to be a unifying spectacle of science, and industry, and might. And still, on the eve of its opening, its buildings are half finished, its grounds unpatrolled, its giant wheel a skeleton. He means to show St. Cloud in its glory, but we fear it will only expose our many weaknesses."

"What are those weaknesses?" someone called.

"Your open borders," the redhead from Livingston-Monroe said, "for one. All those foreigners you accept spilling then into *our* province, taking *our* jobs. Killing folk, acting like animals. It's not right."

There was a flush of whispers at that. Claire was horrified; she looked at Beatrix. "Is the DAC so against immigration?" *Is Livingston-Monroe?*

"Some members are," Beatrix murmured. "Most aren't. I'm not, of course."

"Neither am I," Claire said. "Why are such abhorrent thoughts voiced here, then, and not shouted down? I don't like this, Beatrix—"

Rosa held up her hands for silence but seemed unsure of what next to say. All around the luxurious bathroom, the women bristled at one another.

Finally Beatrix cleared her throat. "I can report that the Barrage will go on as scheduled. My source has confirmed it."

So this was Beatrix's role here. This was how she made herself useful: reporting what she heard from Claire.

"I'd heard the same," Rosa was saying. "And it will succeed?"

"We're not sure," Beatrix said. "It is down to luck now, and perhaps magic."

Beside her, Claire stiffened. Beatrix affected not to notice, but the room was hung with gilded mirrors, and in those Claire could see the guilt playing across her best friend's mouth, reflected over and over and over.

"It will fail," Rosa said, decisively. "And when it does, we will have the support to replace Duchamp. It is true, then?" She cleared her throat. "That Abigail Monroe has arrived in Monticello?"

The room erupted. "The Duchamp cousin?" "The American one?" "The elizabeth herself?" (As though that made any sense.) And into that noise Claire stood, brushing off her trousers.

"Wait," Beatrix said, too loud, pulling at her sleeve. "This is important—"

"Is it?" Claire asked.

Heads were turning to look at them.

"You, more than anyone I know, chafe against the rules of this world." There was a glint in Beatrix's eyes. "This is how we'll take it back."

"All I see here are small dogs fighting for scraps." Claire tugged her arm away from Beatrix and walked, unhurried, out the powder-room door, a legion of eyes on her back.

They had fought before, Claire and Beatrix; this wasn't new. But never before other people. Never over something

Claire had been so sure that they agreed upon.

Lost in thought, she threaded her way through the dance floor. Discarded flowers, soldiers waltzing with their women, a dark pool of something on the floor. She came to herself at the bar. For once it was quiet, no men clamoring for whiskey.

"How was your meeting?" Perpetua asked. Her giant hair wobbled a bit as she cleaned a glass. There were fake butterflies in that hairdo, violets and peonies and little shining moons.

Claire touched her own loose curls. "I didn't mean to go. I was followed by a man who . . . wouldn't take no for an answer. Found myself powdering my nose."

Perpetua stopped polishing. "Is he still here?"

"Does it matter?" Claire sighed. "I don't know. Those meetings—are they always like that?"

"I've never made it through a full one," Perpetua admitted. "*Elizabeths*. It's not my cup of tea."

That name again. "Elizabeths?"

"It's not my place to explain," she said. "Ask your Beatrix. I don't want to step on Morgenstern's toes."

"Tonight," Claire said, tracing a circle on the bar, "I saw a side of Beatrix I hadn't before. She . . . she's invested in whatever it is they're doing there. And I suppose I knew that, but I hadn't realized that she was telling them things she knew about *me*. I don't know if I want to be involved in their business. Some of it is nasty, Perpetua. Though I suppose it doesn't matter. I—"

I'll be gone soon enough.

Perpetua tipped her head to the side, thinking. Her wedding cake of a wig tottered but stayed put. "I'll need to go greet guests in a moment," she said. "May I make an observation first?"

Claire tensed. "I won't stop you."

"That might be the issue."

"Pardon?"

Perpetua sighed. "I don't know what you're afraid of, girl. Or—I don't know why your courage shies back at the precise line that it does. All I know is that you and that hoyden show up here, week after week—which is risky enough, the two of you being respectable ladies and all—and then you watch her throw a punch, find a man or two, and then slip off to foment treason, all while you brood here at this bar."

Claire opened her mouth, then shut it. She didn't have a response ready.

"Think on that," Perpetua said, and left her the champagne bottle.

I'm running away from under my father's nose, she thought, *to marry a man I've never met, all so that I can be safe. Isn't that bravery? Besides, anyone would look like a coward next to Beatrix.* She loved her best friend with a loyalty she hadn't felt for anyone since her mother died. Claire was, by nature, an idealist and an observer (and afraid, her heart whispered, afraid of what you are, what you might be). Beatrix wasn't.

Beatrix had seven siblings and a mother who didn't obsess over her body, her every move. She was adored by every last person she met.

Look at her now, Beatrix, sauntering out of the back room of Perpetua's and directly into a man's arms to dance. As though she believed the best in him. As though she believed the best in everyone. Claire refilled her glass, drank it down. Refilled it again.

While she was distracted, a pair of red-coated Livingston-Monroe men sidled up to the bar. They had that particular look to them—something like mountains, something like a long, clear view to nowhere.

Her future countrymen. Claire gave them a sidelong look.

"The waitress disappears, the barman's gone—what kind of an establishment *is* this?" The blond one fiddled with the buttons on his coat.

"A Levee one," the other said. "You know why we're here."

"None of these fellows knows a thing about that weapons exhibition," the blond one said. One of the buttons came off in his hand. "Son of a bitch."

"Keep buying them drinks, then."

"I would if there was someone to buy drinks from!" The soldier pounded on the bar. The noise was immediately swallowed under the swell of the orchestra.

Perfect, utopian Livingston-Monroe, where the men are all kind. Claire studied her hands intently. Maybe not all the reports are right.

"We'll go to the Governor's Mansion tomorrow. You'd prefer that, anyway, Jonathan. Prettier girls."

Jonathan snorted. "We'll be talking to the scientists. They don't wear skirts." The two of them howled, as though the idea itself was preposterous. Claire thought of Beatrix's glider, and glowered.

"You'll be talking to Remy Duchamp. He might as well, effeminate bastard."

Something about her expression must have drawn them in, because the blond soldier sidled up to her. "That whole bottle yours, miss?" he—Jonathan—asked.

She looked into his eyes. Blue, and guileless, despite what was coming out of his mouth. With her teeth, she pulled off one glove, then another. His eyes looked less guileless then.

Her touch could make a man's dearest wish come true, if her father were to be believed. It had been months since she'd tested it on anyone but Jeremiah Emerson.

Here was someone who wanted to work against him.

Here, Father, she thought. *A parting gift.*

"Let me pour you a drink," she said, and reached out to touch the soldier's face.

FIVE

Claire left the champagne with the soldiers, took her hat from the doorman, pulled on her gloves in the street. In front of Perpetua's, a knot of wide-eyed travelers had paused, and now they watched Claire reassemble herself as though she was one of the Fair's storied exhibits.

"Is this—is this a *brothel*?" the man in front asked.

Claire squinted at his collar. A priest. "You won't find any butterflies here, Reverend," she said, tucking an escaped curl under her top hat.

"Pardon me. Butterflies?"

Claire sighed. "Prostitutes, Reverend. None at Perpetua's, not anymore. No one for you all to save."

This was faddish, now, the reformers walking the Levee at night in frightened clusters, as though they might be set upon at any moment by bandits. Judging by the crowd on tonight's streets, those bandits would have to be can-can dancers, or Alta California men with fat pockets. The Levee wasn't the safest place in Monticello, to be sure, but in the days leading up to the Fair, there was less trouble on these streets than people out rubbernecking for it.

Somehow her day had begun with her supplicating herself to her father and wound its circuitous way here. Claire couldn't help the words coming out of her mouth. "Is this part of your itinerary, then? Dinner at Engel's, then a brief spin through the slums? Have you thought, instead, of taking time to visit the orphans at the Home for the Friendless instead? Or is it part of your calling to gawk at girls in dire straits?"

The beak-nosed woman behind him crossed her arms. "All *I* see is one girl who doesn't know her place. You adventuresses. Lightskirts, all of you."

Claire opened her mouth to unleash another stream of invective—who was she tonight, this girl furious and useless in equal measure? But the priest said, "Peace, child," cutting his eyes over to the woman beside him, a warning. "We're here to save you," he said earnestly to Claire. "You and your brethren. We're here to show you a path back to the sanctity of the home, where you belong. Where you'll be safe."

It was against the common thinking, which held that the city needed its pockets of vice, needed its beer gardens and dance halls, since the sinners would go ahead and sin anyway. There wasn't any saving *those* people. And how inconvenient would it be for the General to shake down his madams for "protection fees" all over town? Better keep them in the one half mile of the Levee.

Even Perpetua paid a monthly sum to the Crown. That's what they called it, paying the Crown, though Claire rather doubted any of the "taxes" got to the official coffers.

"If you were here to save me," Claire said with a tight smile, "you're about ten years too late." She ran her hands down the lapels of her brother's dinner jacket. "My house was never the safest place, Father."

The priest looked at her with something like pity.

Pity: the province of the lazily superior.

"Have a very moral evening," she bit out, and she fled before she could hear any other reply.

Through the streets of the Levee, past the boardinghouses and hotels full to bursting even now, even this late, windows open and ablaze, Livingston-Monroe soldiers dicing outside a shuttered restaurant. *A coup,* she thought, and thought again of the two men at Perpetua's, their interest in her father's Barrage. *Right under our noses.* She watched them for a moment more, the longest she could stand there without attracting their attention. Her face was in shadow under her top hat.

What would King Washington say if his kingdom went to war? West and East Florida had been toying with the idea for decades, but this—this would be something else.

One of the soldiers leaned forward over his dice, looking under her hat, and Claire took off down the street. At the steps to the train platform, she hesitated. Though it was nearing dawn, the El would be running all night—a benefit of the Fair.

She should go home, she knew. Only hours from now, her father would be rousing her from her bed to accompany him to the opening ceremonies. The mayor would speak, and then Governor Duchamp would speak, and then Jeremiah Emerson would have his moment—a display of might the likes of which St. Cloud had never seen. Progress and war-making, hand in hand.

And Claire would be an ornament on that hand.

Gas, shuddering smoke—a train was approaching the station. She looked again at the platform.

"Claire!"

She sighed and turned. "Beatrix."

Her friend was flushed, her mouth a smear in the gaslight. "Aren't you going to ask how many?" she said, weaving.

Claire suppressed a smile. "How many?"

"Two. Two offers to take me away from this miserable place. To show me 'a better life.'" Beatrix blinked owlishly up at the platform, at the waiting train with its open doors. "How many did you have?"

"One," Claire said. "Or one half. Does it count if it comes from a priest?"

"It counts twice!" Beatrix crowed. She clasped Claire's arm with both hands. "It doesn't matter, though. You *are* leaving this miserable place. You aren't going home now, are you?"

Above their heads, the train doors rushed shut. "Not on this train," Claire said, drily.

"No. Of course not. Come to my workshop. Stay the night there."

"The night before the Fair? My father would skin me alive."

Beatrix smiled, tipsily. "He could charge for it. Might make a nice exhibit."

"Don't give him ideas." Claire was tired, so very tired, but Beatrix, as always, fairly burned with energy. When the two of them were out at Perpetua's, drinking and dancing, one often wilted while the other bloomed. "What is so important that I risk my father's wrath?"

Beatrix stepped out into the street to hail a hansom cab. "You haven't forgiven me yet," she said, arm up in the air like a flag.

Hours later, and Claire was clawing herself out from the grip of a dream. She'd been leaning over the starboard prow of a ship, looking for something glimmering in the deep. The salt whip of the air, the low, scraping groan of the anchor hauled from the water, a hoarse shout that land had been spied in the distance.

A strange dream, she thought, stretching, and then opened her eyes to find herself in the stockyard, the smell of blood rich and salty in the air. In the distance, shouting. The terrified lowing of cattle.

Claire had much preferred the ship.

"Hello, little bird," a voice said.

Claire struggled up to her elbows. She'd fallen asleep in her dress jacket. One of the brass buttons had come off in her fingers in the night, and she held it up confusedly like a coin. "Bea," she said, fighting a rising wave of panic. "What time is it?"

There was light outside the window. Her father would have looked for her and found her missing.

He'll kill me, she thought. *He'll kill me, he'll think me dead and when he finds me, he'll kill me for certain—*

But below that voice, another. A new one. *He can't kill what's gone,* the voice said. *And you'll be gone tomorrow.*

Claire forced her muscles to relax, stretched her hands above her head. The idea still felt good. *Let him wait,* she decided.

She distracted herself by taking one last good look at her favorite place in the world.

Beatrix's workshop in the morning was not unlike the girl herself: eccentric, bright, unexpectedly beautiful. It wasn't any bigger than a garden shed, though it had a high ceiling that was ringed with small square windows that caught the eastern light. One could only work here before noon if one hoped to see anything at all.

This morning, the light was coming down in ribbons— across the tools mounted above her small wooden workbench, across the jars of nuts and bolts, the lengths of chain, a leaning stack of stiff heavy paper, the supply of soft red leather Claire had spirited away from her father's study. Blueprints were tacked up above her makeshift drafting table—variations on Beatrix's glider that she had drawn out herself, alongside diagrams torn from books of pelicans and red-tailed hawks, a crumpled pencil copy of Da Vinci's *Vitruvian Man*, and of course, the patent diagram of the first glider model from the much-maligned Wright sisters. Claire had been sleeping on Beatrix's "cot," a sheet thrown over a pile of hay for those nights Beatrix wanted to begin her work with the dawn.

The place smelled of sawdust and spilled ink. It was cramped, drafty, hot in the summer and teeth-grindingly cold in the winter. No matter the season, it smelled like death—of hogs, of cows, of the men with the sharp little knives who slaughtered them.

It was also irrevocably Beatrix's, which was more than Claire could say of anything of hers.

When Beatrix's father had died, her mother had tasked Beatrix to sort through his papers, as Mrs. Lovell couldn't read. Mr. Lovell had been a spendthrift and a gambler, a man who'd win and lose a fortnight's pay in the back room of the bars he frequented, and so Beatrix hadn't been surprised to find, among his papers, the deed for a little outbuilding in the stockyard. It had belonged to one Thompson Gummit of Darling and Company before a disastrous round of catch-the-ten whist.

Beatrix had pocketed the deed to show to Claire, and the girls had decided, huddled together on the street outside the Emerson house, to keep it a secret from all but Beatrix's older brother. Women couldn't inherit property; the place would never be hers. So when she visited her workshop, she told the stockyard workers—startled by the sight of a girl who wasn't somebody's wife—that she was the inventor Barnaby Lovell's assistant, undertaking his more dangerous private experiments while he busied himself running his Edison-esque empire.

And the real Barnaby Lovell—a twenty-year-old freight handler at T&E Fertilizer Works who, like the rest of the known world, had an all-consuming fondness for his kid sister—made an appearance every few weeks to hover in the doorway of the outbuilding, hemming and hawing loudly over Beatrix's latest prototype while the bemused hog butchers watched from a distance.

Such was Beatrix's world, and the means she was making to escape it. "I'm going to give that fancy man Tesla a run for his money," she'd say, bent over a blueprint with a pencil in her teeth. "That boy Edison will *beg* to come work for me."

And when Claire wasn't hatching her own escape plan, all she wanted to do was to be there to watch Beatrix soar.

"The time?" Beatrix was considering, head cocked to one side. Her goggles were perched on her forehead, giving her the look of some blond-haired, many-eyed fly. "Judging by the sun—"

"Please, let's not judge by the sun," Claire said, rubbing her face.

"Then remember to bring your watch," Beatrix said, laughing, and bent her head to continue tracing out a line. "What happened with that redcoat? The one you were fondling at Perpetua's? Wasn't like you. Thought you didn't want romance."

"Who says?" Claire asked, basking in the banter. She would miss this. "My fun's a bit more subtle, that's all."

"I say so," Beatrix said, "and you do too. Remember that poor stockyard boy who kept leaving you candies at the door? He was handsome as hell, and you kept turning him down."

Claire shrugged. She'd never been much for love. "I'm meant for marriage," she said. "And romance has nothing to do with marriage."

She didn't know if she believed that, but she also didn't have the luxury to debate it further. Her family was in debt; her mother was dead; her father was, at best, unpredictable, and at worst the kind of man who'd slit a suitor ear to ear. No one would carry away his blessing, even as a bridegroom.

I've done it correctly, she reminded herself. Arranged a marriage by mail, and by the time my father knows, I'll be someone else's property. And if he's Ambrose's friend, he'll hopefully at least be my friend too.

"Don't go all tough on me," Beatrix was saying. "I was

happy to see you flirting. Well. I didn't quite see it, Perpetua told me."

"Jonathan," she said, plucking the name from the recesses of her brain. "Jonathan . . . Lee? Livmonian boy. I only touched him for a lark, and for . . . an experiment. He had some plan, he and his friend were grousing about wanting to take apart my father's Barrage."

Beatrix glanced up. "Aren't you going to that? Better yet— didn't your father want you there hours ago, to prepare?"

Claire coughed a little; the smell of the stockyard at work turned her stomach. "Let him wait."

"I admire this new leaf you're turning," Beatrix said, pulling the goggles off her head to better squint out the window. "That said, aren't you planning on kidnapping yourself tomorrow? Do you really want him locking you away in your room?"

Somehow Claire hadn't thought of that. She swore. "Oh. I—I really have to go."

"Yes," Beatrix said, "you really have to go."

"Why did I follow you home last night?" Claire moaned as she clambered to her feet. Her trousers were wrinkled; one foot was bare, the other in a delicate sock. "A dress, I need a dress. Do you have one?"

"I do," Beatrix said. "But I don't know if it will pass Jeremiah Emerson's muster."

"Nothing does," Claire said. "So let's have it, or my head on a platter."

Beatrix stood and stretched. "You haven't forgiven me yet," she said, leaning to pull a trunk out from under her desk. With a creak of its hinges, it eased open.

"Forgiven you? For the D.A.C. meeting?" Claire shifted her weight. "Is that terribly urgent? Can we do that later?"

"What later? Tomorrow you'll be gone." Beatrix was tossing things over her shoulder: a feather boa, a slide rule, a stack of tissue-thin pamphlets that fluttered and spun. Claire plucked one from the air. STOP FRENCH TYRANNY. WE WANT MONROE. A woman in a long white dress, white ribbon in her hair, delicately holding her husband's arm.

"You didn't know that I was reporting on your father's activities," Beatrix pointed out. Without looking, she shoved a wad of yellowed cloth into Claire's arms.

Claire unfolded it and held it up. "Bedsheet?"

"Bedsheet." Beatrix grinned over her shoulder. "Early glider wings. See the stitching?"

"Good God. No wonder you crash."

"Pish. What were we talking about?"

"I was forgiving you for spying. And you were fetching me a dress," Claire said. "From that trunk that seems to go down to the center of the earth."

"I was spying for a very good cause, you know. The D.A.C. has plans—"

"End 'French' rule? Hand our province over to Livingston-Monroe?" Claire felt her mouth twist. "Wage war with our neighbors? Though maybe they deserve it, closed-minded as they are."

"Name one thing you've ever done to help St. Cloud. Besides leaving it."

Claire snorted. "How about I name a couple of compromises you're making to get a person in a skirt into office. Like, say, shutting down the American experiment a hundred years in."

"I am *not* against immigration. When I'm a bit older, I'll run for a position in the D.A.C., changing things from the inside. But I'm not abandoning the movement to rot." Beatrix passed her up a box of cigars, then a second. "That's how you do it, you know. Change it from the inside! And for now we'll drag that whelp Duchamp out of office. We'll put a woman in charge of St. Cloud. A *woman*, Claire. How can you not want that?"

"This woman?" Claire asked, juggling her armload to pull out the flyer. She thrust it out between them: WE WANT MONROE. "Looks here like she's standing next to a man."

"How else would we have her rule? Charles Monroe is a milksop, and Abigail uses his money to further her causes. She'd be the true power behind the throne. It's opportunity like none I've ever seen."

Claire looked at the blueprints tacked up along the workshop wall. She let the flyer fall to the floor. "I didn't know you to dream so small," she said.

"Claire—"

"Another shadow government. All these meetings, this skullduggery, these *machinations* to put up another figure-head, one who doesn't believe what you believe. As for the strength behind the throne—do you think the General would go quietly after you deposed Duchamp?"

"Trust that we have a plan," Beatrix said grimly.

"I don't understand why you do it when it's nothing close to what you actually want. What about a woman Governor? What about a woman *King*?"

Beatrix stopped digging through the trunk. She sat back on her heels. "Well, I reckon *you* have a plan, then."

"What?"

"What are *you* doing to get us all the way to a *woman King*?" Spots of color rose in her cheeks. "Other than complain, other than run away from your problems?"

"My father—"

"You're of *age*," Beatrix spat. "Stay. Don't run off to marry some stranger, in a strange town away from everything you know, just to be with a brother who couldn't be bothered to help you stand against your father. Stay *here*. Find a job, rent a room, help your fellow elizabeths. Work for the betterment of others who have suffered like you, and those who have suffered far worse! You think you can tell me I'm wrong for making compromises? At least I'm making something!"

If the arrow hit dangerously close to the bull's-eye in

Claire's chest, she affected not to show it.

"What do you want?" Beatrix was saying.

"I want . . ." Claire swallowed. "I want to go a day without someone looking at me, and wanting things I can't give them. Impossible things. Things that would . . . break me."

"And marriage would give that to you? Marriage to a stranger?"

"It can't be worse. And there's more than one way to disappear."

"I hate your saying that. Claire, I hate that so much."

"You wanted me to come back here to forgive you?" she said, trying to keep an even tone. "Doesn't feel like it."

Beatrix shrugged. She turned her head to dash away a frustrated tear.

"Feels like," Claire said, "you badly wanted to make that speech."

"It was a good speech," Beatrix said miserably.

"Yes," Claire said, "it was," and she'd already forgiven her by the time she finished speaking.

With a sigh, Beatrix plucked something from the bottom of her trunk. She stood, a bundle of white in her arms. "Is this the last time I'll see you before you go?"

"Of course not. The train station. I still need you to see me off tomorrow." Claire took the bundle and shook it out. A waterfall of white crepe de chine, a dress with narrow waist and narrow sleeves. Far nicer than anything else Beatrix owned. "Were you saving this for something?"

Beatrix ignored the question. "It'll be lovely on you," she said, pulling out a pair of matching shoes. "Perfect. Just the smallest whiff of sacrificial virgin."

"Fetch me some hairpins?" Claire asked, already shucking off her suit. "I'm going to be late."

SIX

At first Claire had thought she'd slip into the fairgrounds with the other employees, as she still carried her father's spare pass. But as she approached Washington Park, she and a thousand other fairgoers, the flow of the crowd caught and carried her through the main gate, and she had no choice but to go along.

Claire could hardly see through the top hats and feathered hairpieces, could hear nothing through the roar of a thousand voices speaking languages she hadn't before heard. It had only been a week since she had last met her father here, to prettily bring him his lunch pail while his laborers polished the gun. The Emerson gun, the world's largest gun; a gun that weighed a quarter-million tons and glinted even in the dim light of the pavilion. It would be wheeled out carefully—so carefully; a single shot from the gun cost thousands—for the Barrage, where it would be flanked on all sides by the explosives that were her father's other stock-in-trade.

It was still a surprise to see the Fair as it was meant to be seen. For so long the great white-glossed pavilions had stood half finished, hidden by their scaffoldings, their lawns covered with giant black tarps that bowed under the weight of the endless rain. That was how Claire saw them still in her head; them, and the great wheel that stood perpetually unfinished, a pleasure ride that looked instead like a wooden skeleton.

As the Fair was built, the grounds at times teemed with men carrying pylons and wheeling bricks, architects squinting through their glasses at their plans, bankers frowning at the dubious return on their investments—but more often than not Claire had found herself walking through a ghost town. Now the Fair was a city of its own.

The General wanted the Fair to show St. Cloud's might; Governor Duchamp wanted to show off his province's intellectual power. Claire only wanted to survive it.

She never thought she might marvel at it too.

"Make way!" someone was shouting. Other voices picked up and joined the call. "Make way! Make way!"

Inexorably, the crowd slowed, formed lines. Women fanned themselves against the sun. Mothers tugged their children back to their sides, and she soon saw why.

Soldiers. Lines of them in their best midnight blue, as though they were presenting themselves to their General for inspection. It wasn't clear if they were here for a show of military might, or for the more mundane reason of crowd control.

Maybe both, Claire thought as she shuffled out of the path of a soldier's bayonet, threatening even in its ornamental scabbard. "Make way!" he bellowed, words that were picked up down the line and repeated. Terminating in a broad-shouldered man in an ermine half cape, his mustache a vicious line across his lip.

The General.

Claire wished, not for the first time, that Beatrix had also found her a hat in that trunk. Anything to hide her face.

Or her hands. *My God,* she thought, panic rising—*I'm out here without gloves.* It was the first time in months that she'd forgotten. As the shuffle of her line approached the General, she ducked her face and shaded her eyes as if against the sun.

Not for the first time, she was keenly aware of her body, her waist held tight by her dress like a pair of clutching hands. Her dark curls teased up into a bouffant and tied with ribbons. The wrinkles in the crepe de chine had already fallen out in the heat, and the dress swished against her hips, her bottom, her ankles in a way that suggested, that whispered. She didn't know how she felt about it. This *knowing* feeling, that she was moving in a crowd made up of so many kinds of bodies, that hers was one of them, that it was maybe beautiful.

Knowing that this dress, more than anything she owned, would draw her father's ire.

But here she could pretend to be a tourist. Here she could

be anyone, just another girl from New Columbia or East Florida on an adventure, an attempt to see the world. At that thought, at the brush of silk against her legs, she found herself lifting her chin, pulling her hand down to her neck. *I wonder how I'd move through the world, if left to my own devices*—

And in that moment, a white-gloved hand clamped itself on her elbow.

"Miss Emerson," the General said, his mouth a moue of distaste. He pulled her up against him. She could feel the buttons of his coat pressing into her chest, but when she tried to draw back, he clutched her tighter.

"General," she said, and if she kept her tone even, it was because the man wore a pistol at his side.

He smiled thinly. "Your father," he said, in a voice low and tender, "is half mad with worry about you, and if a slattern in a silk dress is the reason why this Barrage fails—"

Claire struggled back, sweat pricking up on her temples.

"—I will see to it that you are never seen again. Do you understand?"

His fingers would leave purple marks on her arm. Later, she would touch them in a dark, unfamiliar room, after so many awful things had happened that a soldier abusing her in front of the whole of the city of Monticello would be an afterthought.

"I understand."

"Good," he said. Then he raised his voice. "An escort! I

need an escort for Miss Emerson!"

The General may have issued his orders urgently, but there was no fast way to maneuver through the Fair. The guards muscled her along, inch by painful inch, and she had nothing to do but look.

The grounds had been transformed overnight. These lush lawns were like nothing she'd ever seen, and everywhere there were soldiers keeping order, keeping people from dropping litter on the grounds or from walking across the newly manicured grass. The skies were pale blue above them, the rain clouds of the past days swept away as though by a great hand.

The guards were directing her toward a giant stage. The crowd before it had been pressed into two gatherings, like the arrangement of pews in a church, and the aisle running between them had been decorated with streamers and velvet ropes. It was littered with flower petals. Someone had beheaded a hundred roses for this purpose.

For a horrible moment Claire thought she would be marched down that flowered aisle like a girl in a parade, but the guards holding took her around to the side. At the front of the stage, at a flower-bedecked podium, the mayor of the city was bloviating on, giving a speech that he had assuredly not written. The mayor of Monticello was a ceremonial position more than anything, as everyone knew that Remy Duchamp's General dealt with the workings of the city, taking "insurance" payments in exchange for letting

Monticello govern itself.

Claire was brought up the stairs just as the mayor finished speaking, and while his words were met with lukewarm applause by most, there was raucous cheering from the front rows, from the toady industrialists and businessmen who wanted his approval. She was overtaken by all of it for a moment, the smells and the sea of hats like birds thrusting their beaks and feathers into the sky, and then her father's hand closed around her arm, his fingers pressing into the bruises that the General's fingers had left.

He muscled her to the back of the stage, past the schoolboys clustered together in their bow ties, preparing to sing some hymn, past the foreign potentates in their finery watching the proceedings with gimlet eyes. At the far end of the stage was a line of men in chairs, their dark heads remarkable in their similarity. A preacher in elaborate robes, the General tidily taking his chair, and Remy Duchamp, the enfant terrible, thin in his dark blue coat. From where she stood, Claire could see the sharp line of his jaw.

She had never thought to be this close to power. She thought of Beatrix and the machinations of the D.A.C. and shuddered, then shuddered again at her father's hot breath on her face.

Survive this, she thought, *and then you'll be free.*

She waited for him to say something like "Where have you been?" or "I am so disappointed," but his face was drawn with the kind of inward fury that promised a beating later. His eyes raked down the front of her body and Claire found herself trying to cover her dress, a dress like so many other girls wore, with a useless, shaking hand.

"The display is prepared," he whispered harshly, "and I am to light it. Bless me."

Her father, up against all these manicured men, looked all the more like a madman who'd come stumbling out of a forge at the pit of a volcano. Like Hephaestus, the Greek god from her mother's stories: grieving, dirty, unbecoming of a god. Alone and wild with it.

"Bless me," he said again, urgently searching her face. "I need your blessing."

It slipped out of her, then. "No."

He recoiled as though she'd hit him.

Beyond him, the mayor was finishing his speech with a prayer. "Amen," he intoned, the crowd echoing the word back.

There was an interlude—a man took the stage with a blown-glass globe in his hands. Or was it a bulb? The light was blinding. Someone said something about electricity, but her father jerked her back around as she turned to look, and so the crowd gasped at something she could not see. "Bless me," he said again.

Claire shook her head wordlessly.

She would be gone tomorrow. Gone, and away from his consequences. That voice again, rising in her, saying, *Damn him, damn him—*

She opened her mouth and let it speak. "No," she whispered.

That was when Remy Duchamp stood to address his crowd.

"There's no *time*," her father hissed, and spun on his heel, stalking back to the gun on its dais. A crew of men in coveralls swarmed behind him.

Claire turned—to leave the stage, to run—but a member of her military escort stopped her with a hand.

"The ceremony isn't over," he said, and as if on cue, a battery of trumpets blew their fanfare. The boy choir, pinching and prodding one another, fell into line. When they opened their mouths, their faces rearranged themselves into solemnity.

My country, 'tis of thee,
God's chosen monarchy,
Of thee I sing—

All Claire could see was the surprisingly rumpled back of Governor Duchamp's head as he walked to the podium. The crowd, so calm while the mayor had been speaking, kicked up into a flurry of whispers. The General had been right: the people were uneasy about Duchamp's leadership.

As Claire watched from behind the curtain, the General, from his seat, held up a lazy hand to the audience. Even the foreigners among them quieted.

As though Monticello needed any more of a reminder of

who its real leader was.

"Ladies," Governor Duchamp said. "Ah. Gentlemen. Ladies and gentlemen." His voice was soft, his intonation foreign. The sound didn't carry. Claire strained to hear him from the back of the stage. "I welcome you to the Fair." One of his hands stole up to adjust his collar, smooth the back of his dark hair. "I welcome you to Monticello. I welcome you to St. Cloud. I welcome you to the Great American Kingdom." There was grandeur in the writing of the speech, but not in its delivery. Remy Duchamp spoke as though each word out of his mouth surprised him just a little. "Welcome," he said again, clutching his cue cards in his left hand. Their gold edges caught the light, trembled.

The crowd tittered at the Governor. Claire felt a faint, surprising flush of pity.

St. Cloud is doomed.

"I am—" He tried for a smile. "I am to tell you that this Fair will showcase our greatest technological achievements since the steam engine. Which, as you know, was invented in the late eighteenth century. Though some argue that with the invention of the pumping engine, we had its precursor in 1698. . . ." He cleared his throat. "I digress."

"Get to the point!" someone called. Though the front rows were filled with St. Cloud's soldiers, Claire was troubled to see so many red-clad Livmonian soldiers elbowing one another in the crowd. The shout, she was sure, had come from one of them.

This time, the General didn't lift his hand. He let Duchamp bathe in the disapproval.

"As you know, we have worked . . . we have worked very hard on bringing you this Fair to showcase American genius. Our great Nikola Tesla, the inventor, will be conducting electricity before . . . before your very eyes. You saw just a little of that now. The great wheel you see above you will turn to show you the wonders of the city. Our city. That is, it will turn as you ride it. And you will see . . . other things. Cows. Cuisine. Some dancing. And for now, we will fire the very large gun you see behind me."

He took a step back, hesitated. Looked at his seat. It was clear that he knew he must remain standing before this crowd, and that he would rather do anything but.

Into the confused silence, the great gun began to turn. Jeremiah Emerson's men were sweating under the sun as they pulled its turret about with their ropes, heaving with the sound. It made a sound like a great sigh, like it knew the promise of its purpose was about to be kept.

Emerson's eyes seized on his daughter, and Claire shrank back into the shadowy wings. All bravery gone.

If he would just stop looking at her in such desperation.

"On your signal," Emerson called to the Governor.

Duchamp looked faintly ill. He nodded. For the first time since he'd taken the stage, the crowd began to cheer.

Emerson stepped up behind his gun and laid his hands on it, expectantly. It had already been loaded with a one-ton shell; the shell would fire out above the crowd and fall into the great lake, where it would explode. Emerson turned his sweat-glossed face to the crowd, and for a brief moment, in that heavy, expectant silence, he beamed like a man who had been touched by his God's own hands.

The silence continued. Continued. Continued on.

Jeremiah Emerson aimed the gun far above the heads of the crowd, and fired.

Nothing happened.

Remy Duchamp glanced at the cards in his hand, as though the moment of this failure had been written into the agenda.

"And now," Emerson said, "the Barrage!" There was a desperate showman's turn to his voice. Behind him, the General was standing with a look like lightning.

The gun did not fire.

The men did not move.

"My daughter!" he cried out, and it carried to the farthest reaches of the audience. "Bring me my daughter! She is the one responsible for this failure!"

This is what she would remember, in the years that followed. The sun on her shoulders, the slim line of sweat down her back. The soldiers' rough hands bearing her forward. The General, fingers twitching in the pile of his fur-trimmed cape, his face written over with grimmest pleasure. For he had been right in his warnings. Emerson the madman? Emerson had failed. And his willful daughter would be now made to pay in the most public way possible, as daughters were made to pay for the crimes of their fathers.

Remy Duchamp set his jaw and said nothing.

Claire was pushed from one man's hands to another, shoved roughly up the steps to the gun, and though she struggled to pull herself away (though where would she go? How could she escape the entire city?), her father caught a fistful of her crepe de chine dress and drew her close. The crowd howled like hungry dogs. They had come here for spectacle.

This was spectacle.

"Bless me," her father said, and in his desperate grip, Beatrix's lovely dress wrinkled and stained. "*Bless me*, you devil."

She was at the top of the known world, here, higher than any point than the great untiring wheel, and the smallest part of her wondered what the swell of faces before her thought. Who here would imagine that the girl in the white dress had built this great machine? Easier, somehow, to imagine that it was her failure, without it ever having been her triumph.

What else could she say? "I bless this man," she whispered.

"I bless this weapon."

Claire wrapped her arms around herself. "I bless this weapon."

"Take it in your *hands*, child," her father said, and when Claire didn't immediately take up the gunner's position, he took one of her wrists in each of his hands and held them up for display, as though for one brief, awful moment she were offering surrender. Then he pushed them down.

The gun didn't hesitate. It knew her touch, or it knew her father's, or perhaps (as Beatrix would say, always searching for the logic), Claire with her sudden weight had dislodged some heat-swollen gear and sent the thing running along as it should. Did it matter what the cause when it discharged with a great bellowing sound, firing out just above the crowd's heads?

The shell exploded in the lake beyond, kicking up a mighty wave.

There was screaming. Shoving. There was wonder in the voices, fear, the collective wail of boys taking refuge in their mothers' arms. Despite their Governor's warning, no one had expected the gun to fire. For the Barrage to prove something about St. Cloud's might. That it was uncontrolled, erratic. Nothing you could count on.

That it came at the hands of a girl.

Even now, Claire could see the pair of Livingston-Monroe men breaking away to pelt toward the Fair's entrance, so they could report to their masters what they had seen.

Below the blue, white, and red bunting that snapped in the wind, the General gazed up at her, a smile playing at his lips, plans in his eyes. Though that should have been enough to terrify her, it wasn't what set her heart to pounding. What was it that the General had said? Duchamp couldn't care less for Jeremiah Emerson's Barrage. The Governor wanted his Fair to be a show of marvels, of ingenuity. Electricity and great pleasure. Wheels and some dancing. Was that why Duchamp was looking at Claire with haunted, furious eyes?

"Come down from there," Duchamp ordered.

Her father released her wrists. He'd still been holding them as though she were a marionette. "You've brought shame on our house, girl," he said, sorrowing.

She could hear it, then, the sound of her escape plan collapsing.

There was nowhere else to go. Claire drew her chin up high and descended the steps from the platform, the slight wind teasing the skirt at her ankles. A faraway part of her noticed that her hands were altogether soot to the wrists, her nails caked under with her father's powder. The hint of a flame would set her blazing like a Catherine wheel.

"Come," Duchamp said again, as she paused at the bottom of the platform, and when she didn't move, he took two steps forward and seized her by the arm, fingers closing over the bruises the General had left, and she hissed.

Duchamp paid no notice. With an authority he hadn't yet shown, he hauled her to the podium. Another man handling her as though she was his property.

Perhaps she was.

"What you have seen," Duchamp said, "what you have all seen now, is a miracle." His voice carried easily this time—and was it her imagination, or had his accent vanished? His vowels were open like doors to the prairie. "And did I not promise miracles? Did I not promise feats beyond your most distant dreams? You came from Nuevo México, from Alta California; you came from beyond the Atlantic Ocean; you came by railroad and by horse, you came on your own ambitious feet. You came to see what St. Cloud has accomplished. What *America* can do. This is but—a rehearsal for what is to come! We will fire again at the Fair's closing!

"For now, tell me—do you see this young girl? Look at her in her white dress, as though she stepped off a marble pedestal from our great Hall of Wonders." His words belied his ferocious grip on her arm. "Let her be the conduit for our men's imagination! Let her usher in our era of change! Let us open our great Fair!"

His people, the people of the Great American Kingdom, roared.

In this moment, they loved him.

How to square this man with the uncertain boy who had promised cows, and cuisine, and dancing? *Who are you? Who did you just become?* Claire stood, shuddering, stripped bare by the crowd's eyes, and when she tipped up her head to look at Duchamp, she saw his eyes were fixed on her with wonder.

"I will take her to my mansion," he said, wrenching his head back to the crowd. "She will sit in St. Cloud's great room as our angel. She will remain there until the last fair-goer leaves this place, filled with our spirit of ingenuity, off to go into the world, changed! Now go—go and find your own delights!"

Duchamp sliced his free arm through the air, and a brass band stumbled out from the wings. Under the roar of the music, the crowd began to dissipate.

Claire shook herself free from Duchamp's grip, but he reached for her again. "Let me *go*," she said, sidestepping, as he passed a hand over his face and said roughly, "God, who *are* you?"

"I am not your captive," she said. "I'm not your spirit, nor your angel."

Tomorrow, she thought. *I was supposed to leave tomorrow.*

"You?" His eyes were as cold as water. "You are someone who knows something I do not."

In her fury, she stumbled through her words. "You've laid claim on me like—like I was a cow! Like I was a *thing*."

"I didn't plan to do it," he said quietly, "until I spoke the words. And still it doesn't matter what you think, does it?"

Her father. The General. Remy Duchamp. "I will not go," she said, and already she was planning it—she and Beatrix would ransack her workshop, they would take up their bindles and ride the railroad all the way to West Florida and disembark down into the swamplands, they would build a little wooden house in the wilderness and bolt the door. No one would ever see them again.

"You will," Duchamp said.

If it wouldn't have ended in her death, she would have hit him full in the face. "I won't be your *ornament*."

"All you are is *responsible*," he said, his hand against the bare skin of her arm. "For the Emerson gun! Or was it mere luck that it fired, and in the way it did? Tell me, truly—was it your doing?"

"It was not."

"It was her doing," her father rumbled from behind her. Claire stiffened. "All I have laid claim to. It is her doing! And she is *my* child, and you will not have her."

"Oh," the General said, joining them. "I rather think he will. Wouldn't it be fascinating, boy, to learn what Mr. Emerson has been keeping from us all this time?" He raised his hand again, crooked his fingers. A pair of soldiers surged past him and seized her father by the shoulders.

"You cannot *do* this!" he yelled. "You cannot take me from my girl! Claire! Claire! My girl! I am coming for you!"

Claire flinched, but she did not turn to look. The General canted his head as he watched his men pull Emerson away. And Remy Duchamp, slim shouldered, straight-backed, every inch now the prince he hadn't been before, paid them no attention. He studied Claire's face as though she were his muse.

Ambrose, she thought, mourning. *Orleans. An escape*—

Today, of all days, she had forgotten her gloves. Why had she forgotten her gloves?

"Claire, is it?" the Governor asked, in a voice like silk. "I have so very many questions for you."

SEVEN

It wasn't until the next morning that Claire fully understood
the complexities of her situation.

The process of transporting her to the Governor's Mansion
had been achingly slow, as Duchamp and the General had
duties to attend at the Fair for the rest of the day. And yet
the General, in particular, didn't want to let Claire out of his
sight. With a nervous sergeant in tow, he'd marched her to
a pavilion at the far side of the Fair, an icebox of a building
devoted to St. Cloud's dairy industry. Past the display of
mechanical churns, past the electric lights beaming down on
the show Holsteins tended by pink-cheeked, picture-perfect
farmhands, past the clusters of tourists sipping new cream
from glass pitchers. Up a side set of stairs into a little office.
The General gestured brusquely for Claire to sit at the desk,
and he and the guard stepped outside onto the platform
overlooking the pavilion.

"There's nothing uncanny about that girl," she heard the General mutter, "but her father's gone and lost his mind, and he'd stop at nothing to get her back."

"Pardon my asking, but why do you bother with Jeremiah Emerson, sir?"

Claire leaned forward to peer through the cracked door. The General was adjusting his cape, thinking. "Fanatics work long hours for little pay, and this one is smarter than most," he said, finally. "The trick is in knowing when to cut 'em loose, son."

"But won't taking his daughter just enrage him?"

The General sighed. "Tell that to the Infant. Duchamp's grown himself a set of iron balls overnight." With that, he shut the door, and Claire watched, horrified, as the lock turned behind him.

She spent a good eight hours in that little room, cooling her heels, covering her mouth when the rich, round smell of the buttercream below was too much to bear on an empty stomach. No one had thought to feed her, but that seemed to be the smallest of her problems. She had gone without food before.

Instead she thought over the morning again, and again—had there been a time she could have resisted? Run? Her brother would be waiting for her at the station tomorrow. Waiting with flowers in his arms, a key for her room in his pocket. A chance to choose her future—and even if, somehow, both of her brother's friends were cruel tyrants, at least she could have had a say in her new captor.

It wasn't safety, but by God, it was closer to safety than where she was now.

They came for her at dusk. The Fair had been trimmed with streetlights, and they glimmered against the darkening sky as the soldiers put her into a carriage and set her off to the mansion.

Claire knew where the Governor's Mansion was. Everyone did. A few years before Claire had been born, the city of Monticello-by-the-Lake had been decimated by a fire. Three square miles of the city had been taken, including the old residence, home to Remy Duchamp's father, that had overlooked the great sparkling lake that the city's name had laid claim to. The Duchamps had taken the fire as an opportunity to move their home inward to a more defensible position, and now the mansion sprawled down Prairie Street.

Tonight their carriage passed the smaller homes of the mayor and the General (three-storied and turreted, still too much house for anyone) that clung sycophantically to the end of Prairie until they could see the mansion rising in the distance. It looked like a castle. Not just in style, but in how it had clearly been built to be defensible—small windows, small doors, great swaths of undecorated stone. No wood, not even in its shutters. The fire had taught them that. The mansion went on for what should have been blocks, its walls swelled out to the edges of the sidewalk, and in the gathering dark Claire felt a prickle of fear begin behind her eyes.

"I don't have any of my things," she whispered as the carriage pulled up out front. It was an idiotic thing to say, but maybe, just maybe, they would let her go home first, and as she packed her bag, someone would turn their head for a moment and she could change her ticket, take a train to Orleans tonight—

The soldier snorted as he hopped out the door. "You won't need your things," he said, and hauled her down to the ground.

Soldiers everywhere: soldiers opening the mansion's doors, soldiers milling about in the hall inside. She only had a brief, confused impression of the mansion's foyer—polished pale marble floors, a white-armed statue of Hera, all the ceilings inlaid with a mosaic tile that gleamed like blackfish below the water—before she was ushered upstairs and into a room at the end of a long hall of doors.

"I don't have any of my things," she said again, as the soldier produced a set of keys and fumbled with the lock.

The lock. They could lock her in there.

At that, he looked her full in the face. Dark eyes, dark hair, a generous mouth that right now was turned down at its edges. His skin was brown from the sun.

"Sir," she said again, and he frowned.

"My lady," he said, with exaggerated courtesy, "my name

is Sergeant Miller. And you are a guest here. We will give you what you need."

The door clicked open. Miller waited until she took a step inside, and then he shut it firmly behind her.

She was a guest. The room was beautiful. In the achingly graceful mirror, Claire counted the bruises on her arms, and then she cried herself to sleep.

When she awoke to the clawing of her stomach, it was scarcely hours later. The sun hadn't yet risen. As she looked around, remembering where she was, she was tempted to fling the covers over her face and weep—

No. Enough of this. I'm not without two hands and a will.

She forced herself to stand, and then when she was on her feet, she found she couldn't stop moving, pacing the length of her room, looking for something she could use as a weapon. She laid out the possibilities on the mussed-up sheets of her four-poster bed—a fireplace poker, a planter, two decorative swans with pointy beaks and of a surprising heft. But there was no one to use her weapons on, and after a minute, she put them all back.

At a loss, she took off and hung her white crepe de chine dress, stained and wrinkled and utterly impractical for any move she was about to make, and stalked about in her combination undergarments. There were no other options, nothing fit to make an escape in. There was an armoire full of dresses too small for her and shoes that didn't fit her feet. All of these were sized as though for a child, but there was nothing else of a child's in this room, and she wondered at the mystery of it for a half second before realizing it didn't matter. She wouldn't be staying to find out.

How much time did she have to concoct a plan? *I suppose that question depends on what Duchamp truly intends for me.* Because she didn't believe for a moment that he merely wanted her as some ornament to polish on the throne in front of his court. She was attractive, but not so attractive; she could do calculus, read Latin and Greek, rig a glider's wings, but he had seen none of that. All she had done this morning was put her hands on a faulty gun before it had fired of its own volition.

Still, Duchamp might wake in the night and remember that he had a young woman under his power and just down the hall and—

She blanched, bent over the tiny escritoire in the corner.

No. Think it. Think the words. He could try to have his way with you. This is no time to be delicate.

But why? If it was sexual relations he wanted, there was no reason for him to publicly steal away one of his inventor's daughters. *There are still plenty of ladies of the night in the Levee who would warm his bed for the price he would pay them.* What was it, then—her father's war knowledge? He could have requisitioned Jeremiah Emerson's papers. Or better yet, kept *him* under lock and key.

Perhaps she was a whim he'd already forgotten about.

You're looking for an excuse not to act. If Duchamp doesn't steal you away to his bed, the General will. She ran a hand over the writing desk, a place for fine ladies to maintain their correspondence. Could she somehow get a letter out to Ambrose? Had Beatrix heard of what had happened to her? Had Perpetua?

No one is coming for you. She dressed herself again. Then she crossed to the window and, with a whispered prayer, put her hands under the sash.

It opened into the night.

So get yourself out.

Claire caught her breath. From what she could tell, the window let out over the mansion's pleasure gardens. Below her were dogwood trees, rosebushes, a statue standing tall and white in the night. In the distance, another roof—for what building, she couldn't tell, she didn't know Prairie Street at all—and beyond it the faintest wick of light on the horizon. Soon the house would begin to awake.

Her room, on the second floor, wasn't so very far off the ground, and though she'd never scaled a building before, she had stood on the roof of Beatrix's shack by the slaughterhouses and watched her friend, strapped into a glider made of little more than cloth and wood and mathematics, throw herself out and into the air. If Beatrix could do such a thing just for the love of it, Claire could climb out a window to save her own life.

With quick, dispassionate hands, she yanked the blankets off the bed and began to knot them together. It wasn't terribly original, she knew, but she'd never needed original before. *That's the thing about clichés. They work.* When she had a makeshift rope long enough, she tied one end to a bedpost and flung the other out the window. It would hardly take her halfway down. Cursing, she hauled it back up and began taking the dresses from the wardrobe, starting with the sturdiest looking. *Who on earth stayed in this room before? Some young Duchamp cousin? There's winter wear here, summer dresses, and all of them exquisitely done—*

No matter. She tied one final garment, a plaid day dress, to the end of her rope and tossed it down again. From what she could tell, it would take her most of the way to the ground.

Well, she thought, peering out over the edge. *Here we go.*

Gingerly, she eased herself out the window, both hands on the rope, her bare feet finding purchase on the stone. The first few steps were simple enough, and the night air stirred her loose hair as she felt her way down the wall. But it took patience, and time, and her arms trembled with the strength it took to brace herself.

And then above her, in a hideous parody of her scheme with Margarete, the four-poster bed began to slide. She could hear it more than feel it, and before she had time to react, all the tension went out of the rope in her hands. Slack now, a useless ribbon—and for a horrible moment, her toes lost purchase and she scrabbled against the stones, desperate for any kind of hold, and as she pulled at the rope she took the bed with her in a long, disastrous shriek—

Oh God, she thought, *it isn't any good to escape if I wake the whole house,* and she pushed with her knees and released the rope and let herself fall to the ground.

With a suppressed cry, she landed on her bottom on the grass, inches from one of Duchamp's overgrown rosebushes. Still, she had to gasp to catch her breath from the shock of it, and as she pushed herself to her feet, she felt the complaints of her hips and legs.

I need to get to Beatrix's workshop. She'll know what to do. She'll help me get to the station in time.

The only light in the garden came from a trio of electric streetlights set down the center path. It was easy enough to avoid them, staying to the shadows alongside the mansion as she picked her way across the gardens. To her relief, she saw that no lights had come on in the house at the sound of her clumsy escape.

I didn't realize the mansion was shaped like a horseshoe, she thought, the grass soft under her feet, *and that building before me, built in that matching fieldstone—is that part of this same complex?*

But as she neared it—

No.

The mansion had been built in a perfect square with a courtyard in the middle. An ideal spot for a garden, a place for pleasure protected from the city that surrounded it.

A place with no way out.

She pressed the heels of her hands against her eyes, unable to think. When she withdrew them, she found herself gazing up at the statue that stood in the middle of the park. Claire could see now that it was the goddess Athena, stone-eyed, laden with knowledge. She gazed down at Claire with a godly sort of pity.

And to think I was so confused to see that they had left the window unfastened. . . .

"Psst! Claire!"

Her head snapped around. There—on the roof, opposite her. Someone in trousers, one arm in the air. "Claire!" they said, or it *sounded* like "Claire," anyway, and before she could react, the figure had tossed a rope ladder off the side of the house like they were snapping out a tablecloth to dry. It must have had weights attached to its ends; when it fell, it stabilized, and the figure bent to pin it to the roof before they began to climb down.

Claire was too fascinated at first to be afraid, but moments later, when the figure had hopped off and was trotting across the garden, she found herself shrinking back into the shadows.

"Claire!" the voice hissed again as they neared, and this

time, on the left side of the figure's face, Claire caught a glimpse of gold.

"*Beatrix,*" she said, and fairly flung herself into her friend's arms. "How did you—"

"Grappling hook, rope, but first a rope *ladder* I added another ten feet to, and I had to tack it into the slate roof and who knows if it will hold, utter five-alarm panic—*the whole city* is talking about you. . . ." Beatrix pulled back, her hands on Claire's shoulders. "*Dammit,*" she said, "your *goddamn* father," and then she hugged her again.

"Tell me you're here to rescue me," Claire said into her shoulder.

When she pulled away, Beatrix's face was grim. "Not quite," she said.

"Not quite—"

"Listen, it's almost gone day, and I don't have much time. The D.A.C. sent me. No, don't look at me like that—I would have come anyway, but they have a better plan than I do."

"Let me be the judge of that," Claire said darkly. "I'm supposed to leave for Orleans in a few hours, Beatrix."

"I *know,*" she said, "but I'll tell you the honest truth—I think it's worse out there for you than in here. Soldiers all up and down Prairie Street, it's like that all the way to the Fair. And they're not out carousing, they're *posted* there, on orders."

"And they're there because of me? I doubt it."

"I wouldn't," Beatrix said. "You're the only good headline

from the opening day of the Fair. The Governor's trying to keep peace in the city after what happened this afternoon."

"This afternoon? What happened? I was locked away in the dairy building."

"The dairy building? Did he tie you to a cow? Did he—"

"Beatrix. Focus."

"Fine," she said, and sobered. "Official story? Some drunk-and-rowdies got into Tesla's lightning exhibit when it was empty, started a fire."

"A fire?" Claire shuddered. After the conflagration that had decimated the city twenty years before, Monticellans took arson seriously. "What's the real story, then?"

"The D.A.C. has word from a source that it was a pair of Livingston-Monroe soldiers. They were dressed in St. Cloud colors. So many of the Fair buildings are marble, you know, shored up to last, but Tesla's pavilion had all this wooden scaffolding, which is frankly a design flaw that someone should have noticed—"

Claire raised her eyebrows.

"Focus, I know," Beatrix said. "Listen, rumor has it that the General hedged his bets. Your father's gun wasn't the only weapon he was researching. He was keeping something in reserve. Something bigger, and worse, and you've heard what Tesla can do, the man is a magician. I heard that it could level a *city*. What if he levels it at Livingston-Monroe? Wouldn't matter if you ran away to Orleans."

"That can't be true—"

Beatrix looked at her steadily. "If we want Abigail Monroe in charge of our province, we can't begin by destroying huge swaths of her people. The General wants control of St. Cloud, and the easiest way is for him to make himself a war hero, blowing holes in Livingston-Monroe. And he's going to do it all under Duchamp's nose while that boy is distracted by shiny little inventions."

"Either way," Claire said, "giving St. Cloud over to Monroe or the General, it's going to end in war."

"No, *one* of those options is a war. The other is a coup, and a bloodless one, and it ends with the Monroes on the throne. Our people will go anywhere to get out from under the Infant's thumb." Beatrix paused. "Love, I'm here to make you an offer."

"An offer?" She swallowed. "Please tell me it's a ride to the train station."

"The D.A.C.—they want you to stay here. At the mansion. To gather information."

Claire couldn't quite believe what she was hearing. "Stay," she said. "As that man's prisoner. When the borders are about to close. When my brother will be waiting for me."

Above them, the sky had gone dawn white, red at the edges. A cockerel was crowing somewhere, and at the sound a flock of starlings took wing from the trees.

"Just for two weeks," Beatrix hurried on. "It's enough

time to find out exactly what Tesla's building, to get some intelligence on the General, to gain Duchamp's trust—"

"For your cause," Claire said, edging forward. "For *your* cause. And what happens if I refuse? *When* I refuse. Beatrix, you know full well this is my last shot to leave!"

Beatrix wiped the sweat from her brow, lifted her eyepatch, and dashed away the sweat there too, or maybe it wasn't sweat, maybe Claire wasn't giving her enough credit, but she also hadn't ever thought that her only friend would betray her. Her good eye fixed on Claire, but the other was milk white, and when she finally spoke she said, "Willie LeGrande."

"No," Claire said. "No," something rising in her chest until it was choking her.

"Willie LeGrande," Beatrix said hoarsely. "I'm calling it in. I would do it again, Claire, I would go back ten years and I would get between you and him, I would lose the eye all over again. But now you need to do this thing for me, because it's right, and because I know that you can."

Claire shut her eyes, briefly.

It had been such a simple thing. She and Beatrix had been children, playing cards on the floor in the Emersons' kitchen in the tenements. Claire's father had been working, her mother asleep in the next room. Neither of them had heard the cat screaming in the next flat over. But Beatrix had, and she'd run out the door, Claire hot on her heels, to find the neighbor boy thrashing the stray with a switch he'd made from a branch. At twelve years old, Willie LeGrande was already thick necked and evil. But Claire and Beatrix had been fearless then, the both of them.

At least when they were together.

They hadn't made any kind of plan. There hadn't been time. Beatrix had rushed the boy while Claire threw herself down on top of the cat, protecting it, and in the midst of all the yelling, the boy had raised the switch and taken it to Claire's back. She'd screamed, then choked on it, the fear and panic and the all-consuming pain, and the cat below her screamed too and scrabbled its nails against her skin.

He had only whipped her once. When he lifted his arm again, Beatrix had put herself between them.

It was a simple gesture; it hadn't been simple at all.

Willie LeGrande brought the switch down across her face.

She'd lost the eye, or the use of it, anyway, and the boy had been stunned enough by the force of what he'd done that he'd frozen, and then smiled, *smiled*, cocking his arm back again, and that was the first time that Claire had understood that there were people in the world that would hurt you because they wanted to. Because that was how they found their pleasure.

Their screaming had woken Claire's mother, who burst into the flat before Willie LeGrande could land another blow. By month's end, the boy was sent away—to Australia, they had heard, on work detail, or maybe off to the Home for the

Friendless. In the years after, Claire had wondered sometimes how LeGrande had come to be cruel. Was he born rotten? Or had he learned it the usual way, at his father's knee? She never decided; the LeGrandes left for West Florida not two weeks after their son disappeared.

As for the cat, the old tabby had spent the rest of its life trailing Beatrix around, meowing for scraps and purring on her lap. When it died two years later in its sleep, Beatrix was already wearing the black velvet eyepatch that Claire had sewn for her from an evening dress of her mother's. "I won't wear it again," Susannah Emerson had said, thrusting the fabric at Claire. "Make that girl something pretty."

That was that. It wasn't a day they relived or even mentioned. It was a fault line in their friendship, and still it was the ground that friendship was built on. And now it all rushed over Claire in a second—the terror, Claire's shame at being unable to stop it, and they *were* speaking of it. They were speaking of it now.

"I want you to do it for me," Beatrix was saying, "because . . . because if you don't, I don't know if I can get you out. The D.A.C. sent me here. They'll hunt you until they find you, and they'll lock you up themselves until they decide what to do with you, and we'll be here again, having this conversation, only I imagine you'd be in a cell."

"These are your allies. These are the women you call friends."

"Friends, no. More like bedfellows. The bed being our eventual liberation."

Claire made a face.

"Fine, it's not a perfect metaphor, but listen to me. Love, if you can't make yourself stay, I understand. I truly do. But tell me—how is this gilded cage any worse than the one that waits for you in Orleans?"

"Because I asked for that one! Because I would be with my brother, who loves me—"

"Who never once came back to see you—"

"And I would have a home, and marriage."

"To some Jehoshaphat goddamn First Baseman that you don't even know! Claire, you aren't sure what the Governor wants of you. He could marry you tomorrow. Unify the city. At least until we take it from him." Beatrix shrugged. "And he's not bad looking, if you like them bookish and dreamy eyed."

"You don't?"

"I want a little more fire in a woman," Beatrix said, then cleared her throat. "In a man. In anyone. Listen, we don't have time. If you're going to stay, there are things you have to tell me—"

"I knew some day you would call it in," Claire said, "but I always thought it would be to—to make me stay. To not go to Orleans, to find an escape here. But you're calling it in for a *cause*, not for our friendship. Willie LeGrande."

"Willie LeGrande," Beatrix said steadily.

"You want the Monroes in power." Claire couldn't quite look her in the eye. "Duchamp deposed. And the General?"

"Dead," Beatrix said. "You don't lock up a viper, you take off its head. But that's not our business, that's Rosa Morgenstern's and the D.A.C.'s, and anyway we're not asking you to hold the gun. If you're sitting at Duchamp's side, you'll hear things. That's all the D.A.C. wants."

"That's it," Claire said. "You say that's it."

Slowly she held up her bare hands between them.

Beatrix swallowed. "I haven't told them everything about you."

"You haven't."

"I swear. I haven't. But it doesn't mean you can't . . . I mean, you could touch them, if you wanted. The General. The Governor. The inventors that report to him—"

"No," she said again. "Even if it isn't a delusion, even if there's something to it, I have no control over that power! That leaves me to the mercy of what those men want. Those *men*, Beatrix. Think of what you're asking of me, you and your women who want so badly to be rid of them!"

"I know what I'm asking," Beatrix said, and pulled her eyepatch back down. Claire looked at her friend, her face dirty, her hands dirty, her trousers ripped at the knee from breaking into the mansion to offer a choice that wasn't a choice at all.

Because the day they hauled Willie LeGrande away, all

the neighbors whispering about the chain gang waiting for him across the ocean . . . Claire remembered something about that day.

Not a week before the incident with the whip: Willie LeGrande, tracing in the dirt with a finger. Claire and Beatrix had been walking home, their hands sticky with rock candy. They'd bought it with a penny they'd found in the street; they had two sticks for later. When they saw Willie outside the tenement, Beatrix had wrinkled her nose and run upstairs, but Claire lingered, wanting a better look at the design he was drawing.

He looked up at her. "Give me your candy," he said, and since he was big and awful and Beatrix had the rest upstairs, Claire gave him the half-eaten stick.

"What is that?" she asked, braver now that she'd given him what he wanted.

"A kangaroo," he said, gnawing at the stick. "I saw it on a poster downtown. It was drinking a beer. I want to see one someday."

"Well, maybe you will."

Something possessed her to hold her hand back out for the candy. Glaring at her, he chewed the rest of the rock candy off, then gave her the wet stick to throw away.

For a minute, their fingers had touched.

And not a month later he was, they said, on a ship bound for Australia.

Beatrix knew that story. She knew the story about Ambrose

too, and every last fear Claire had that she was a weapon waiting for some man to pick her up and aim. Beatrix knew all that, and loved her despite it. Because of it.

Looking now at Beatrix, she knew that whatever scraps of loyalty she had left demanded that she stay. Willie Le-Grande. Beatrix's love. She could take those scraps and mend them into a cloak, something to protect her against the way her heart hurt now.

The sun was fully up in the sky, windows opening all over the mansion, and they both knew that Beatrix had stayed too long. She led Claire back through the hedges to where the rope ladder dangled from its pegs on the roof, shaking a little in the wind.

"Two weeks," Beatrix said. "You have two weeks until the King arrives to tour the Fair. We'll find a way to get word to you. And then we'll get you to your brother."

"*If* you can sneak me across the border. *If* I'm not caught and hung as a spy first." *And if,* Claire thought, *I get away with telling lies to the D.A.C.*

"You don't have to. Say the word, and I'll take you with me. I'll take you with me right now. But I think—I think you see the worth of this."

Claire shook her head.

"For what it's worth"—Beatrix mounted the first step—"I'm sorry."

"I am too," Claire said.

For a half second, her friend looked back, her face blanked out by the rising white of the sun. "Claire," she said. "Take off your gloves."

But Claire had already turned from her to walk inside, her head held as high as she could.

EIGHT

The heavy door back into the mansion opened into the great hall. She walked inside as though she had only been out for a predawn stroll, nodded to the posted guard, and without hurrying in the least took the stairs to her bedroom and pulled in the tied-together rope from the window, undoing the knots one by one until, exhausted, she fell asleep in the nest she had left on the floor.

When she woke next, it was full noon. Her train to Orleans had left an hour ago; her stomach reminded her that she hadn't eaten in a day and a half. No one had left her a tray. No one had come in to tidy her room. The ewer held the same water from the night before. Half-heartedly, she splashed her face, washed her neck and under her arms, put her dirty feet into shoes. *Why hasn't anyone come?* she wondered. Were they planning to lock her up and starve her?

She stepped out into the hall, and found, somehow, that

she wasn't afraid anymore.

Everything in the hall was black and cream—the floors pale, the ceilings pale and cut through with black beams, the walls darkly patterned with fleur-de-lis. Though it was full day, the mansion was lit with electric lights, and Claire counted them as she walked down the hall. Her head swam. *Food*. She would ask for food, politely, and she would gather enough information to satisfy the women who were helping to keep her captive, and then she would leave this city behind her.

The rooms in her wing did appear to be bedrooms—their doors were thrown open, and the staff inside were taking down curtains and fluffing pillows. Down the stairs, the foyer was empty but for a guard on the door. She nodded at him with this new confidence that had come on her from nowhere, then smoothed her dress and ducked through a doorway. A parlor with a fireplace sized for the gods, burning away though it was full summer. Another parlor with a harpsichord, and chairs too delicate to sit on. An open door to a pantry, laden with bushels of fruit, garlic hanging from the rafters, three braces of rabbits beheaded one by one by a man in a bloody apron. Behind him, a housekeeper gave notes to a deliveryman, and when she caught Claire's eyes, hers narrowed.

No friendly cook here, then, to take pity on her and let her raid the larder. Not even instructions as to how she could conduct her day, where she should go, why she was here.

Nothing but headless rabbits.

The domestic wing of the mansion gave way to the public areas—a great cavernous dining room, a salon with a piano inlaid with tile, two giant doors that led into the great hall—and then past that, a wing whose use she couldn't quite suss out, not at first. The doors here were locked, heavy, but there was noise behind them, a great amount of noise, and as Claire hesitated by a keyhole, wondering whether she should step closer to look, the door in front of her crashed open.

A group of liveried workmen appeared, carrying a ladder between them, and beyond them the darkened room crackled with something bright and dangerous. She could see that the ceiling inside was far higher than those in the other parts of the house.

Here, up into that emptiness, stretched a pair of giant metal poles. They were ridged like beehives, and between the finials at their tops they tossed small sparks back and forth. As Claire watched, transfixed, the workmen pushed past her, muttering among themselves.

"Duchamp brings a sorcerer into his house," one was saying, "who arrives with a hankering for *fig salads*. Eats better than the General. Nobody says boo."

"Can't fathom it."

"You all find that odder than that witchery in there?" Another laughed. "Or that basket of animals he totes around?"

"We're going to be overrun with Livmonian men by

Christmas, mark my words."

They rounded the corner and disappeared. Claire's stomach seized with hunger, but she crept back to the doorframe and peered into that darkness once more, trying to make sense of what she saw. The poles were quiet now, waiting.

"Girl," a voice said, amused. "Young girl. Perhaps you'd like to stop lurking there in the hall like a sad little cat? Come and help me with this bulb."

Claire stepped through the door. Past the poles was a pair of long worktables laden with books and charts and maps, and standing behind one of those tables was a man. As she stood, her eyes adjusting to the dark, his face was suddenly illuminated from below—his mouth bright, his eyes in shadow.

She blinked rapidly, but the image remained—a man with a large glowing sphere, held chest level, where his heart should be. Rising up beneath it was a metal coil mounted to the floor, vibrating merrily away.

"Come," he said, with greater impatience. "I had asked for a hand."

She looked up at the poles between the two of them, at his hands holding a bushel of light. "Is it safe?"

"It's quite safe."

She squared her shoulders and obeyed, stepping over the giant snaking wires on the ground. Above her, one pole sent a shower of sparks to the other. All the hair on Claire's arms stood at attention, and she swallowed a cry.

"Safe?" she said, her voice just this side of polite.

The man watched her with warm eyes. "Safe," he said. "Not inactive." He inclined his head, and she stepped forward, and he put the light into her hands. "Stand there. Don't move."

With a brisk hand, he reached over to turn up the gaslight, but Claire couldn't stop looking at the bulb she held. It trailed no cords. No wires. Its light was generated from her own body, from the warmth of her hands. Her skin prickled, and as she watched, sparks began to fly from her dress as though she herself was a kind of filament.

The man saw her looking and smiled. He had dark hair parted in the middle, an elegant mustache. On the table before him, a map curled in on itself in a leather case. "You are surprised by the means by which I light my laboratory? I want nothing to interfere with my greater project."

"I am less surprised by the gaslight," she said, trying to keep her hands still, "than the fact that I have become a . . . candelabra."

"A poor candelabra, that only has two arms." Without further ceremony, he took the bulb back from her. "Thank you," he said, and when he set it on the far end of the table, the light extinguished itself. Reaching behind him, he threw a switch. The coil between them stopped its vibrations. "Those men, I can never persuade them to assist me with this. And yet I cannot do it alone. A man only has so many hands."

Claire had spent enough time around Beatrix to know

when to ask questions and when to keep quiet and watch, though she was fairly burning for an explanation for what she had just seen, and done. The inventor—for surely that was what he was—smoothed down his suit jacket, and the linen threw off a shower of sparks. It bothered him not at all.

He pushed aside a mass of copper wire on his desk and pulled up the map case, flinging it across the table. It curled at the edges, threatening to snap back together. "Since you are here, you can help me. Yes? Here, little cat—put your hand here." He took up a pen from a cup on his table and leaned forward, squinting in the dim light.

It was a map of the Fair such that Claire hadn't seen before, illustrated in a hand that looked quite similar to the one making notes on it now. *Voltage,* he wrote, and a series of numbers, and then drew a dotted line between two buildings, between another and the lake. He put the end of the pen in his mouth and chewed. As he thought, a tiny calico cat jumped up onto the table and strode across the markings he had just made, smearing the ink. He didn't seem to notice.

Claire bit her lip against her questions; she could still feel the energy in the room, could sense it crawling down her arms. "I shouldn't be in here," she muttered as the kitten butted her arm with its soft little head. She gave it a scratch behind the ears.

"Where should you be, then?"

Claire laughed despite herself. "At home. Or, I suppose,

in the great hall, posing like one of those statues—"

"Ah, so you are the girl I heard tell of. You are Duchamp's chosen figurehead?" The man made another mark on the page. "The girl brain behind the Barrage, or so he thinks."

"God help me. I suppose so."

"And I am his sorcerer, if the men of this house are to be believed." He spared her a sidelong look. "Neither of us, then, are what we are said to be. This does not mean we cannot continue our work and let the tongues wag as they will."

Claire kept her face still. She was beginning to have a suspicion as to who this man was who had given her his implicit trust, and if she was right, he had much to fear from the kind of "work" the D.A.C. had asked her to do. "Why do they call you his sorcerer? This"—she gestured with a hand—"is all very awe-inspiring, but I thought Duchamp was a man of science."

He snorted. "I am a foreigner. It is easier to call my work magic than to consider an alternative."

"Than to give you real credit, you mean. To call it genius."

"Well." He seemed pleased, in an absent sort of way. "I see many things differently, yes, little cat? For example, I see that you are very much in need of a wash. I see that no one has thought to feed you. I see that you have clever eyes and hands that no one here has yet to put to use. That you do not ask questions to derail the work. These things are not genius, but they are nonetheless truths that others are ignoring."

For the first time in days, Claire felt a flicker of hope inside her. "And I see," she said, finding her voice, "that you could have placed that cup here to keep your map open. You didn't need me to stay."

The man grinned. "For the map, no. For many other things, perhaps yes. You have more than earned the right to ask a question." He gestured to the grand poles, to the coil before him. "What would you like to know?"

What has the General ordered the inventors to do beneath Duchamp's nose? Beatrix had wanted to know, and if that was the question at hand—"Are these weapons?" she asked, and feared the answer.

He considered her. "No. Or—they are not intended to be. My other project . . . well and so. I should not say. As to why I am here, I have worked for many years in America; for many years, I have made my laboratory in the Duchamp-Westinghouse company. And then—there was a fire. Much was lost. Much that I could not replace." He shut his eyes briefly.

"I'm sorry about your laboratory," she said, meaning it.

"Thank you," he said. "I cannot go back. Now, I am to set up my own company—private, not under the aegis of the Crown. Our building, it is not ready until next year, and so when Governor Duchamp asked for bids to light his Fair these next few months, I said, yes, I will do this thing. I have nothing else pressing."

Claire glanced up at the poles above her. They didn't look like marquee lights to her.

He followed her gaze. "Ah. What you see here—these are old inventions. These are magician's tricks. I am to stage them for the benefit of the King when he comes to see the Fair, as I was also to do yesterday. But there was a fire, they say, and so I did not go on. I am cursed by this, fire. It follows me."

"I'm sorry," she said again, as she put together this man's identity.

He smiled tightly. "You did not hear of this before now? You must have been occupied, with your soldiers."

"With the *General's* soldiers."

"Yes," he said. "And some of the work of which I do not speak is because of the General."

Claire studied his face. He gave up this information too freely to be in on any kind of plot. Or perhaps he thought her harmless. "Because of the General? Or for him?"

At that, he laughed—a real laugh. "I have given you many answers that you do not need, nor care about," he said, a neat sidestep.

"May I ask you a question, then?" At his nod, she continued. "Does Duchamp . . . invite many women to his mansion?"

He considered her frankly. "No," he said. "He lives as a monk does. I think sometimes our Governor might have enjoyed keeping bees on a faraway hillside. Solving mathematical equations with the great minds in Mount Vernon.

But he has been called to rule. So rule he does."

"Ah," she said. Some small comfort—*Duchamp doesn't sound like a man with plans to ravish me.*

He frowned. "Do not suppose he is not dangerous. For all that I admire him, and his ambitions, he is not safe. Him, and your General, and the man who may bring you your meals. We are in a state of war. You have been brought here for a reason. I would like you, please, to be wary. And perhaps to lock your door, for there are monsters here that you have not yet met."

Claire felt her stomach curdle, and the man, studying her, patted her arm in consolation. "Do you like figs? We shall have them, and new clothing for you, and then we shall work. I am called Tesla."

Her surmise had been correct. Tesla the magician. Tesla, constructing something secret under the orders of the General—he had admitted as much. Tesla, the fancy man Beatrix so admired, and she felt a tightness in her chest again at the way her best friend had put her into a position where she had to lie to this man.

But I'm doing the right thing—aren't I?

He was extending a hand to shake. "Yours is quite clean? Forgive me for asking."

She wasn't wearing gloves. "Not clean," she said, relieved for the excuse. "I need a wash, remember? But I'm Claire Emerson."

With a wry smile, Tesla shook his hand in the air between them, and at the fizzling sparks from his fingers, Claire laughed aloud. "In here, we ourselves are the conductors of light. Could anything be better?"

At the ring of his bell, they were brought lamb chops, and new potatoes, and a salad with figs and pears, the dishes laid down in haste before the servant sketched a bow and left. Tesla took the salad and left the lamb for her. He worked steadily as he ate, but his papers remained fastidiously clean. When she had cleared her plate, Tesla rang again for food, and for the first time in days she was full.

Under his direction, Claire refilled his pens, alphabetized his papers, made fair copies of the documents he gave her. None of them seemed to be for any kind of weapon, but she tried to remember their specifics anyway. Electricity was dangerous, she and the whole world knew it, but they also used it to light their streets and their homes. The diagrams she held looked only like lines to her.

It was silent work, and she enjoyed it, and yet she felt the weight of guilt on her shoulders, and the fear that snuck in behind it.

Tesla had told her to trust no one. Was it safe for her to trust him?

Hours passed. He threw a switch on the wall, then the other, watched the strange bright dance between the poles with impassive eyes. It was close to suppertime when the housekeeper she'd seen earlier came to the door.

"Your wash is here," Tesla said, sparing her a smile. "Come back later if you so wish."

The housekeeper took Claire away to the wing of the house where the bedrooms were, down a hall she hadn't yet seen. There, she opened a door to a pearl-bright bathing room with golden fixtures that put Perpetua's to shame. In the center of the room, a bath had been drawn, and beside it, a selection of oils and ointments had been laid out on a tray. Claire needed no prompting. She shucked off her dress and hung it to let the heat press out the wrinkles, and then she eased into the water with a sigh.

"I have sent for a bath attendant," the housekeeper said, lifting a white hand in shock. Perhaps she wasn't used to women doing for themselves.

"Oh, I'm perfectly fine," Claire assured her, stretching out her toes. It was a long bathtub.

The housekeeper went to a closet in the corner and began pulling out large fluffy towels. "Mr. Tesla was very upset to hear you had no maid. He of course didn't know that *we* didn't know of your arrival until the Governor decreed it—"

Claire sat up, sending water over the sides of the bath. It had been easy, for these few minutes, to forget that she was a prisoner. "As you would have preferred notice of my captivity, I would have preferred not to be a captive. I apologize that my kidnapping has inconvenienced you. But

I assure you that I do not need a girl to wash my hair."

The housekeeper continued as though Claire had not spoken. "Well, I've just gone and gotten my instructions from the Governor as to you." She set the towels down beside the tub. "He has visitors today, some ambassadors of some kind. Not sure from where. But we're to fancy you up and make you beautiful for display."

Claire opened her mouth, then shut it. She stared at her toes through the water.

"For now, we'll make do with our own staff, but we've sent for a maid for your daily needs, and that bath attendant—ah, yes, here's the girl!"

A girl of Asian descent, no older than twelve, slipped in and curtsied. Her face was a perfect blank. Looking at her, Claire thought again of Margarete, taken by her father from the orphanage with the promise that he would give her a home. And then he put her to work.

"Go on, child," the housekeeper said, taking Claire's dress off the hanger with a small frown. "Get a pitcher of water and do milady's hair. I'll find something to fit her. This isn't much good but for rags, now."

The woman took Beatrix's dress away then, but the girl stayed. Her hands were gentle in Claire's hair, and Claire took a breath and let her do her job.

NINE

Despite her discomfort with being waited on, Claire watched the maid's progress in the mirror. She'd never been served like this before; who had, in the tenements where she was raised? *Maybe* from time to time a family hired a charwoman, but more like than not, it was the neighbors of Claire's childhood who had taken in the laundry of the better off. Her mother would have considered it an insult to have someone else cook their family's meals.

After her death, when their fortunes had changed and her father had taken little Margarete from the Home for the Friendless, he had thought that the girl would tend to Claire like a lady's maid . . . in addition to doing the cooking and the washing and all the other chores about the house. This would have been difficult enough, but Jeremiah Emerson had refused to pay the girl, insisting instead that she was a "part of the family."

Claire had tried to take that at face value, sharing Margarete's chores until her father had caught her sweeping out the kitchen and thrashed Claire, then Margarete, with the broom. After that, the girls kept their distance from each other. During the hour each morning that Margarete was to tend to Claire's toilette, Margarete slipped in and slept on Claire's bed while Claire put up her own hair. They had, over the years, reached a sort of détente, though Claire could still feel Margarete's seething resentment under every word the girl said—and why shouldn't Margarete despise her? Though Claire had desperately wished for a sister, for any ally in her strange, lonely home, the gulf her father had created between the two of them was wide and seemingly uncrossable unless Claire had the means to pay Margarete for her help.

"Are you paid well?" Claire asked the maid, abruptly.

She started at that, her hands full of Claire's hair, a clutch of hairpins between her lips. "Yes, milady."

"I am no one's lady," Claire said, with a smile to soften the words. "In point of fact, I might want to take a job such as yours when I finally leave this place."

"A job is a job, milady." She began twisting Claire's curls into a bun, pinning as she went. "I make three dollars fifty a week, and room and board, to help with the Governor's lady guests when they come. My sister doesn't make half that. She's a knitter for silk stockings, still lives at home with Ma. Going bat blind, she is, while I sit here and paint ladies' faces. Lots of faces, now, with the Fair on and all."

"I suppose that isn't bad—"

The girl laughed. "Bad? It's *good*, is what it is, and I aim to hold on to it. I got three brothers, milady, and all three lost their work to machines. The oldest, he runs a factory floor now, but the other two left for Livingston-Monroe and the railroad. Plenty of work out that way for a person with two hands. Though they're a lot less friendly to those that look like us, and now they're saying the borders will—" She bit her lip. "Well, I shouldn't say more. Only that I'm lucky that the Governor hasn't found some man to invent a machine that does hair."

"He wouldn't see it as important enough," Claire muttered. The girls shared an amused look in the mirror.

"Well and so. No one knows what'll happen next. War? Machines that think and eat and talk? But whatever comes, I'm hanging on to this position tooth and claw."

"I'll keep that in mind." Claire dropped the maid's gaze. "My father hasn't let me take a job."

The girl snorted good-naturedly. "Then you *are* a lady, milady, whether you think so or not. 'Tis a privilege to choose not to work."

It was hard to take the step back to see her upbringing as a privilege, but Claire knew the girl had the right of it. She chewed on the thought as, in the mirror, the maid's clever hands arranged the curls at the front of Claire's bouffant so that they framed her face. It was a fine thing, that mirror, a spread of silvered glass that had surely cost a fortune, and it was supported on either side by golden statuettes—angels, by their wings and harps and by the gold-leaf wreaths they wore.

The young maid caught her studying them. "There's an idea," she said with a touch of glee.

"An idea?"

"An idea." She scurried over to the wardrobe.

"Nothing in there will fit me—"

"We'll make it fit."

Claire looked down at her figure, more generous than any of those dresses allowed, then looked up again at the metal angels. Were they smirking at her? "You're not planning on making me carry around a harp, are you—"

The maid reemerged with an armful of fabric, satins, and silks piled up to her chin. "You seen that statue at the edge of the Great Basin, at the Fair? The girl all in gold?"

"Oh, no. No. Don't tell me—"

"From what I've heard, Duchamp wants a show, milady." The maid sounded much, much older than her face suggested. "So let's give him a show."

In the great hall, in the carved throne at Governor Duchamp's right hand, sat a creature that was not—precisely—Claire Emerson.

This creature was the height of Gibson girl fashion, with

her halo of teased dark hair, the touch of color on her lips. Her dress was a shot of gold against the black-and-white backdrop of the room; the bodice was cut daringly low over her generous bust and tied, Grecian style, at her shoulders. The slippers she wore beneath peeked delicately out from the folds of her skirt. Only if you looked closely would you see the toe of that slipper worrying the velvet rug laid under the chair she sat upon.

For the girl beneath that girl *was* Claire. The girl in a swan-bill corset that emphasized parts of her she'd until yesterday never put on display, the girl who had been sewn directly into this dress by three giggling maids, swatting at her to keep her still. The girl wearing rubies at her ears, bangles at her wrists. More wealth than she'd ever seen, and all of it hung about her body.

The girl who didn't like the eyes on her now. Not at all.

"Why, boy," the General had boomed to the Governor as a soldier escorted Claire into the hall. "She looks like the bloody Statue of the Republic!"

The conversation in the hall quieted, then ceased.

"I'll remind you that you are speaking before the angel of this house," Duchamp had said mildly, from his chair in the middle of the dais. Then he had turned to look at her.

Had she imagined it, the brief flash of terror on his face? And what on earth could have put it there?

But he raised an eyebrow, and the moment broke. She

couldn't tell with him what was meant to be satirical and what wasn't. There was an insouciance written in the lines of his body—his dark hair tousled, his suit of clothes starkly tailored—that gave his words an edge they wouldn't have otherwise.

Maybe it was how he sat, long limbed and careless, on his throne. Perhaps it wasn't quite right to call it a throne, but it wasn't *not* a throne either, not by Claire's reckoning. It was flanked by a pair of chairs less grand in size but not in construction.

At the moment, the left held an ordinary-looking man who sat so gingerly, Claire thought he might bolt at any moment.

"Ah, yes. An *angel*." From the floor below the dais, the General had made a mocking bow. "How do you fare tonight, my angel?"

"Sit," Duchamp had said to Claire, gesturing to his right.

Her face burned. She sat, like the marionette she had recently discovered herself to be. The crowd began to talk again, but in a new, toothsome tenor.

Claire had arranged her face into the mask she wore when her father was at his most unpredictable—the face she wore that gave nothing away. She took stock of the court before her.

For that was what it was—a court, like something out of a story.

She had heard tell that St. Cloud's gatherings were one of the least impressive in the kingdom. Those wags must have seen more of the world than she had, though, because Claire was flummoxed by what lay before her. This court reeked of power, so many kinds of power that she hadn't ever considered. At first she couldn't make sense of who exactly was invited to a court such as this—there were no minor noblemen in the Great American Kingdom, not like in the British histories that her mother had set her to reading.

But that wasn't where the money was in Monticello-by-the-Lake. *That* was in the businessmen she saw before her, the developers and architects, the factory owners, the advisers to the Governor on finance and railways and war. In knots they gathered, sleek in their fine suits, their neatly trimmed beards. Waiters floated between them, proffering trays of crudités and oysters on the half shell, and the men ate these and drank their champagne and still they looked hungrily about them, the hunger of men who were not easily satisfied.

She was sure that some of these men were the patrons of the artists who gathered in their own colorful knots at the edges of the hall; she knew that Duchamp himself sponsored the scientists whose laboratories took up their own wing of his mansion.

From what Claire saw, Duchamp paid them little mind, glancing only now and then at their numbers when a group of them laughed heartily (*and performatively,* Claire thought; *they want his attention*) at some joke.

Claire knew that to be a mistake. The acoustics of the

room were brilliantly constructed; they threw the words of the milling crowd up to the dais while keeping the conversations of the leaders who sat there at a whisper. Within the first few minutes, Claire had heard "weakling" and "foreigners" and "the largest standing army," and it didn't take a brilliant mind to know that they were speaking of war. Duchamp didn't blink an eye at them, or at the women, peacocked and plumaged, who hovered in their own circles. Jewels glinted at wrists, at throats, at all the delicate parts of a woman's body, as if to outline them for a weapon's blade. Some would seem to be the wives of the men in suits, some seemed to be their daughters—

As I'm Jeremiah Emerson's daughter to the outside eye, she thought, tugging subtly at her dress, and nothing else. *These women have their own lives, their own agendas. If I don't remember that, I'm doing myself no favors.* A fair few of the women kept an eye on the dais, on the Governor or Claire or both. Some of those glances were pointedly jealous (a tossed head, a drawn mouth), but most were simply assessing. There was a new power here.

Little do they know I'm more of a puppet.

And if Claire read them right, a few of those looks were longing ones, directed at the young Governor by girls her age and younger. He wasn't an ugly young man, by any means—he was tall and slim, and he didn't have a wife. Or a mistress, at least not that she'd heard tell of. He didn't seem to have eyes for anyone, honestly, and there were some beautiful people in this room.

Duchamp paid less attention still to the soldiers. Not only the pair standing at attention on the dais, rifles strapped to their backs, but those in the crowd who clustered around the General like baby birds awaiting their supper. Almost all were bluecoats, St. Cloud's men, but to the General's left she saw a pair of red-uniformed soldiers.

Livingston-Monroe men, wearing enough expensive trim on their uniforms to put them at a rank equivalent to that of the General. And the one with the blond hair, fiddling with the buttons on his coat, leaning over to say something in the General's ear—

Is that the soldier I touched two nights ago at Perpetua's? Jonathan Lee?

As though he'd felt her looking, the soldier's head swiveled slowly up toward her. Before he could catch her gaze, Claire turned away, to the Governor and the man he spoke to.

"—I am not saying it is wrong," the man was saying diffidently, "just that I can't personally imagine myself participating. Or maybe it's my spirit. I worry what my mother would say about this. What she would say *Jesus* would say about this. You know what I mean."

Though Duchamp had his back to her, she could see him incline his head, thinking. "But you carry a gun, do you not?"

"No, sir. Governor, sir." The man shifted in his seat.

"Never saw the use for one, being protected here and all. More soldiers here than I ever saw in my life."

"But surely, before you came to work in the laboratories in the mansion—"

"Begging your pardon, sir, but before I came to work for you, I was just copying designs out for Thomas Edison and his boys. Every now and then, I'd get a word in edgewise, maybe someone who'd put down my idea, test it out, like, but it wasn't till I came to St. Cloud that I got a fair shake. Developing this . . . project is the first time I've been put in charge of something, and, sir, I've enjoyed myself mightily, but the thought of turning that thing westward . . ."

The Governor tensed. Claire watched his fingers tighten on the armrest of his throne. "Keep your voice down, unless you very badly want to muck out my stables."

The scientist (*for that's what he is,* Claire thought, *an inventor like Tesla*) blanched. "Sorry, sir, begging your pardon, sir," he said, beginning to rise from his chair.

"Sit," Duchamp said. "I did not ask you here to discuss strategy in earshot of the most dangerous men of my province."

"Yes, sir, of course, sir." The groveling was beginning to turn Claire's stomach. She would look away, but she was too afraid to see Jonathan, the Livingston-Monroe soldier, staring her full in the face. Even now a part of her mind was spinning out the problem—*nothing too terrible could have happened after I touched him, even if I granted his wish to*

*make something bad happen to the Fair or to Duchamp;
the Governor's still alive and the mansion's still standing
and that scientist might be a chowderhead but he's certainly
alive* at least *and—*

"I invited you to here to celebrate your accomplishments.
Now you stand." Duchamp climbed to his feet, and the man
followed suit.

The conversation in the hall grew quiet, all but for the
General, who kept gassing on—some story about a runaway
horse—until he came to the end of his thought.

A waiter hurried over with a tray of champagne flutes, and
Duchamp took three in his hands, shuffling from side to side
to offer drinks to Claire and to the scientist. She wasn't sure
if she should stand as well; Duchamp hadn't introduced her,
had said nothing to her, in fact, since she'd been placed beside
him. She ended up crouching over her seat, not standing, not
sitting, until she gave up entirely and flopped back down onto
it like an ungainly animal. Someone in the crowd snickered.

Fuming, Claire took a long drag of her champagne.

"Friends," Duchamp said. "Soldiers. Everyone else. This
man beside me is brilliant, and as it is Sunday, I will be telling
you of his accomplishments. Please put up your hands if you
are familiar with direct current."

One of the blue-coated soldiers looked around and then
pushed his hand halfway into the air. No one else moved.

"Good! Excellent!" Duchamp's expression sharpened, as

though he were stepping into his body for the first time that night. "Many more of you should be reading the newspapers, for when we talk of electricity, more specifically, I think, we are talking of direct and alternating current. Mr. Tesla, of this court, is the pioneer of alternating current, and this man here, Franklin Michaels—"

Michaels nodded his head. He clutched his glass in both hands, like he was a royal cupbearer.

"I have brought him here to work with Mr. Tesla. We are working on something very exciting, very . . . dangerous." A few of the glazed-over faces in the crowd blinked back to attention. "But today, I am telling you about direct current, which Thomas Edison would have you know is better than alternating current—yes, he is even going about killing dogs, and cats, and sometimes even horses on stage at his demonstrations. The horrors of it . . . his audience watches the animal foam horribly at the mouth and then fall over dead—"

At that, a man took himself discreetly out of the hall, presumably to empty his stomach.

Duchamp brightened momentarily. "But though it can do that, alternating current is far safer than direct. Here, let me tell you why." And the Governor rattled off a series of facts and figures with the confidence that they would be met with rapt attention.

Claire might have found the lecture interesting had she been sitting across a table with him, able to refer to notes, diagrams, able to focus her attention entirely. But then, Claire liked nothing more than to sit down with a complicated problem, and not everyone felt the same way. Especially on a night like tonight, the hall heavy with summer heat and the jasmine-scented candles lit in every windowsill. In this, the hour after the court had dined, people could not pay attention to a lecture like this, not without a pressing reason for that attention.

Even Michaels, the scientist, could feel their boredom— he was beginning to dance a bit from side to side, almost as though he needed to relieve himself.

"Of course," Duchamp was saying, slowly, "your understanding the *importance* of this distinction assumes you have an interest in science, which is not a given—"

"Oh, come now, sir," a voice called out.

Heads turned, and Claire sat up in her chair to see better. Michaels took the opportunity to absent himself from the dais. At the back of the room, one hand still on the giant doors to the hall, stood a woman shaking her head.

"You speak to us as though we are children," she said as she strode up to the dais, "when you are no more than a stripling yourself."

"May I assume," Duchamp said coolly, "that you are one Abigail Monroe, late to join her fellows who arrived this afternoon?"

The woman's eyes flickered from Duchamp to Claire and

back again. She was wearing a suit jacket of unadorned black over a skirt of the same. It was day wear, working wear, and to Claire it seemed as though the woman's goal was to make the other women here, in their flounces and ruffles, look frivolous by comparison.

Abigail Monroe. Claire smoothed her face into a smile. He invited her here? Interesting.

"I am, sir," she said, folding her hands before her. Though she spoke ostensibly to Duchamp, her voice carried to the corners of the room. "Unlike my entourage, I refused to take the railway. They say, you know, that the construction of the railway has created work for those who needed it, and perhaps it has—but those who look to science to solve our problems are shortsighted. Look to our factories, our laborers replaced by machines! We have still not recovered from the crash of our economy, sir, and with this influx of *immigrants* from Europe, we must think of the work of our own peoples—"

Duchamp held out a hand to Claire, and the woman stopped, blinking.

Claire tried not to do the same. When she didn't take his hand, he turned to her and offered it again with exaggerated courtesy. She put her gloved fingers in his, and he pulled her to her feet.

Then he took his hand, his bare hand, and placed it just below the nape of her neck, on her flushed, prickling skin.

"I suppose you want to introduce me to your lady," Abigail Monroe said. "Forgive me."

Before Claire could spit out "I am not *his*," Duchamp said the words for her.

"This," he said, in a French accent that deepened as he spoke, "is not my lady, though I suppose she is, in a sense, *all* our lady. See how she is dressed as the muse of our great fair? She is both a person and an idea. It is interesting, to be a thing and not a thing, all at once. I am sure you know that."

"I don't take your meaning," she said.

"Ah," he said, dropping his hand down to Claire's waist. "Shall I put it this way? I am not an immigrant. I was born in this country. And still something about the way I speak is not pleasing to you? So, in the interest of politics, then perhaps you speak of foreigners, you speak of immigration. Tell me, Miss Monroe, when did your people come to this country?"

"My great-grandfather came to fight during the War for Independence."

"As did mine," he said. "As perhaps you know. Cousin. And then, humor me—what office do you hold in Livingston-Monroe, the province that bears your name?"

"My husband," she said, "rules Livingston-Monroe. As perhaps you know."

She gives as good as she gets, I'll say that, Claire thought.

"Which makes *you* both a politician and not a politician," he said. "Yes. It is good, you see, when we are clear with one another."

"Clarity," Abigail Monroe mused, tilting her head to the side. "Interesting. You see, your province—note that I do not say *you*, sir, I know you aren't the only power in St. Cloud—"

Claire winced.

"—but your *province* has an entirely different set of laws regarding European immigration. Much different than those patriots who are your neighbors in Livingston-Monroe."

Duchamp barked a laugh. "Madam, I had thought it a basic right, for each province to pass and enforce our own individual laws that did not conflict with the American Kingdom's."

This had clearly been the opening Monroe had been looking for; now she raised her voice. "It is no secret that our country needs laborers. And of course we can't expect natural-born Americans to do that work."

Claire's stomach turned. *This* was the candidate that the D.A.C. supported to run St. Cloud? This prejudiced, short-sighted person made a better choice simply because she was a woman?

"We need to import that labor somehow. It makes sense to have some—*some*—foreigners come in. But St. Cloud has no reasonable cap on its immigration policy! So they come into your province and sneak over to *ours*, because you don't enforce your borders"—she was talking faster now, even as the crowd began whispering at her impudence—"and then they take our jobs!"

"I thought you wanted them to work for you," Duchamp said mildly.

"Not as skilled workers, or as tradesman! Not *running* businesses! Just working to do—"

"—to do the things you yourself wouldn't deign to do. No, I see your point quite *clearly*." He stood. "I wish I could say well met, Mrs. Monroe, but indeed, I can only say we've . . . met. I assume your husband is here as well?"

"He's just freshening up," someone said in a carrying whisper, and the court tittered. *They love their Governor again,* Claire thought. *Just like that.*

"He is seeing personally to the stabling of our horses," Abigail Monroe said, anger striping her words. "I came straight here."

She's trying to shame this man in his own court. And he's shaming her for the fact of who she is: a woman with ambition. Claire bit her tongue. *I think I hate them both.*

"You mistake me, perhaps," Duchamp was saying. "This court is not a place to hear petitions. I will be glad to have more conversation as to your thoughts on . . . immigrants in private, yes? Excellent." He took Claire's hand in his. "We shall speak more tomorrow, Mrs. Monroe. I shall retire now for the night."

And to the surprise of everyone in the room, not least of all her, Remy Duchamp swept out of the great hall with Claire on his arm. Heads turned, hands covered mouths. The General tossed his half cape over his shoulder and nodded to her with a look vile enough that Claire knew she would double-check the locks on her room tonight.

Tesla warned me about this.

And the Livingston-Monroe soldier, the one she knew from Perpetua's—he paused, as she and Duchamp paraded past him, staring up at her for the briefest moment with a look of deepest hatred.

My God, Claire thought. *What is going to happen to me?*

TEN

The door to the great hall thudded shut behind them. Even behind its massive weight, Claire could hear the stir that they had caused, the hullabaloo of voices. But now that they were out of sight, they were running from the hall as though it had been the scene of a crime—Remy Duchamp's legs were long, his stride fast.

"I'm sorry," she said to this man, to whom she'd only spoken a handful of words, "but where exactly are you taking me?"

He said nothing. They rounded the corner into the hall of Grecian statues—Apollo with his lyre, Poseidon rampant. Claire pulled her hand from his, and he stopped to stare at her. "*Where* are we going?"

"My study." His face was a study in contrasts—elation and fear. Above him, a god Claire didn't recognize lofted a bow and arrow. "Come," he said, taking up her hand again.

"I must speak with you, and soon we will be followed."

"By *who*?" Claire asked. "Dear God, can you just give me an answer?"

"The General," he said, his voice low, and this time when he started down the hall, Claire ran after him.

They passed through the wing that housed Tesla's laboratory. It was one of several, the doors all hung with name plaques that Claire was moving too fast to read—she must have missed Tesla's before, when the workmen were walking through—and then around the corner the doors began to run closer together. Small rooms. *Sleeping quarters?* She could feel Duchamp's pulse in his hand.

His study was the final room, and what looked to be the largest. He ushered her inside and then bolted the door.

"Are you well?" he said, flicking on the electric lights. Claire had taken a step away from him.

"I am well," she said, and swallowed. "Though I am a girl locked in a strange room, in a strange house, with a strange man."

Duchamp moved to sit behind his desk. It was grand, and cluttered, but he folded his hands over the mess as though he was about to make a pronouncement. Behind him, bookshelves laden with texts in French, hand-painted wallpaper in blue and green and gold.

"Is it propriety that gives you nerves?" he asked. "I did think we were past that."

"How do you know so little about polite society?" she asked, realizing even as she spoke that she knew the answer. Remy Duchamp didn't know that you couldn't be alone with a young woman without besmirching her reputation because he didn't need to. It meant nothing to him.

"No," she said, "not propriety."

"No?"

"Self-preservation." She moved slowly to one of the chairs across from him and sat, her absurd dress rustling around her ankles. "You see, this strange man seems to think he has some ownership over me."

She had never thought she would speak so casually to such a person—such a man—as Governor Duchamp. She'd dressed him down after the Barrage, that was true, but she could argue that she had been under extreme provocation. *Well, I could surely argue I still am,* she thought, *but this is a man who has the power to do what he likes with me. As I've now had ample occasion to notice.*

But he watched her avidly as she spoke, and the hunger there was nothing like the men in the hall. It had nothing of possession to it.

He looked at her as though she kept some answer he desperately wanted. *The Barrage,* she thought, nauseous. *He's on the verge of war, and he thinks I know how to fix his greatest weapon.*

And she needed *his* secrets to pass on to the D.A.C. Why,

then, did she find herself baiting him?

"You understand my problem," he was saying. "I have no wish to own you."

"No?"

"No." His dark eyes were burning. "I wish to know why your father's gun worked for you. I wish to know why, when you are near, I can find the words that . . . elude me, otherwise. You heard how poorly I addressed the crowd before you arrived."

"I have no idea." She could taste blood in her mouth. "I thought both your speeches were excellent. All three. Every speech that I've heard."

A hint of a smile. "You aren't a good liar. You heard what I said to Mrs. Monroe."

"I heard it."

"I have—" He swallowed. "I have never spoken like that. It was . . . exhilarating."

They stared at each other over the desk until the Governor dragged his eyes away.

In the taut silence, Claire dug her fingers into the armrest. "I—" How could she get him to trust her? *Get him comfortable, get him talking.* It was what she'd always done with her father. "I didn't realize that this would be so much of your role, as Governor."

"Dressing down emissaries before my court?" He had turned in his chair to look out the window. Night had settled on the courtyard beyond.

"No," she said, with a hint of cheek. "Questioning young women in your study."

"How are you to know how I spend my nights?"

"Talking, I mean. All the talking you have to do. It doesn't seem to have all that much to do with governing."

At that, he swiveled to face her. "Did you think that governing happened entirely by written decree? Or that I gave orders for my aides to carry out while eating rice pudding from a silver urn in my bed? It's expected that I give speeches."

"Expected by who? Certainly your court doesn't want them."

To her surprise, Duchamp huffed. *Was that a laugh?* "Why, did they not seem to enjoy my discussion of alternating and direct currents?"

She started to smile back at him. Stopped herself. Then—*he needs to trust you*—made herself smile again. "Your scientist Michaels surely wanted the ground to swallow him up."

He shuffled a pile of papers into a folder. His desk was a rococo marvel, its sides carved into leaves and roses, and it was piled with the sort of distraction Claire knew from Beatrix's workshop—tinkerer's toys, curiosities. The things that restless hands played with. As she watched, he lifted the lid of his stamp box, then let it fall heavily shut. Claire eyed it. It was gold plated, inlaid with jewels. If she stole it, she could easily sell it for a train ticket to Orleans.

It wasn't even the fanciest thing on his desk.

Duchamp sighed. "The Sunday-night speeches are expected by the General. He is, as you've gathered, a dangerous man."

"Did your father do that? Give speeches on Sundays?"

"Yes," he said.

"About . . . science?"

Duchamp stiffened. "No."

"Ah." Claire didn't know what to say to that. "And it's expected that you govern as he did?"

His dark hair spilled onto his forehead as he leaned forward, spreading his hands across the desk. "I give speeches. I draw up the budgets. I protect our borders. I tend to my people. I do not swan about from chair to chair in a dress as a woman does, waiting to be plucked and placed in someone's parlor and kept there for the rest of my life. I can't sit with a book in the *gardens* without being bothered. I have duties."

"Poor you," Claire said with asperity, and watched his face redden. "You certainly sound as though you enjoy them. Your duties."

"And so my enjoyment matters to you?"

"How on earth do you want me to respond?" She couldn't believe herself. She couldn't believe, either, how he responded— his eyes bright, his body taut and tense under his jacket. "Have I been plucked and placed in your—your garden? Do you *envy* my position?"

"Tell me this instead. Did you *want* to return to your

father? I have come to know Jeremiah Emerson. Perhaps I have done you a favor in taking you away."

She bit her lip against her sudden tears. They came from frustration, from being passed between men's hands without any say-so in the matter.

Still, she knew she looked to the Governor like a lost little girl missing her father. *None of us are what we seem,* she thought.

"Don't cry," Duchamp said quietly.

As she wrestled her composure back into place, he sighed. She watched as, bit by bit, he relaxed the muscles in his shoulders. It was a minute or more before he spoke again. "There have been philosopher kings throughout history. Wise men, who used their wisdom to govern their people. Men who knew when to guide, when to listen to their advisers. 'Defend,' those advisers say, and 'Build trade, and innovate, and make a home for your city's spirit.' I had hoped to be one of these men. But I'm not their idea of this leader. I can see that in their faces when I speak." He studied her. "I can see it in your face when I speak. And then Abigail Monroe walked in tonight, and I was a different man."

Without thinking, Claire hid her gloved hands in her skirts. "Who *is* their idea of a leader?"

"The General. As you well know." He thought for a moment. "Abigail Monroe, or so my advisers say. And I—"

"What *about* you?"

"You don't think I am preparing for war?"

"I don't," she said. "Or rather—your people don't."

"You don't." He stood, and his slim frame made a dark line against the wall. "I must know all you know of the Barrage, and its failures. I must . . . quantify this effect you have on me. Our real work, then, will begin in the morning."

She lifted her chin. "I am not yours to experiment upon."

"You are not mine," he said mockingly. "You have said this many times. But, if my working theory about you is correct . . . well. In this place, you must belong to someone, and it is better me than anyone else."

She opened her mouth to protest. *Fat load of good that's done you so far, Emerson—*

"Sir!" A hammering at the door. "Sir! The General wishes to speak with you, urgently, about Livingston-Monroe! We have new intelligence from the—"

Duchamp spread his hands wordlessly, as if to say, *you see, we have been found.* "I am otherwise occupied," he called back. "Tell the General I will meet him in the war room in one hour."

A confused silence. Then: "Sir!" His footsteps retreated down the hall.

"So," Claire asked, not without some irony, "what are you going to do with that hour?"

"I am doing a thing that has just tonight occurred to me," Duchamp said, and he flung himself back down in his chair.

Idly, he picked up a wire-and-bead sculpture from his desk, expanding it between his hands as though he was knitting himself his own personal galaxy.

"What's that?"

The Governor stared at her with the avidity of a man tracking his north star. "I am going to make the General wait," he said, and collapsed the sculpture between his palms.

They played chess, running the clock down until the page returned.

Claire hadn't known the rules. Even if she had, who would she have played with? The Governor taught her with a patience she hadn't expected, and after she'd learned the names of the pieces, he ran her through a game at half speed, explaining each of his moves before he made it.

The strategy he favored was a slow one, defensive, plucking her pawns from a distance and then retreating. His queen, the most powerful piece by his reckoning, stayed always next to his king.

"You're not using her at all," Claire said, taking a rook of his that strayed too close to her bishop. "What good is she doing back there?"

With a nimble finger, he traced a path above their pieces—diagonal one way, diagonal the other. "Look," he said. "In three moves, I will win. The queen comes out at the end, and the end only. I reserve her for that moment."

"You only win if I make the moves you predict I will," she said, offended. "Isn't there a chance I could surprise you? And then what? Your queen has gone to waste."

Duchamp spared her a dry smile. "It's very difficult," he said, "to work against he who taught you how to play," and in three moves he had her in checkmate.

The page came as they were putting away the pieces.

"You will come," Duchamp said. It wasn't a question.

Claire shut the box, and he took it from her and tucked it under his arm. She said, "I'm about as much use beside you in a strategy meeting as I am next to you on a dais."

"Precisely," he said. "You're of tremendous use," and since Claire didn't want to be dragged through the halls again like a small, uncooperative dog, she lifted her chin and followed.

In the crowded war room, the General swept an arm from under his ermine half cape and said, "I see you brought your plaything."

"Miss Emerson," Duchamp said, "stays."

He put the chess box under his chair. Then he waved a hand. Another chair was pushed in beside him for Claire. After the Governor sat, the other men did as well, and a pair of footmen placed an enormous sandbox in the center of the table. It had a line of white stones that ran down its middle, like a river. After a moment, Claire saw it for what it was: the border between St. Cloud and Livingston-Monroe.

One of the advisers looked unhappily at Claire. "We will

be discussing sensitive information."

"The girl stays. If I must say it again, this meeting will become much smaller." Duchamp leaned to flick the little flag that stood in for Monticello-by-the-Lake. "Report."

The adviser looked at the General. The General looked at him. This was, Claire surmised, not the way these meetings usually ran.

"You will meet with Abigail Monroe tomorrow," a weedy-looking man said, consulting his notes. "You had asked to combine that meeting with the delegates from the society of women, being Madame Isabelle Bogelot, treasurer of the International Council of Women; Mrs. Fredriksen, of Denmark; Contessa de Dubernatis, of Italy; Signorita Esmeralda Cervantes, of Spain; and Dr. Marie Popelin, of Belgium—"

"A lady doctor," the General huffed.

Claire hardly heard him. She knew those names. Delegates from the D.A.C. meeting.

"I assume now," the man said, "given the Livmonian threat, that you will choose to meet with Lady and Mr. Monroe separately. You have rather more pressing things to discuss than how the women's society arranges their parasols."

Another cleared his throat. "If I can draw your attention to the sandbox. You'll see that the Livmonian soldiers have made significant gains in the Gateway region," he said, indicating with a hand. "It's good farmland. They've taken it peacefully, ten miles' worth, and claimed it as their own. Then they stopped, fortified, and began checking papers. American-born citizens only, and with proof. They're calling it the new border."

"And what of your ships, Vice Admiral?" Duchamp asked him coolly. "Did they not stop them at the river?"

The man paused. "I can't account for it, sir. Our flagship's here for the Fair, as you well know. But the Livmonians should have been challenged many times over. We're investigating what's happened with the Gateway fleet, but by all accounts, they've disappeared."

It went on that way. Troops missing, troops surrendered in the night, gains up and down the sandbox so insignificant that they could be nothing less than a test of St. Cloud's border. They hadn't managed to take much of the northernmost border—"Wardenclyffe Tower," the Vice Admiral had said, and Duchamp had nodded as though that were explanation enough. The south, though? The bridges? He continued asking them questions, each in turn, the Vice Admiral and the Exchequer and the Minister of Commerce, and in turn they gave voice to the rumors that had reached even Claire Emerson living in her little house in Lordview.

They were losing their land. They were losing their men.

"You've sent word to King Washington," Duchamp asked, for what must have been the third time, and at last Claire could hear the panic rising in him.

"Yes," the Exchequer said miserably, the man who hadn't wanted Claire there at all. "We have once again sent word. You will be notified the moment he responds."

St. Cloud was like—*like a dinner,* Claire thought, laid out at a royal table. The bone china, the silver, the tablecloth embroidered with stitches so tiny you couldn't see them. And laid out on it was the most beautiful, the most *correct* feast. Oxtail soup or consommé. A side of beef, or filets of salmon, pink and ridged, with a little pitcher of hollandaise at each setting. The world's most perfect pecan pie to finish.

And then you sat down, and you lifted your fork, and you saw that every last bit of it was rotten.

One of these men is a spy, or all of them.

Duchamp studied the sandbox as though there was an answer there, touching the line of the Jeffersonian River like he might shift it by desire alone, wipe all of Livingston-Monroe's progress away.

The General kept his face blank.

"Well?" Duchamp said. "Will you make your report?"

"We need men," the General said. "Are you finally ready to consider the workhouses?"

"No," Duchamp said immediately. "No, I am not."

The Vice Admiral looked around the table. "Sir," he said, "though I'm also uncomfortable with the notion, you must admit a certain amount of sense. John here can tell you that it is our soundest financial option"—the Exchequer nodded grimly—"after the . . . lack of tax funds in our coffers."

Empty coffers? Claire thought of the taxes leveed on the Perpetua Club, on the neighboring dance halls and restaurants, by the General and his enforcers. *Where is that money going? Does Duchamp even know about it?* She opened her mouth, then thought better of it. *How could he not know?*

"The Fair was, and continues to be, a drain on our resources," the General was saying. "A return on that investment will *only* come from a proper show of might. Which we had thought we'd have with the Barrage." He waved a hand at Claire. "You saw the results there. God help us. No new weapon, and a little girl sitting in on our meetings."

Before Duchamp could speak, the General barreled on. "We need to pay our army. Barring that, we need soldiers we *don't* have to pay. Take the men on the chain gang and give them muskets instead of hammers—"

"No," Duchamp said again. "No one deserves to risk their life without compensation. Our nation was *founded* on that principle."

"Then be prepared to lose your territory, boy."

Duchamp stiffened. "I've been working on my own weapons," he said, but like a boy caught out at shirking his duties.

"No matter." The General stood. "You come in and demand answers, like you give a damn. Or like you want to make a show of it. This girl worth all that talk?" He looked at Claire, quiet in her golden dress, and his lip curled. "No. Her brute of a father, he's the only one who can win you that land back. Don't talk to us. Get *him* to fix up that gun."

"I'll take it under advisement," Duchamp said, his eyes glittering as he got to his feet. "As I said, we're working on our own weapons."

"*We*," the General said, his eyes flicking over again to Claire. "Well, then, boy, you don't need us," and he took himself out. The other men stood, and only the Vice Admiral had the decency to nod to his Governor as they scurried out the door.

In their wake, Duchamp was staring down at the sandbox, his hands folded tightly before him. Then he reached under the table and took out the box of chess pieces and emptied it, a black and ivory rain, over the border of St. Cloud and Livingston-Monroe. He lined up pawns along the river—soldiers, she imagined, though he chose the colors indiscriminately—and spaced them a finger's length apart.

Then he pulled three black pieces back. The rook went north, where the Vice Admiral had pointed out the place called Wardenclyffe Tower. The bishop went to Monticello, edged up against the blue-rock border of the lake.

Claire pulled in her chair to take a better look, and Duchamp startled. As though he'd forgotten her there beside him.

"I'm sorry," she said. "Can I help?"

"You can go," the Governor said softly, but there was steel in it, and she nodded to him and left him there, in the long spill of lamplight at an empty table, turning the queen over and over in his fingers.

ELEVEN

In the morning, after a breakfast Claire had been too anxious to eat, she was led to a laboratory across the hall from Tesla's.

Inside it was her father's gun.

"Please ring if you need any materials," the butler said.

"Materials?" *For what?*

"Er . . . pens. Paper. For calculations and the like. Gun oil?" He glanced at her. She knew she looked nothing like the scientists he must usually serve. Even Beatrix had a jaunty, piratical air, for all that she was a girl.

Claire was just a defeated child in a dress. "Gun oil," she said.

The butler nodded. "Anything like that," he said, and dismissed himself when Claire didn't do it for him.

She stared it down for a long while, the monstrous Emerson gun. Someone—or, more likely, many, many someones— had hauled it from the pavilion where it had spent so many months half built.

Its mouth was a long telescope, its body a box on wheels. Her father had labored over it for years, and now she was meant to fix it in the span of a morning. And how on earth was she to test it? Was she to fire a half-ton shell into the walls of the mansion?

The door clicked open behind her. "Hello, little cat," Tesla said. "So this, then, is my competition?"

"What competition?" she asked, unkindly. "I thought you only made light bulbs."

He looked at her sidelong. "Then you are very stupid," he told her, and reached up to the gun's muzzle. Tesla stood above six feet, but his hand hardly grazed the barrel.

"I'm sorry," she said. "I've been given an impossible task. Rumpelstiltskin's locked me in here, and all this needs to be turned to gold."

"Ha. Well, what do you know of this dross, then?"

She sighed, rubbing the back of her neck. "Only what I've overheard. I haven't been trusted with the details. It's called a gun, but it isn't—it's a cannon, really. A howitzer, if you're German. It costs more than a thousand dollars to fire a single shot. It could tear a hole in the wall of the universe, if you listen to my father, and if you keep listening, he'll tell you that the King is going to buy about a million of these from him and make the two of us rich. At least, that's what the General's been making him think."

"And what do you think?" Tesla asked, crossing his arms.

"I'm not often asked that."

"Well and so."

"I think—" Claire squinted up at it. "I think it took four wagons and sixteen horses, or maybe a magician's railroad car, to bring this thing here. I think it's oversized, finicky, and too expensive for what it is. I think it's odd to order these up for a country that's supposedly peaceable. What would St. Cloud do with a million of these, other than line them up at the border between us and someone—"

She cut herself off. What kind of awful spy was she, if she spilled everything the first time someone flattered her for her opinion?

But Tesla's mouth was grim. "Someone we are not yet at war with?"

She nodded tightly.

"Ah," he said. "So you, then, are in . . . a pickle? This is the expression? For the General speaks often of this gun. It was meant to be a deterrent to those who would harm St. Cloud. But to be a deterrent, it must be famous. A showpiece, yes?"

"But they saw it, at the Fair," Claire said, following his logic. "And it *did* fire. Eventually."

"So perhaps we put the lie about. You are the only one who may make it fire. You whisper to it in its own language." Tesla stroked his chin. "It will do, for now."

"It means the Governor has reason to keep me here," she

said, "if I'm so talented." *Which is the last thing I need.*

He circled the cannon, studying it, his shoes clicking on the floorboards. Finally he said, "It is a behemoth, and unnecessarily so. Nothing elegant here."

"No," she said, tired now. "My father is not an elegant man."

Tesla gave her an unreadable look. "Perhaps you would do well to have the Governor keep you, as you say."

From one man's hands to another's. Marriage, without its protections. Claire set her jaw. "And what shall I do for the Governor? What use am I if I can't fix this gun? Without it, he doesn't have the—the mighty weapon he thinks he needs."

Tesla smiled thinly. "Anything can be a weapon, Miss Emerson," he said.

Back in her room, Claire spent an anxious, empty few hours waiting again to be summoned. *Like a dog,* she thought. She kicked off her shoes and wrapped herself in an afghan on the bed, stewing. *What next? More chess? More theatrics in front of the court?*

It could be worse, she found herself thinking. You could be married to a stranger by now.

When the knock came, she startled.

"Miss," said the boy at the door. Maybe eight years old, with a missing front tooth. He wasn't wearing the Governor's livery. "Do you have a message for me?"

He's from the D.A.C., she realized. "No," she said, then "Sorry," even though it felt ridiculous to apologize to a child in her enemy's employ.

He chewed his lip. "I'm meant to tell you I know you was in there with that inventor man, with the big weapon. And in with the big boss last night, they said."

"It doesn't work," she snapped, feeling more ridiculous still. "That's the message. The gun doesn't work, and the Governor beat me in chess. Go away."

"Miss," he said, eyes lowered, and Claire swore and found a nickel that she could tuck into his pocket.

She hesitated, then rumpled his hair with a bare hand. "Now get," she said. "Those aren't nice people you're working for. You shouldn't want to help them." *He's a man, even if he's a little one; maybe I can . . . bless him. What meager power I'm allowed—*

"Miss Emerson." Sergeant Miller's voice carried down the hall. "Who is this child?" he asked, striding toward her.

The boy ducked under his outstretched arm and tore off down the hall, the unglued sole of one shoe slapping the carpet as he ran.

"Wanted money. Thought someone was supposed to be guarding this place." Claire was aware she sounded surly. It felt good.

Still, her attitude meant nothing to Miller. "Governor Duchamp requests your presence," he said. His eyes drifted down her rumpled dress, settling on her bare feet sticking out under its hem.

"When?"

He was still looking at her toes. "One hour," he said. "Perhaps that will give you time to change—"

Claire shut the door. It was satisfying. It also meant she knew nothing of what Duchamp wanted. She'd hardly stepped away when Miller rapped again.

"For pity's sake," she snarled, but when she wrenched it open, she saw Margarete instead. "Oh."

"Oh," Margarete echoed, and pushed into the room, a bucket in her hands.

Claire swallowed. "Margarete?"

Over her cotton frock, she was wearing a starched white pinafore, and her hair was pulled back severely and pinned into a mob cap. A little frill bounced when she walked.

"Margarete," Claire said carefully. "Why are you dressed like a maid?"

"Because Duchamp's housekeeper didn't believe you when you said you didn't have one." Margarete poured water into the ewer, then balanced the empty bucket against her hip. "She sent an errand boy to Lordview. He found me."

"Why—"

"I'm to tell you there is a shower bath for your usage, if you would like. They're all a-titter belowstairs—you don't want bath attendants?"

"I, ah—"

"I never thought you to be so modest, Claire."

Surely she imagined the twitch at the corner of Margarete's mouth? "Please tell me they didn't force you to come," Claire said.

"They're paying me," the girl said. "Your father never paid me. As you know."

"And he just let you come?"

Margarete shrugged, one-shouldered, and shifted the bucket to her other hip. "I'm here, aren't I?"

Her sister and not her sister. In the absence of her father, Claire could see a glimmer of a truce forming between them, but she knew the wrong word would dispel it for good.

"I can dress myself," Claire said. "You don't have to do that."

Margarete's face reddened. "Will you please just sit down at your vanity table like someone who wants me to keep my job?" She took the bucket into the hall and returned, wiping at her forehead. "The air in this room isn't moving at all," she said, crossing to the window. "I—"

She stopped. With her hands under the sash, she pushed up again, then bent to peer at the wood. "Claire," the girl asked. "Has this window always been nailed shut?"

Claire went white. It was the window she'd climbed out of two nights before.

"I see. No matter," Margarete said, straightening. "We

don't have time. That child maid is going over your gowns I brought with me. I need to take stock, make a few things over. What's in that wardrobe there, anything useful? Come on, we don't have all day!"

Before the soldier returned, Margarete had done Claire up in the way she recognized—a neat dress, a workaday hairstyle, a clean bare face to greet the world. She took care to cover every last inch of her body with fabric. The nape of her neck. Her wrists.

No one would be able to touch her. Not even Duchamp.

Claire hardly noticed. All she could do was stare into the mirror, her hands gripping the arms of her chair, wondering who had seen her with Beatrix.

Who had seen her with Beatrix, and nailed shut her escape.

When the soldier returned to rap at the door, Margarete was pinning Claire's last curl into place.

"Come," the voice said, knocking again, and with shaking hands, Claire took up her jacket from where it hung and turned to Margarete to thank her.

The girl had a peculiar look on her face—stricken, almost. Claire had only ever seen her composed, or furious.

"I should tell you," Margarete said, the words dragging out. "Your—Jeremiah has left home. I was alone in the house when they found me."

"Left?" Claire said, her stomach curdling. "Left for where? How long ago? What are you—"

"Miss Emerson," the soldier boomed from the hall, and Margarete rattled her fingers against her stomach and said nothing else.

"I want to know more," Claire said. "Tonight, you have to tell me, Margarete."

Margarete's mouth crimped at the corners as Sergeant Miller, exasperated, stalked through the door and took Claire by the arm. "Women and their toilette," he said under his breath, and Claire was too shaken to make any kind of a reply.

He fairly pulled her down the hall, down past the guest quarters and to the laboratory wing. *My father—the window—the Governor—am I wanted as an experiment?* she wondered, sick and dizzy still. *After what Duchamp said last night—*

But they were passing Tesla's door, the other doors too, and the soldier propelled her down the back stairs and up to a carriage waiting outside the livery stable.

"In you go," he said as the coachman held open the door into the plush interior.

Clinging to the shreds of her composure, Claire snarled, "Shouldn't you just tie me to the roof, then, if I'm the sort of cargo that doesn't need to know where it's off to?"

"I don't know if your simple female mind can comprehend this," Miller said, as pleasant as though he were discussing the weather, "but us? The ones at the bottom? We follow orders. I go where I'm told. *You* go where you're told. Stop acting like a martyr—you're wearing jewels."

Before Claire could respond, he picked her up by the waist and shoved her inside as though she were a tantruming child, slamming the carriage door behind her.

As she pushed herself up on her hands from where she had sprawled on the seat, she could feel the clatter and sway as Miller swung himself up next to the coachman, and before she could right herself completely, the carriage jerked into motion, hurtling off toward another unknown.

Duchamp was waiting for her by the Fair's main gate, beneath the banners crackling in the air, red and white and blue. An honor guard idled behind him.

"Miss Emerson," he said. *He looks well,* she thought. She was certain she was still a rumpled mess from her ignominious carriage ride. "I have many marvels to show you."

Was this part of his experiment? Did he have her father locked away? Would she be thrown in alongside him, the two of them locked away until they created a weapon that worked?

Get him *to fire up that gun,* the General had said, but he'd been looking at Jeremiah Emerson's daughter.

Duchamp was offering her an arm, waiting. She swallowed and slipped her hand into his elbow. *Breathe,* she thought. *You know nothing yet.*

The two of them pressed along with the crowd, his guards

thick around them, and while the occasional dusty traveler turned to gawk at Duchamp, they were the least of the attractions around them. This suited Claire just fine. To her surprise, it seemed to suit Duchamp as well. He hummed to himself as they approached the Transportation Building, Claire's hand still tucked in the crook of his arm.

"This is a great favorite of mine," he said, holding the door for her. Inside, the crowds were made small by the great hulking shapes around them. Claire blinked against the sudden cool darkness.

"Is that—a ship?" she asked, drawing nearer to its prow.

"It is," Duchamp said from beside her. He reached up to place a palm on the white-painted hull. "An ocean liner. But not a complete one—take, say, twenty steps to your left."

Frowning, Claire complied. "Oh!" she said, peering around the side. "It's a cross-section. Those are passenger quarters?"

"You know the term?"

She blinked at him. "Passenger quarters?"

One of the soldiers behind the Governor discreetly poked the other. "No," Duchamp said, pacing toward her. "Cross-section."

"I learned geometry as a girl." She disliked his scrutiny, and looking for a distraction, turned again to the cabin of the ocean liner. It was the approximate size of a hatbox, and still it had a sofa trimmed in velvet, a table and chairs, an armoire. . . . "Is there a bed? Or do you sleep on the sofa?"

"There." Duchamp pointed. He stood right behind her; she could feel his breath on the nape of her neck. "Do you see the lines in the wall? The bed folds up when it isn't in use."

"Clever."

"What else did your mother teach you?" Duchamp drew her away to the next exhibit.

The crowd was pressing in, and Claire had to raise her voice to be heard over the din. No one yet had interrupted their conversation to make a fuss over the Governor. No one had even pointed and elbowed a friend. But Claire saw that they were beginning to attract some notice—women, mostly, eyeing first Duchamp and his soldiers and then turning a more critical eye on her.

"Mathematics," she shouted over the noise, feeling deeply ridiculous. "I studied mathematics." He raised his eyebrows, and she decided to equivocate. "Oh, don't look so impressed. I learned the usual things you need to run a household. Keeping accounts. Making sure the grocer doesn't cheat you. . . ."

This talk of her mother, even though it was lies, made her think, inevitably, of her father. *Missing*—

She pulled ahead of Duchamp, dodging through the crowd.

"You shouldn't play coy," he said, jogging up behind her. "Your father already revealed you as the real genius behind his work. Surely you would need to know something of mathematics to make a machine like that work."

She nodded, jerkily. "I was taken in to see the gun this

morning. I don't—I don't think it will. Work."

"Oh, come," he said. "You fired it yourself."

"Work with any regularity," she said, aware of the crowd pressing in around them, "and be worth its cost—it's an inelegant design." Tesla's words, not hers.

His eyes dropped to her mouth. "Inelegant," he repeated.

She took a half step back. "Surely there's a better weapon." *Let me go,* she thought. *I'm no use to you.*

"But it's your father's work," he said. "For which, I'll remind you, this province has paid dearly."

"Take the money back, then." She thought of her father's creditors sneaking round to shatter his windows, the debt he'd dug himself into at the butcher. "Or don't. I think you got what you paid for: a big, massive brute of a weapon that speaks to St. Cloud's power. Doesn't mean you need to fire it."

Duchamp looked momentarily startled. "A showpiece, then."

"Why not?" Claire asked. "Isn't that what all this is, you boast—er, exhibiting your province's smarts and know-how to the world?"

"It is a boast," he admitted, and surprised her by laughing. "Come, Claire the Mathematician. I have another boast to show you."

The exhibit before them announced itself with a banner that read THE ROYAL LIMITED. Claire studied it without really seeing it. *What would he think was worse,* she wondered, *being caught out as a spy or as an incompetent scientist?*

"The King's train," Duchamp said, a note of apology in his voice. "It was a bargaining chip of my father's to win the Fair to Monticello."

She took a breath and made herself look. It was beautiful, that train, navy blue with gold gilt touches, KING AUGUSTUS WASHINGTON and THE ROYAL LIMITED written in fancy script over and over. Claire stood on tiptoes, but all she could see over the crush of the crowd was a line of lit-up stained-glass lamps in the windows of the car before her.

"That's one of the dining cars," Duchamp said into her ear. "There are five altogether, just one of its extravagances. When the King travels, his whole court comes along. If they're in northern New Columbia, they stop to pick up lobsters and a chef to prepare them. In the Floridas, grilled alligator. They eat with forks of solid gold. He has a new train now. Fancier, supposedly. I can't see how."

He had a good speaking voice, a baritone, rich and sound. "You know all the details, then," Claire said. She couldn't help thinking of her feast from the night before, St. Cloud lying rotten before them.

Maybe the whole American Kingdom's moldering away.

She could feel more than see him grimace. He was very close now, the heat of him warming her even through her jacket. "The King asked that I oversee every detail for his pet exhibits myself. If you'd like a reason for why the Fair went up so late . . ." He huffed. "Well. Grief, I suppose, is the real reason. Grief, and the King's gold forks. You can see them through the window. Shall we shove in, elbows out, to get you a glimpse?"

"No," she said, laughing. Some of the tension slipped from her. "I believe you. What else did he demand?"

As before, he pulled her away. The movement was gentle, but it was still more commanding than she would have liked. "A baseball field, just outside the walls of the Fair."

"Baseball!" Her brother's name was on the tip of her tongue. But—*you don't know this man, Claire,* she reminded herself, *and speaking of Ambrose brings you very close to telling one of your secrets.* "I love baseball," she said instead.

"You do?" he asked. "Do you play?"

She looked down at her long, heavy skirts. "Yes," she said. "Every day. Can't you tell?"

Duchamp laughed. "I don't either. To be honest, I don't quite understand sport. But the King is mad for it, baseball especially, and that team of his—he treats them almost like his own personal traveling fair. I think he loves it when he rolls into a place like New Teshas with his team in tow, and they trounce the locals."

"It's like war," she said. "Purposeless war. War for . . . well, for the bored."

They stopped at the great golden doors at the back of the Transportation Building, and Duchamp drew her aside, out of the way of the passing crowds. "Exactly," he said.

"Why are we stopping?" It was hard not to look into his eyes; something made her keep her gaze on the ground. She fidgeted, then forced herself to stand still.

"We need to wait for the guard to find us."

"They lost us?" Claire asked. She hadn't noticed. "They're not very good, then."

"No," he said. "Or they don't much care. I don't keep a personal guard. The General sent these men along as a precaution."

Claire didn't understand him, not at all—this man who was proud and yet self-effacing. With what felt like great effort, she brought her eyes up to meet his. "You speak freely of the King's failings."

He considered her. "You've studied geometry."

"And calculus," she heard herself say.

"And calculus." His gaze was warm and bright. "Of course. Shall we talk about functions and exponents?"

"We shall not," she said, looking away with difficulty. The first of Duchamp's soldiers had arrived, looking somewhat put out. "We shall go find lemon ices instead."

After his men reassembled, they all wandered back out into the sun. Claire found herself unaccountably tense. She wasn't sure if it was Duchamp's interest in her or the keen eyes of his soldiers. She ate her lemon ice quickly before it melted. Duchamp declined his. *He's too fastidious for public dessert,* she thought.

He didn't speak for some time. Finally, as they passed yet another grand pavilion, he gestured toward it. "That might be of some interest to you," he said.

"By virtue of my sex?"

He shrugged, loose and relaxed, her opposite. "You have many virtues, I imagine. But you are a woman who is interested in unwomanly things."

Functions and exponents. She should have known he'd use it against her. "What is its function? The building?"

"The Board of Lady Managers, those other women who look beyond their station—they have convened a congress that will meet soon in that building."

He spoke without judgment, as though a woman's place was determined by the universe itself, and he were simply acknowledging it. On the steps of the Women's Building, Claire watched a woman with a grim face and a clipboard soliciting signatures from the passersby. None stopped. "I haven't heard of the Board of Lady Managers," she said, choosing her words with care. "Were these the women mentioned last night? Who is their leader?"

"A woman named Rosa Morgenstern," he said. "You two don't know each other?"

Through sheer force of will, Claire kept herself from startling. "No. Why would I?"

He shrugged. Had Claire not been watching him closely,

she would have taken the question at face value. "You seem to have many interests in common. You can speak with her, if you'd like; after I declined her meeting, she requested an audience with Abigail Monroe this afternoon."

The D.A.C. has a long, long reach, she thought, *and many names*. "I would enjoy that," she lied. Morgenstern would surely find a way to ask again about her progress, and she had no progress to share.

"Then," he said, "we must get you home, so that you may prepare your thoughts for Miss Morgenstern."

Home, she thought, as the Governor ordered Sergeant Miller to bring round the carriage. She arranged a smile on her face.

Claire was growing accustomed to this, her sullen entourage. "Thank you," she said to Sergeant Miller as he lingered at the entrance to the salon. Inside she heard the rustle of skirts, someone softly playing Chopin.

Miller looked as though he had something to say to her, then thought better of it. "I'll return in an hour," he said, in a voice that made her think he'd be listening at the door.

For a moment, she flushed with anger—*How dare he mistrust me!*—before she remembered he had the right of it. But it had become uncomfortably easy to forget, this afternoon, whose side she was on.

My own, she thought, forcing herself to smile up at him.

I am on my own side.

"Miss Emerson, is it?" A voice was calling. "I hear you're to come in and meet with our guest of honor."

The salon's windows faced east, so it was cool and shadowed in the late afternoon. On the low, pillowed benches, ignoring the tea set before them, a pair of women sat with their skirts fanned out around them. Abigail Monroe and Rosa Morgenstern, two incredibly powerful women who looked for all the world like a pair of old biddies discussing their daughters' marriage prospects.

And if that wasn't enough of a surprise, the piano in the corner was being played by a man.

Though men performed on the great stages of the world, it was women who played most often in private company. It was their position to entertain, prettily, while around them and behind their backs, men rearranged the world.

"Is that a Chopin étude?" she asked.

"Yes," Abigail Monroe said. "My husband plays very well."

Claire nodded to disguise her discomfort. The Governor of Livingston-Monroe, serenading his wife on the pianoforte.

"Please, join us," Rosa said. "Have a sandwich."

Claire nodded again, then cursed herself. *Take action,* she thought. "The Governor is sorry he cannot join us," she said, sinking into a chair. "I'm sure he didn't know Governor Monroe would be in attendance."

The women were too intelligent to glance at each other,

but they may as well have. "Speaking to my husband is as good as speaking to me," Abigail said crisply. "Isn't that right, dear."

Governor Monroe didn't pause in his playing. "Yes, of course," he said.

It was like nothing she'd ever seen, the two of them. It would have been refreshing if she didn't find their politics so odious. "What was it you wished to discuss with Governor Duchamp?"

"I simply wished to continue our conversation from court," Abigail said, "in a more private venue, as he'd suggested."

"Ah," Claire said. "Your discussion of immigration."

"The immigration *problem*," Abigail said.

Rosa paled; clearly this was not where she wanted this conversation to go. "You must have gotten to know the Governor quite well these last two days, to speak for him as you did," she said, in a neat misdirection. "Why, I heard he's even given you unprecedented access to his advisers."

Abigail Monroe looked at Claire with renewed interest. Behind her, her husband flung himself into the opening chords of Beethoven's "Moonlight Sonata."

"I am nothing more than an ornament," Claire said. It felt unreasonably good to state the truth of her situation. "An amusement, at best."

"Oh," Rosa said, smiling. "Amusements are never unimportant. Especially those that fascinate a powerful man."

Claire tried hard not to look at Abigail Monroe. "Charles," she was saying over her shoulder. "You know I hate that infernal song. Could you go back to the Chopin, from before? I like his music, for all that he was a frog."

"I think he was Polish, not French, Abigail," Rosa said, "though one could understand your confusion, with that name." With her eyes, she fixed Claire to her seat. *Say nothing,* those eyes said.

"Abigail," Claire asked anyway, "have you ever been to France?"

Abigail snorted and reached for her teacup. "There is more than enough of this great kingdom to keep me entertained, young lady. What about you, Rosa? Have you gone and eaten their snails and stared at their pictures in that old château?"

"I went to the Louvre," Rosa said. "It was to be expected, studying at the Sorbonne."

Abigail stopped sugaring her tea. "The Sorbonne?"

"I made pictures, as you say." Her hands were delicate on her lap. "Paintings. Rather good ones, if I may toot my own horn. I had studied for a very long time."

"What made you give it up?" Claire asked, forgetting herself. It was easy, somehow, to imagine Rosa's determination refocused—her scraping a failed painting from a canvas, her furious hands cleaning brushes.

"Who said I gave it up?"

Claire raised her eyebrows.

"I had no openings," Rosa said evenly. "In galleries. I had my technique copied by the men in my mentor's atelier, and those mentors would not claim me in public. I was . . . I was very alone in France. For a time, though I made things to look at, I found myself invisible. And so I returned, and saw my project change."

Abigail looked at her sidelong. "What's that project?"

Rosa smiled. "Visibility," she said. "Of course I still paint in the evenings. Only for myself, you understand. Though I have heard that one or two of my works may find their way to the Palace of Fine Arts before this Fair is over."

"I would like that," Claire found herself saying.

With her painter's hands, Rosa refilled her teacup. "We will have further correspondence about that," she said, "and other matters. Through our usual channels. I expect to find it . . . useful."

"Do you," Claire said. Her sympathy only stretched so far.

"Charles," Abigail called, clearly bored. "Play something fun! These songs are going to make us weep."

Claire left the salon feeling considerably worse than when she'd arrived. *It's as though I'm being asked to lug a giant block of ice,* she thought, *in a rainstorm, only I don't know where I'm supposed to drag it to. Like—like I'm being tested, but I haven't been given the rules.*

The feeling didn't wane, not the next day or the day after

that, not even as a week slipped into a second week. She woke to Margarete drawing back the curtains; she breakfasted alone, not with the court; she sat abed until she was summoned. If she didn't sit and wait, if she instead stole down to the library or to the kitchens or, heavens forbid, to the front door, Sergeant Miller was waiting. Each time he caught her and returned her to her room. "General's orders, miss," he'd say when she pressed him. He didn't look any happier about it than she was.

Nursemaid duty, she thought, as he frog-marched her up from Tesla's laboratory. The laboratory door had been locked; it was a waste of an expedition. *I hope this is a demotion for him.*

"The sooner you're gone," he said under his breath, flinging open her door.

"You could just lock me in," she said, panting.

"I asked," he said. "The Governor said no." He shut the door in her face.

What the Governor said, what the Governor wanted: Duchamp's desires ran like invisible lines through the mansion. For three days, the household ate nothing but Brussels sprouts because Duchamp had read that they "massaged" the brain. The maids all suddenly began wearing yellow. (Margarete shrugged when Claire asked her. "I hear it makes him happy," she said, "and now I have a second dress.") On a Tuesday night, extravagantly bored, the Governor read

Jane Eyre in silence. On his dais, in front of his court. Every now and then he chuckled to himself.

Margarete brought the whispers of the court back to her. "He's never been this strange," they said, or "He was strange before, but he seemed ashamed of it then" or "Who does he think he is?" And, every now and then, "Did you ever notice how handsome he is?"

Claire noticed. She tried very hard not to. But what the Governor always desired most was Claire's company, and so, after the interminable waiting each morning, he sent a soldier to collect her.

Duchamp would be waiting, and the days followed the same pattern—every afternoon at the Fair, Claire dolled up and dangling from his arm. They spoke of little of importance; there was so much to look at, all of it new to her. It was enough to comment on what they saw. There were buildings devoted to science and industry, to the arts, and to the various nations across the globe, all of which were staffed, Duchamp said, by representatives from their own country. "We'll go to the midway some other night," he'd said, with the sort of ease one had while planning a date with his sweetheart.

She had been careful not to touch him, despite her gloved hands, and still she wondered a bit at her hesitation. *What if Father's right, somehow, and I grant men's wishes? What would a man like Duchamp want most? What is it that I'd bring out of him?*

The Fair, and then court, some nights, and some nights dinner alone in his suite. And after that, a game of a chess that, one night, Claire was flummoxed to discover that she'd won.

Until she looked up to see that Duchamp had been studying her, his gaze hot and searching.

Claire didn't know the extent of her power. *I likely never will,* she thought as Duchamp glanced quickly away, *if it exists at all, but if it does—*

If she did in fact have any influence, she needed to exert it now, in the moments before they went into the war council. Most nights she helped him pack up the chessboard, brushed his hand accidentally as they gathered the pieces. Touched his wrist to get his attention. There was no way that he didn't read it as flirtation. *Let it be flirtation, then,* she thought, angry with herself. *What good does propriety do me, anyway? The world must think I'm his mistress.*

That was the horrible thing. That he was handsome; that he was kind to her. And still he kept her as some kind of figurehead, or some kind of punishment to her father, and he gave no indication that he planned to set her free.

But have you asked to leave? the voice in her head asked. *Or are you too afraid he'll say yes?*

"Are you ready?" Duchamp asked, the board under his arm. "They'll be waiting for us."

She took a breath and went to him. Gently she pulled an invisible thread from his dark hair. "A bit of something," she said, at his look. "We want you to look presentable."

"Yes," he murmured. "Thank you."

They walked side by side to the meeting.

"I have a question." The words were out before she considered them. "The General. He says a lot of things about . . . St. Cloud not having money."

Duchamp nodded. "He does."

"But . . . what about the taxes that he—that the Crown collects from those businesses in the Levee?" Duchamp didn't respond, and Claire barreled on. "Doesn't it have a name? The vice tax? Something like that?"

"There aren't any particular taxes on businesses in the Levee," Duchamp said, looking at her.

"Are you sure?" she pressed. "Not on the dance halls, or the brothels? Not on the gambling halls? No one is collecting *specific money* from them?"

Duchamp stopped to look down at her, mouth set. "What are you implying, exactly? Is this just a fit of feminine imagination run wild?"

At that, she lifted both her eyebrows. "St. Cloud is flat broke," she said, "and from what I can tell, with my *feminine imagination,* we're also in some danger. I've sat in, what, a half dozen of these meetings, silently polishing your halo? Will you *listen* to the one significant question I've asked you this week that isn't about how to castle in chess? What use am I to you?"

"What use?" His eyes dropped again to her mouth.

Claire took a ragged breath. She hated him; it was like electricity inside her, the way she hated him. She wanted to push him against the wall and—

"I'll go without you," he snapped, and left her there, half panting, alone.

In the morning, Sergeant Miller. "You're going to the Fair," he said. He frowned. "Perhaps wash your face?"

Claire hadn't slept; fury and something else had kept her bitingly awake. "My face?" she asked sweetly. "Is there something wrong with it?"

Miller immediately realized his mistake. "I'll be back in an hour," he said, and made himself scarce.

This was the boy's appointed hour to show up, demanding news for the D.A.C., whereupon Claire would give him a penny and some misinformation and send him on his way. Today, though, he didn't show. Claire found herself missing his company. *At least he knows our talks are transactional,* she thought. She was still stung by Duchamp's dismissal the night before. *At least I'm of some use to someone, even if it's just as a girl with a sack of pennies.* Even then, she'd had to ask Tesla for the money; she told him it was for an experiment on copper. He'd believed her not one bit, but had gotten her the coins anyway.

All I am is a pack of lies, she thought, grimly dressing her hair. A pack of useless, self-serving lies, while this country marches merrily off to hell.

She rode alone to the Fair. Duchamp, as was his custom, had arrived before her, to meet with the Fair's managers; he spent his mornings going over safety and security, the week's take, the most popular attractions. *Useful things*, she thought.

"Governor Duchamp," she asked, as formally as she dared, "may I ask why we're here?"

They were walking the path that led to the Palace of Fine Arts. It had rained that morning, and the Fair was quiet, though the sky had begun to clear. The usual soldiers ambled behind them, a few steps out of earshot.

"Here? At the Fair?" He glanced down at her.

"Yes," she said, as evenly as she could. There were redcoats on the path, Livmonian men. More than usual. Claire tried not to make eye contact.

"Do you think, then, that we have seen everything there is to see?"

We are pretending, then, that that conversation didn't happen. "I don't, sir."

"Sir," he said. "That's terrible. Don't say that. Instead tell me a thing you wish to see."

"The Women's Building," she said. "I would be happy to see that."

"Ah. You do not wish to see a model of King Washington made entirely out of plums?"

She couldn't help it; she choked on a laugh. "Plums?"

"Yes. As he is a *plum genius* leader—"

"No," Claire said, lifting her skirts with her free hand. Someone had spilled a carton of spiced nuts across the path; even as they passed, a janitor was hurrying over with a push broom. "You're joking."

"I'm quite serious," he said, enjoying himself. "Though if that isn't to your liking, we can visit the dairy pavilion. I hear they have made spectacular things out of butter."

She felt her face harden. "I've been there already. The General . . . kept me there after my father's Barrage."

"Ah." Duchamp's pace quickened. "How well do you know the General? This is something we have not discussed."

She looked sharply up at him, but his eyes were guileless. *What happened in that meeting last night?*

Claire was aware, again, of their honor guard behind them, all those individuals in uniform pretending to be of one mind, devoted to their Governor. Even if the crowd wasn't paying attention to Duchamp, his soldiers certainly were—and Claire had an inkling of who they *actually* reported to.

She caught Duchamp's eye, inclined her head, hoped he'd understand. "I don't wish to speak of the General," she said, giving her best impression of a silly society girl. "I wish to know why you were just now telling jokes. I thought you an entirely serious man."

Had the penny dropped? She couldn't tell. He glanced

down at her but didn't slow his pace. "Perhaps I wanted to impress a lady," he said, in the same jocular tone.

"I see no ladies here."

"Pity," he said. "Let's go find some," and he led her up the grand staircase to the Women's Building. Here, at last, the crowd recognized their Governor, stepping aside for the man and his honor guard.

"Will you be allowed in?" Claire teased him, still in character. "It's the *Women's* Building."

"Not if I bring all fifty of these louts along with me," he told her. Then, over his shoulder: "Boys, wait on the steps. The worst that could happen to me in here is that I'm bludgeoned by someone's parasol."

Some of them grinned at each other. "Thank you, sir," said Sergeant Miller, unsmiling. "We'll send a pair along behind you. At a discreet distance."

"They think I'm taking you here to ravish you," Duchamp murmured. They had ascended to a terrace straight from the Italian Renaissance, trees and hedges designed in sweeping patterns, and he led her to a stone bench beneath an arbor.

Claire blushed as he sat. *As any silly society girl would do,* she told herself. "I believe we're safe now," she said, smoothing her skirts as she sat beside him. "You don't have to act anymore."

"Ah," Duchamp said, studying her. "Well and so, if we are not acting. Tell me. How did you know of that . . . extortion?"

She stared back, unashamed. "Is that an apology?"

"It might be," he said. "I have my Exchequer looking for the money."

"But the way he looks at the General—" She stopped. "You really don't see it?"

"See what?"

"He . . . admires him. And not in a way that can be used. It's not envy. He looks at the General like he's a god. You asked the *Exchequer?*" Claire groaned. "You'll never find the money."

Duchamp frowned. "I don't see any of that."

"I know you don't," Claire said miserably.

"But the Exchequer admitted to knowing about the extortion—"

"Everyone knows! He doesn't want to lose his position after you ask *any other person in Monticello.*"

Duchamp snorted. "I should have let you handle it, then."

"Yes," Claire said, "you should have."

To her surprise, he laughed. "Miss Emerson," he said. "All this time I thought you weren't paying attention."

"Yes, I just wander behind you with cotton stuffed between my ears."

"Where did it go, then? The money?"

"The General's buying himself a skyscraper. Just you watch." *Or a country,* she thought, but did not say.

"Tell me," Duchamp said, "what you did not before. How

well do you know the General?"

"He kept a close eye on my father as he developed the Barrage," she said after a moment. "Coming to our house all day and night, surprising me around corners. He . . . he told my father he wanted my hand in marriage."

"*Your* hand?" Duchamp's eyes narrowed.

Claire bristled at his disdain. "I may be lowborn, but it is hardly a ridiculous notion," she snapped. "My father is—was an asset to the Crown."

"I see."

The sun came striped through the arbor, drew patterns on Duchamp's suit, on his clasped hands. Claire felt hot with humiliation. *This should be the least of my worries,* she thought, *and yet—*

"It scarcely matters what he said." She avoided Duchamp's gaze. "He would have proposed in secret, then . . . ravished me, as you say, and broken off the engagement, having gotten what he wanted. A man like that does not honor his word."

"You would have accepted him, then?"

"I wouldn't have had a choice," she reminded him. "He's a powerful man, who my father—another powerful man—is indebted to. If it eases your mind, I don't think he has any such designs on me now."

Her father. Her father who had disappeared. Was he working himself to the bone to fix what was broken? Had he fled St. Cloud in fear of the General's revenge? Was he even still living?

What did she even want to be true?

"Absurd," Duchamp was saying. "You are only more attractive to the General now, having gained my ear." His eyes went far away. "Listen to me. Absurd. All of it is absurd."

"What is?" she asked, trying to catch up, but he shook his head. The air hung hot around them. Claire resisted the urge to strip off her gloves; her palms were beginning to sweat. "When did this antipathy begin, between you and the General?"

"When I returned from France," Duchamp said, kicking out his long legs like a schoolboy. "My father had sent me to Paris for an education. Monticello is often likened to Paris, you know; that was the excuse he used to justify my absence. I would learn Parisian ways, and I would return with them to the Paris of the American Kingdom."

"Did you like it there?"

"Did I—" He halted. "I went with my mother and with my younger sister. She had always been delicate, and so she was meant to take the sea air in Biarritz for her lungs. Sometimes I wonder . . . I know I could have had a fine enough education here, in St. Cloud. But Clotilde didn't want to be alone. So I studied with my tutors from the Sorbonne, and as often as we could, my mother and I joined Clotilde there."

A sister? I don't remember a sister, from the papers. Duchamp must have seen it in her face.

"Clotilde had always lived very quietly at home. She was unwell. Fragile. My family did not speak of her in public.

She was an embarrassment to them."

Gently, Claire touched his arm, then drew her hand away.

His eyes followed her fingers. "So you see, it was no hardship for them to send her to Biarritz. I still remember her wrapped up against the chill, in hat and mittens and coat, sitting on her balcony in the sanatorium to take in the air. She was ten years old, a year my junior." He shook his head. "The consumption took her quickly, when it came. It was two years before Robert Koch discovered the root of the disease. My father rushed the vaccine into production."

"No one has consumption anymore," Claire said quietly. "Hardly anyone, anyway."

Duchamp nodded. "My sister's only legacy."

"I'm so sorry," Claire said. It was inadequate.

"After Clotilde died, my mother chose to stay in France. My father had first met her abroad at an ambassador's ball. She is exquisitely Parisian. From what was said of me in the papers and on the streets, I had assumed I was Parisian as well, that I would take to it as fish to water . . . I don't know how I would feel about France if Clotilde and I had never gone. If she hadn't died there. As it stood, all I wanted in this world was to come back to my city on the lake to grieve. And here I am, still a stranger."

Claire didn't know what to do with this feeling, like someone had put a hand around her lungs. The last thing she had ever imagined was that she would have some sympathy for this man. She thought of the clothes in her bedroom, all beautifully made, all sized for a child.

In the silence, Duchamp sneaked a look at her, so fast she might have imagined it. "I stayed in Paris five years. There seemed little urgency to teach me to govern; my father was young and hale and would certainly rule for decades more. In France, knowing he was watching from afar, my interests in industry, in mathematics and scientific pursuits, were encouraged by my tutors. I thought he would be pleased when I returned. He built skyscrapers, kept inventors on retainer. He worked to modernize his city. He and the General."

"So when your father died, you came home."

"Quite suddenly. Everything was upended. A shambles, as they say . . . the General, who had always been my father's right-hand man, was working to consolidate his power. He was looking to expand our borders. My father had spent years trying to thwart his schemes, but whenever he gave in to the General, he found they had the city's approval. He . . . he changed, after a time. My father was a popular leader. He would do nearly anything to remain a popular leader."

Unbidden, Claire thought of the headlines hawked on the city's street corners. DUCHAMP FIDDLES WHILE CITY BURNS! DUCHAMP'S FOLLY: FAIR FIVE YEARS LATE! ST. CLOUD ASKS: WHERE'S MY FIVE MILLION DOLLARS? "Not that popular," she said. "Your father bit off more than he could chew, trying to keep up with the times.

He put together an impossible bid to host the Fair, with his citizens' money, and then couldn't get his act together. And you know as well as I that he drove our economy into the ground."

"Everything crashed in the eighties," Duchamp said, rubbing his face. "The General pushed for this Fair, and my father saw opportunity there. In that, and in his other programs, he hoped to bring our city into a new age, one of automation, of progress. That he had to do so kicking and screaming speaks ill of our citizenry, not its leaders."

Claire was aghast. "People lost their jobs to machines," she said, "to your father's precious toys. He decided to hold a *Fair* while Livingston-Monroe eats at our borders! And you're just following in his idiot footsteps—"

Duchamp was watching her, brows knitted, as though he was bent over a mathematical proof. "You feel as though you can speak to me this way. With so little respect."

"Yes," Claire said mutinously. How could she have gone so quickly from aching for this man's losses to wanting to drown him in a bucket? Her captor. The man who kept her as an experiment. She was too hot to think; she tugged off a glove, then the other, and then in a fury put the gloves back on. "I suppose I do."

"Perhaps I have encouraged too much familiarity." He got to his feet. "I refuse to believe that the fruits of human genius, our railroads and telephones and cameras, our great industrial machine, will bring our race to ruin."

"Then you are ignoring the evidence of your eyes. Of your borders. What a poor scientist you are." It was like spitting into the wind, arguing with this man.

Duchamp, finally, was outraged. "You would tar your own father with that brush."

My father, dead in a run-off ditch, dead like my mother, carried out the front door—

"My God," Claire said, her voice spiraling up as the terror swept over her. "My *father*? You don't know anything about me, do you? Why did you even bring me with you today? Why do you bring me with you at all?"

He stared at her; his eyes dropped to her mouth, then just as quickly to the ground. Claire could only stare at him. She willed her heartbeat to slow, for her to focus on what her eyes could see.

He was a strange cosmopolitan figure against the green of the garden, even as manicured as it was. His morning jacket, cut close to his slender body, was a sober black, the white points of his starched color rising above it, and unlike the middle-class men Claire knew, who wore black bow ties most every day, Duchamp's was stark white, as was the style for America's aristocracy. There was a song about it. *How did it go?* she wondered. *Something like "King Washington's white-tied neck . . ."*

Despite the heat and his wool suit, Duchamp looked

pristine, his pale skin untouched by sweat. He was slender, long necked, every bit of him made for the library rather than the battlefield. It was tempting to think one knew all kinds of things, looking at him, especially knowing what she did about his bookishness. Claire had to fight against the urge to extrapolate.

But she had dressed herself in a tweed ready-made suit that Margarete had brought her from home, the sort that working girls wore, complete with a wide-brimmed hat worn sideways over her teased hair. She looked every inch the bicycle-riding, loud-laughing agitator, the kind of girl Beatrix was. The kind of girl Claire wasn't. She had wanted to borrow that armor for today.

She could not be susceptible to what this man wanted—to being his experiment, or his sounding board, or his favorite ornament. She would not give in. She needed him to trust her, and she needed to use that trust against him so that she could escape.

She had to remember that.

She had to try.

"I brought you," Duchamp said, dragging his eyes back up to her face, "because Nikola Tesla's laboratory went down in flames yesterday, and I pledged him I would examine it today so that he could continue with his work."

Claire raised her eyebrows, waited.

"I also brought you so that"—he looked pained—"the

crowds might see you on my arm. As you well know."

"Ah," Claire said. "And how have you been enjoying that?"

"Next time, I'll bring a rabid bear," he snapped. "I might enjoy it more."

Claire barked out a laugh, then began to laugh in earnest, and after a moment, Duchamp joined in, wiping his brow. The heat had finally gotten to him.

"Well, *I've* been enjoying it immensely," she said.

And then she realized that she meant it.

Armor, she thought. She needed better armor.

TWELVE

Relenting, Duchamp offered her an elbow. "Come. Let's tour the Women's Building. I hear there is a pavilion dedicated to your sex's accomplishments. One wonders if it is the size of a rabbit hutch."

As they strolled through the Women's Building, past the model kindergarten, the mock hospital, the rotunda devoted to women's reform work, Claire listened with half an ear to Duchamp's explanation of the building's design and wondered. *Every exhibit here pictures the woman as helper,* she thought. *How we help men, children, the sick and dying—but if we say one thing about helping ourselves, we're branded as revolutionaries.* Duchamp pointed to the grand hall that would house the First Women's Congress in a week's time.

"And what will they discuss?" Claire asked as Duchamp led her back down the grand staircase to the lobby. "How to change bedpans, perhaps, or how best to entertain a child on a rainy day?"

"You mock your sex's accomplishments." He paused on the landing as fairgoers streamed past them with little regard for Duchamp's status. "Many see this Fair as a show of might, or patriotic folly. Or as a mere entertainment, something to take their minds away from the drudgery of their lives. No. I intend it to be educational. You travel for miles and miles. You pay a pittance at the gate. You loft your parasol, you drink your lemonade. You walk through magnificent buildings, laid out according to law and reason. And in these places you learn about the world."

"But *you* determine what they learn about the world," Claire said, surprised at the desperation in her voice. *Why is it so important to me that he understand this?*

"Of course," Duchamp said. "I'm their Governor."

Claire let go of his arm. "Will you show me the rest of the Fair?"

Frowning, Duchamp took a step back, nearly trampling the two men behind him. He didn't seem to notice. "If I have offended you, I'm sorry."

She nodded. "I'd like to see the damage to Mr. Tesla's pavilion. On the way there, perhaps you can tell me more of what the women's congress will be discussing."

It was clear that the Governor could tell she was upset, and that he didn't know what to do about it. "We'll stroll together," he said, as though to himself. "We don't need to give anyone a show."

The congress would discuss many things, he told her, from the ethics of dress to the role of the woman banker, the woman scientist—all those things of special interest to women. "The goal is to imagine a new world, I think. The endeavor is led by the Daughters of the American Crown. You might be familiar with the work they do in the Home for the Friendless, or in the poorer districts of the city. They are forward-thinking women. People. Forward-thinking people."

"Yes," she said. "I'm familiar with the D.A.C."

"I thought you might be," he said. "As I said earlier."

It hadn't come up, in all the time they'd spent together— her loyalties, that meeting with Abigail Monroe and Rosa Morgenstern. He'd never asked.

There was, now, something sorrowful in his eyes.

My God, she thought. *Does he know? Does he just not want to admit it to himself?*

But Claire said nothing. After a moment, Duchamp looked away.

They were skirting the man-made lagoon at the front of the Women's Building, filled with little pleasure boats and children splashing about in bare feet. At a safe distance trailed their honor guard. The sun hung hot in the sky, the day now as cloudless and bright as a sheet pulled across a bed, and underneath all that white the city glowed in answer. She could see the light bulbs that lined the railings and the arches and the eaves of the grand buildings, all evidence of Tesla's spectacular power. At night, this miniature city would glow as though it were itself dreaming.

With all the wonder around her, Claire was surprised to see what little crowd there was thinning out so close to midday. But when she asked Duchamp the reason, he just grinned.

"The continuous clambake begins today," he said. "I imagine they're getting lunch before their afternoon explorations."

She snorted. *Perhaps what he wants most is to torment me,* she thought as they crossed the bridge to Tesla's pavilion. It wasn't an unfounded guess.

"Mr. Tesla!" Duchamp called out cheerfully, as the man himself approached from the facing path, hat in hand. He had a leather bag slung over his shoulder that bulged with unknown objects. "I'd thought you stayed at the mansion."

"Governor." Tesla executed a neat bow. "My apologies if I have caused confusion. My anxieties got the best of me, and I could not keep away. I must see the extent of the damage for myself. Hello, little cat," he said, and bowed again.

"Hello, Mr. Tesla," Claire said. "How are you feeling, after the fire?"

He shuddered. "It follows me, this fire."

Duchamp glanced between the two of them. "You've met?"

"Claire is an able pair of hands. I see they are clean, yes?" She held her palms up for inspection. "Excellent. Now we shall soot them up together. Governor, if you do not mind, I would appreciate several more intelligent eyes on this problem. Six are better than two, yes?"

There was a pair of guards keeping out the public, a barricade placed before the door. Beyond those, past the lobby, Tesla's pavilion was set up in the manner of a magician's stage, with drawn curtains and a curved proscenium and a wealth of wooden chairs in rows.

At least, that was what the shapes suggested, underneath all the soot and smoke. The place was a shambles, the walls licked black, the curtains in tatters. A small army of boys with buckets and rags worked furiously, scrubbing at the floors.

At a word from Tesla, a pair of them ran up to the stage and ducked under the curtains, and after a moment, she heard the great creaking as the curtains began to open. Beside her, Duchamp crossed his arms.

"What's behind the curtains?" she asked, as it tugged slowly out, and out.

What was there was a generator. A great beast of a generator, its wheels and gears gleaming. It must have weighed several tons, and Claire turned to Duchamp with a question on her lips.

Tesla shook his head. "Thank God."

"Tesla's polyphase alternating current 500 generator," Duchamp said, as though in prayer. "The engine that lights the Fair."

Tesla watched him with a casual pride that seemed to Claire both familiar and unfamiliar. "That's correct."

"I wish—" Duchamp stopped. "I wish there was world enough, and time, for me to learn from you while I still have you here. Instead of these distractions. If I could only look over your shoulder for an hour or two each day . . ."

Tesla gripped his shoulder. "My doors are open for you," he said, "always," and Duchamp smiled at the ground. There was a real affection between the two men, the inventor and his unlikely protégé.

"Today, we will look over the generator together, yes?" Tesla asked. "Perhaps you can lend me your little cat to help? Many hands, light work."

Duchamp pulled his watch from his waistcoat. "I wish we could," he said. "It is growing late—"

"Have one of your many fine men there bring us sandwiches," Tesla said, nodding to the soldiers behind them. "You hardly have need of an army. And Remy, dear boy, I would always like your help. I only know you have many demands on your time."

It was clear that Duchamp wanted nothing more than to escape those demands. "I was meant to meet with Abigail Monroe, but surely I can ask the General to do so," he said.

I don't think putting those two in a room together is a good idea, Claire thought, but said nothing.

"Yes," the Governor said. "We will assist however we can."

The two of them looked the generator over as, around them, the boys continued to clean with their cloths and push brooms. Claire leaned against a wooden chair in the audience. She felt a wave of déjà vu pass over her. Here she was, in a dark cool pavilion, waiting for someone's orders while men did the real work.

Sighing, she turned to the honor guard that had followed them inside, and was surprised to see that only two remained, standing at ease at the end of the aisle.

One was Sergeant Miller. The other she didn't recognize, but that was the thing about soldiers—the uniforms rendered them faceless. "Can I ask one of you to find the Governor and his scientist a picnic basket? Bring enough for three."

Miller muttered something to himself.

"I'm sorry?" Claire asked, her temper fraying. "Did I interrupt you in the middle of an important matter?"

They glanced at each other. Miller set his jaw. "Right away, miss," he said, and smartly exited. To her surprise, the other soldier followed.

Now that she had found a way to feed the men, she was made entirely superfluous. She tried picking up a cloth to assist the boys in cleaning the walls. After all, the largest of them was scarcely four feet, and so even with a ladder he couldn't begin to reach all the tall places where the plaster was stained. But after a moment, the eldest of the boys rushed over.

"Begging your pardon, ma'am," he said, clutching his

cap to his chest. "I mean miss. Ma'am. Uh, you see, us boys are paid the amount of time that it takes us, and while we 'preciate your help, we—"

"Need the money," she finished. "Yes, I understand. I apologize."

He bobbled an awkward bow.

Which was how Claire found herself in the third row of the theater for quite a long time. She was used to the quiet, with little to do, long afternoons sitting while her father worked or while Margarete cooked dinner or while Beatrix launched another glider in the air—but rarely did she feel as ornamental as she did now. And then she realized that Tesla and Duchamp had already inspected the generator and were talking about something quite different.

She stood and moved to the second row of ruined chairs, as though she was looking for a more comfortable seat, then stretched and moved up another. She could nearly hear them now. One of the boys had produced a table, and the two men hovered over it at a far corner of the stage, their heads bent together. Tesla had unrolled one of the map cases from his bulging leather bag. Duchamp, pencil in hand, made annotations, and Tesla made vehement counterpoints, gesturing with his elegant, vehement hands. Then Duchamp glanced over his shoulder at her in the front row, and the two of them dropped their voices.

What she could hear: "power," certainly, and maybe

"aiming" and "ray," though it could also have been the word "named," or less likely, "amiable." A gun? Were they the designs for the Barrage? Hardly enough to report to Rosa Morgenstern when she came for her rescheduled meeting with Duchamp. Claire was certain that Morgenstern would find a time to pull her aside to report.

Strange, she thought, watching Duchamp through the heavy haze of uselessness. *He seems different.* The Governor had been so unaffected by the heat earlier; now, in the much cooler pavilion, he was beginning to sweat. His neat suit was wrinkled, bagging at the ankles. The aristocratic lock of hair that always fell over his forehead looked different, somehow—rattier. And his voice. Had it always been so strident? Even Tesla leaned away as Duchamp spoke.

It was like watching a copper penny go shineless and old before her eyes.

Behind them, the great doors opened, then shut. A soldier—the one Claire had spoken to?—placed the picnic basket on the ground and flopped down into a seat beside it as though he were off duty. He looked angry, and ill-used.

Perhaps he was; she knew nothing of how the military worked. She shook herself awake and stood, her rumbling stomach clearing out the rest of her cobwebs. Still, the soldier's behavior was odd enough that, as Claire approached him, she could feel her scalp begin to prickle. He sat with his hands clutched in his lap, his lips moving without any sound.

She couldn't see his face beneath the shadow of his cap.

"Thank you," she said, hanging back a bit, and when the soldier didn't look up, she snatched the basket and trotted back up the aisle and onto the stage. This time, neither of the men noticed her.

"It is a ridiculous exercise," Tesla was saying, "and quite beneath you. How on earth could you hope to study this effect? No. I am happy when my cats are near. I am less happy when they are not, this is not a hypothesis—"

"It isn't *happiness*," Duchamp snarled, this man who not an hour before was desperate for Tesla's attention.

Claire inched forward. This close, it was clear she hadn't imagined the Governor's . . . disintegration. He listened impatiently, mopping his brow with a crumpled handkerchief; he looked like a molting bird, nothing like the elegant gentleman of this morning.

It was as though he read her mind.

"Look at me," Duchamp was demanding. "Have you ever seen me in such a state?"

Small sounds from back by the entrance: a man muttering to himself, wanting to be appeased.

Compulsively, Claire whirled to look back to the door. The soldier was rocking slowly back and forth, his head in his hands. It sounded as though he was crying. The boys were staring now too; a few of them edged nervously toward the stage.

"Something's wrong," she said, loud enough for the men to hear but not loud enough for her voice to carry. "Something is very wrong."

Duchamp turned, and Claire drew in a breath at the sight of him. His face was sallow, drawn, his hands shaking. "There's a problem with your lunch?" he said, mocking.

"No," she said, setting the basket on the floor. "Look—"

But before she could speak, she heard the unmistakable sound of something smashing.

The soldier raised the chair above his head again and slammed it against the floor. Wood splintered, broke. At the foot of the stage, the boys exchanged panicked glances, and a number of them climbed up and dashed past the two men into the rooms behind the stage.

"Soldier! Stop what you're doing!" Duchamp yelled, his voice breaking at its ends. There was no authority in it; he sounded petulant, childlike. The soldier ignored him; with a heave of his shoulders, he pushed one of the broken chair legs between the handles of the great doors, barring it.

Duchamp looked outraged. Behind her, Tesla hurriedly wrapped up his materials and stuffed them into his bag. Claire felt herself begin to back away into the wings. She knew better than to trifle with the anger of men.

"What is the meaning of this?" Duchamp said, clambering down from the stage. "Soldier! Where is the rest of the guard? I demand that you call them at once!"

The soldier turned and stepped forward, into the light. Claire swallowed.

Jonathan Lee, the Livingston-Monroe soldier from Perpetua's. The man who had stared her down at court.

Holding a gun pointed directly at Duchamp's chest.

"You useless child," he said. "You traitor. You *foreigner*. I have wanted to do this for so long."

His chest rose as he drew a steadying breath, and he fired.

THIRTEEN

The soldier had stumbled backward through a mess of chairs, his rifle clutched in both hands. Before Claire could speak, before she could move, Sergeant Miller shouted through the doors, "Apprehend him!" And the boys swarmed the soldier like hornets shaken from a nest.

My fault, my fault, the voice in Claire's head chanted. She moved as though in a dream, down the stairs from the stage to Duchamp's bleeding body. He was folded in on himself, a stick snapped in half.

Claire got to her knees. Took off one glove, the other, her hands shaking with the effort. Where had he been shot? There was so much blood. She touched his forehead, his cheek, white as quicklime. Then she steeled herself and, with the lightest possible pressure, ran her hands down his suit.

There. His torso, below the fine linen of his waistcoat. The shot had gone through his side, and even as her fingers searched him for damage, her eyes found the path the bullet had taken when it had passed through him. A scattering of red against the veining of the floor. The shot had embedded itself into the proscenium, leaving a splintered cavity in the baseboards.

Below her hands, Duchamp coughed, shifted.

My fault, my fault, my fault—

And the worst was that they weren't yet in the aftermath. Even as she cursed her lack of medical training, she could hear a scuffle by the auditorium doors. The shooter hadn't been apprehended yet, though it sounded like someone—several small someones—were trying their damndest to comply with Sergeant Miller's shouted orders. The boys were yelling, high-pitched and young, but underneath Claire could hear the soldier's voice, that same voice she had heard in front of Perpetua's cascading tower of champagne. "Monroe," he said, the words growing clearer now, "For Monroe," and then another gunshot, the sound of a heavy something hitting the marble floor.

A heavy someone.

"Miss Emerson," whispered Duchamp, under her fingers. "I hope I haven't upset you."

"This is immensely upsetting," she told him in the brightest voice she could muster, her fingers trembling over the buttons of her jacket. Once she finally wrested it off, she balled up the cloth and pressed it to his side, hot and wet now with blood.

His hand crept up from the floor, brushed hers.

She clasped it. "Don't move. You shouldn't move."

"Pity," he said, "I was planning on . . . jumping jacks. A marathon."

Pale and shivering, he lay minutes away from slipping into a sleep from which he wouldn't wake—and still in this moment he was as bright and sleek as a star through a telescope. Even his whispers were handsome.

Had that been true a minute ago? Had he changed since he'd taken her hand?

She shied away from the thought, but her free hand crept up again to touch his cheek. *Take strength from me, then,* she thought. *Your killer did.* Though what she said was aloud was, "You are far too obnoxious to die." Then, turning her head blindly: "Some help—"

"I'm guarding the door," Sergeant Miller called. "We don't know if he was working alone," and Claire was absurdly grateful.

There wasn't time to consider how to cover it up. Tesla had sent a boy for a stretcher, for a doctor, for the rest of the Governor's guard, and while they waited he took a turn putting pressure on Duchamp's wound so that Claire could mop the blood from her hands. Her skirts were striped red.

When the boy returned, trailed by Duchamp's soldiers in their midnight coats, Sergeant Miller dismissed those he didn't know by sight. Claire didn't know if he had the rank to give orders, but it seemed the soldiers were too shaken to argue. They took themselves away—*To report to the General,* she thought grimly, *so he can begin planning his coronation.*

There was nothing she could do about it now. Instead, she kept a hand on Duchamp's damp forehead, whispering the most ridiculous things she could think of to keep him awake. She knew too little of medicine, but she knew she should keep him awake.

The boy was telling Tesla that he'd found a physician at the medical pavilion. The doctor was packing his kit, and he'd be on his way. But the boy shook a bit in his worn shoes. "There was a reporter there too, from the *Sporting Gazette,*" he said. "In the hospital place. I—I think he heard me when I asked for a doctor?"

Tesla pressed a fistful of coins on the boy. "It is not your duty to keep this secret," he said, without conviction. His eyes darted to the doors to the lobby, as though they were under siege.

"Once, at the Perpetua Club in the Levee," Claire was whispering into Duchamp's ear, as fast as a thoughtless prayer, "my friend Beatrix took on one of your fat-cat advisers in a drinking contest and he didn't catch her tossing her whiskey shots over her shoulder until she stood up and slipped on the wet hem of her dress and fell into his arms and all he said was, 'I lose the contest but I win the war!' and not only paid her the forfeit but they waltzed for hours and he ordered the both of us a carriage home—Duchamp, keep your eyes open—"

"Stupid man." A thread of sound. He was still awake.

Above them, suddenly, the doctor in his frock coat, bag under his arm, as harried as though he'd been through the wars. The doors swung back shut, but not before Claire saw the army of flashbulbs assembled behind him. Voices calling: from the *Crown*, the *Sun*, the *Sporting Gazette*, the Yiddish and the French papers, from every last two-bit tabloid rag in the city.

"Get *back*," Miller was yelling, struggling to shut the doors against them. "By the order of the Crown!"

Duchamp strained to turn his head toward the commotion, but Claire shifted to block his view. "Governor Duchamp—"

"Remy."

She swallowed. "Remy. Your adviser was a *smart* man," she said, and when Tesla stood to whisper something in the doctor's ear, she took over putting pressure on Duchamp's wound. "He took a risk, with Beatrix. He won even in his losing. That's worth any price."

"I was . . . it was me. I was stupid." His eyes blinked open. "The pain. I don't. Do I feel it?"

"All right, miss," the doctor said, his shadow falling over the two of them. "You'd best let me take it from here."

But when Claire stood, a change swept over Remy's face, sudden as thunder. *"No,"* he said, the words bitten out of his mouth. He thrashed upward as though in a seizure.

The doctor took Claire by the shoulders and brought her back down to the ground. "Calm yourself, sir. It is imperative that you remain calm. You'll only further injure yourself."

"Your hand." Remy reached up to draw her back to him. "I need her—hand. When she lets go—I can't—"

"You heard the man," the doctor said. As she replaced her palm on Remy's forehead, Claire recognized the doctor's bluff, cheerful tone; it was her own, from just minutes ago. "He needs his angel now more than ever. Child, if you could just give me some space to examine him—excellent. Well, sir, if we're going to do this right, we'll need to get you into surgery here shortly. They're pulling up your carriage now. Feel like driving us back to your palace?"

"Not a palace," Remy said, with difficulty. He didn't take his eyes away from Claire's. "Too . . . European. She doesn't like that."

"Yes, well, 'mansion' really does have quite the democratic ring, doesn't it," said Claire as the doctor dispatched a pair of boys to lift him to the stretcher, and then to take that stretcher to the carriage. As she trotted alongside, her hand in Remy's, she tried not to stare at his contorted face, at the tears running freely down his cheeks. It was all she could do to stay present, what with the rolling heat, the shouting for their attention, the lights. All around them, the photographers' flashbulbs were firing off like a hundred exploding stars. Where was Tesla? She'd lost him in the crush.

"Call it what you want," he whispered, after they wedged his stretcher into the waiting carriage, after she slammed the door on the shouting reporters, after the doctor called for the driver to run his horses. "Call it a hovel. Better yet," he said, his eyes searching her face, "call it your home."

"Keep him talking, missy," the doctor said as he mopped his brow. "You certainly have a gift for it."

At this rate, Duchamp would be dead soon enough. Claire stared down into the beautiful, besotted eyes of her captor, the man she planned to betray. Then she pressed a kiss to his forehead and said, "Anything, Remy. I'll do anything you need."

The carriage rattled down the cobblestone walkways of the Fair, and though Claire and the physician tried to keep their patient steady, he groaned with every judder and jolt of the wheels.

It was hardly midday, plenty of time for the story to circulate, and Claire knew that the news of his assassination would be called from every street corner tomorrow. That her photograph would be beneath the headline for the second time in weeks. Beatrix would be proud that she was ingratiating herself with her target. Her father—wherever he was—would be furious that she was tending to another man.

And you, Claire? How do you feel?

But there wasn't any time for that. Already they were

rambling down Prairie Street. She could see through the glass windows of the carriage that the soldiers had barricaded the side streets to allow them to rush unimpeded to the mansion.

Even while she let Remy clutch her hand, as she murmured to him that he would be all right, a part of her was far away, in the tenement home of her childhood. Her mother, in the throes of typhus. Her mother, sweating, feverish, her arms reaching up from the bedclothes for an angel that wasn't there, while her eight-year-old daughter watched sobbing from the doorway. Jeremiah Emerson had rushed out to find a doctor. He'd found one. But he hadn't been able to pay, and when he returned, he put his fist through the wall while his daughter cowered. And the next day her mother was tied up in a sheet, her skin still blotched purple from the fever, and taken away to somewhere Claire would never be able to follow.

And here they were, speeding down blocked-off streets in a three-thousand-dollar carriage, doting doctor in tow, to save a man whose life surely couldn't be worth more than her mother's.

Her hand tightened on Remy's. Too tight. He paled, and she looked away.

"Now, don't cry," the doctor said. "I promise you he'll be right as rain."

Claire bit her lip against her tears. *Aren't we at the mansion yet?* Before she could say the words aloud, the carriage swerved, hard. A horse screamed. By instinct, Claire clutched at Remy's stretcher to steady it, but an explosion of light burst through the windows. Flashbulbs. Reporters yelling.

The carriage door swung open into the cacophony. Before Claire could get her bearings, a pair of soldiers took up Remy's stretcher, leaving her and the doctor to follow in their wake. She threw up her arm against the photographs, but the crowd of reporters was thicker here than at the Fair, more insistent. "Miss Emerson!" they yelled. "Miss Emerson!" And before she could tell them to politely go stuff themselves, she realized that she knew one of the voices.

It was her father's.

He stood at the top of the steps, in symmetry with the mansion's jewel-box facade, as though he'd been made part of the architecture. Her father had always been fond of pageantry. Did that explain why he'd dressed himself in an itinerant preacher's outfit, all black worsted cloth frayed at the edges, a beaten-up Bible tucked under his arm? Did that explain the forbidding-looking woman beside him, her lips curling up as she gazed down onto the mayhem below her?

Claire went still. The soldiers thundered past her, Remy wrapped in the stretcher between them, and only one spared a look over his shoulder for the girl they'd left behind.

Sergeant Miller.

"I am here," Jeremiah Emerson was thundering, "with the reformer Miss Anna Wilman, who has of late led me to salvation! I have given up my sinful ways, given up the work I have done for a sinful Crown, to better examine my conscience, and today, I am ready to answer the question that has been put to me by the *St. Cloud Sun*! The question that has rung in the ears of those by Monticello-by-the-Lake! The question that asks—has my daughter, Miss Emerson, fallen prey to the gravest of sins? Has she given herself over to Governor Duchamp's . . . perverse French fascinations?"

Treason. It was purest treason.

Many rumbled against the Crown, yes, but in private, in bedrooms and boardrooms, in the women's powder room at Perpetua's, and *no one* spoke this way to a reporter.

Much less to every reporter in the city.

The noise was deafening, but as always, her father was louder. The sneer on Miss Anna Wilman's face began to slip.

And every face turned toward Jeremiah Emerson's daughter.

"Yes, I tell you! My daughter has been made into the Governor's whore! I have learned that he has groomed her for this for months—that she has been seen in the city's darkest dance halls, sitting on the laps of men! That she has ridden every carousel in this city, that she is the worst kind of adventuress, leading upstanding men to their doom!"

It was fact, liberally salted with falsehood, and Claire could feel the color rising in her face. She was surprised to hear her own voice say, "Do you have a point, sir?"

Emerson took one step, then another. He glowed like Hephaestus at his forge under the punishing noontime sun. "I will make it known now that I *refuse* to continue working on a weapon for that whelp Remy Duchamp, who values himself so little that he will take in such a woman as my daughter! We all know that war is imminent, that St. Cloud, this city of vice, deserves to fall to the likes of Livingston-Monroe!"

The speech was rehearsed; it clearly did not account for "that whelp" being at death's door. "And what if the Governor dies, sir?" a reporter called, his white-bill tucked into his hat.

"Then I will take my daughter back," Emerson thundered, "if she will repent, and cleave again to her family."

A hush fell over the crowd. The crush around Claire eased; people were giving her room to speak. Before she could retort, her father flew down the steps between them and grasped her face in both his hands. "Repent, child," he said hoarsely, his breath hot on her face. "Tell me I haven't sold my only treasure to that whoremonger."

He had touched her. Touched her skin. She knew, after today, that his wild supposition of her divinity had been true. Any moment now, he would achieve whatever it was he most wished for. What agency did she even have against such a power? What move could she make that wouldn't play into his hands?

His treasure. His family—

Remy Duchamp's gleaming eyes. In this place, he had

said, you must belong to someone, and it is better me than anyone else.

Claire straightened her shoulders. She pulled her father's hands from her face gently, as though she cared dearly for this poor, misguided man. More than ever before, she was aware of the picture she presented—the pale, shivering girl in her bloodstained skirts, following a stretcher up into her home.

Claire let her lower lip quiver.

"Gentlemen," she said, choosing her words with precision, "and lady reporters. We had wanted to make this announcement on our own terms, but it seems as though that choice has been taken away.

"I refuse to respond to my father's accusations. He is unwell. Only this month, he was expelled from the Fair's grandest stage to contemplate his great failure. A man this beaten down and broken is no threat to me. I choose to pity him. I choose to ignore his ugly words. I am thrilled," she said, "to announce that I have accepted the Governor's proposal of marriage. I belong to this man no longer. I am proud to belong to Mr. Duchamp instead.

"I must go tend to the man who will be my family now, in this hour of need. I trust that my fiancé's guard will help my father find the care he needs?"

In the ensuing silence, she lifted her bloody skirts and swept up the stairs into her mansion, pausing just before the door so the photographers could get the best possible shot.

✳ ✳ ✳

"Miss Emerson is to be given everything she wants," the housekeeper said as the bevy of maids stared at her, eyes disbelieving above their cotton masks.

Behind the housekeeper, in the overstuffed chair by Remy's bed, Claire kept her face still. It was a look she'd taken without thinking from the marble that presided over the grand foyer. Not compassionate, not forbidding—just hard, gleaming perfection. A girl with her wings bent over the man she meant to save.

A girl looking to save herself.

Around them, the mansion thrummed, electric with worry and with suppressed excitement. Word was, Jeremiah Emerson was dragged away to a sanatorium by a bunch of bluecoat soldiers, but they'd let him talk to reporters before they locked him up. Word was, the moment Claire had let go of his hand, Governor Duchamp had cried out and slipped into unconsciousness. Word was, it was only through the ministrations of his mad scientist Nikola Tesla that Remy had made it through surgery at all. Tesla had insisted that Dr. Sanderson operate using the latest medical research about wound hygiene; he had sterilized his laboratory, then the doctor, and then Remy's wound itself. Anyone who entered the Governor's sickroom wore cotton gloves and cotton masks as an extra precaution.

"We do not know why it works," Tesla had said, scrubbing

his arms with carbolic acid so that he could assist the doctor if needed. "We only know that it does work. It is enough for me."

Word was, now Remy Duchamp was resting in his bed after his operation, still very much alive, and the common girl who no one had known he'd intended to marry was at his bedside. Come to think of it, though, he *had* been acting strangely, sneaking her into the mansion, parading out of the hall with her on his arm. And the poor thing *did* seem beside herself; she wouldn't leave his side, had her hand bound up in his.

No one had seen the General, except for one wag who claimed he'd been spotting riding hell for leather for the military barracks on the west side of town.

That was the gossip. But it didn't quite get at the truth of the matter.

If Claire was to get out of this alive, she only had a matter of hours—if not minutes—to consolidate her power. For all she knew, the General was just outside the door with a pistol and two dozen men.

If he was at all intelligent, he would be.

Claire smiled at the maids with an exhaustion she didn't have to fabricate. She kept Remy's hand clasped in hers; he was still unconscious underneath the pile of blankets, and the maids all assiduously avoided looking at him. "Tell me again your names?"

They glanced at each other. "Ellen, miss," the first said, then Sarah, Bess, and of course, Margarete. The latter narrowed her eyes at her over her cotton mask, but the rest seemed pleased to be asked.

"Ellen, will you fetch me a bowl of ice and some washcloths? I aim to make cold compresses in case he starts another fever, and for now I can give him water from the cloth if he's thirsty. Bess, I doubt he'll be up for broth anytime soon, but can you have the cook begin gathering chicken bones for a pot? I'll want it as soon as he's ready. Sarah, I'll need extra blankets and pillows, and sterilized bandages too—I don't want to keep disturbing Mr. Tesla, but he'll know the proper method to . . . purify them? Is that the word? Dear me, I'm in over my head!" Claire waved a hand airily. She couldn't quite tell through the mask, but she thought that Sarah smiled at that. "And Margarete," she said, in the same tone, "will you fetch Sergeant Miller? I'd like to set a guard on the door. Lord knows if there are any more fanatics out there looking to hurt our Governor."

It was intentional, slipping in the request for arms at the end of an otherwise feminine list. "Yes, miss," the girls chorused, including Margarete, and they filed out in a line.

Claire sagged against her armchair. "Mrs. Firth," she said to the housekeeper. "I confess I know nothing about running a house of this size, and I wouldn't presume to give you any orders."

The housekeeper inclined her head. "There'll be time enough for that, I reckon." Her eyes strayed to Remy in the bed, ash-white and still. "Poor thing. I've known him since he was in short pants. He's had a terrible time of it."

Claire bit back an unbidden swell of guilt. She certainly wasn't solving any of Remy's problems.

Mrs. Firth came over to kneel by her chair. "It'll be all right, dearie. You're his inspiration. That's what he keeps saying." She tucked a lock of Claire's hair behind her ear. "All this for him, and nothing for yourself. I'll send a girl with sandwiches and a change of clothes."

"Thank you," Claire said, with real gratitude. "Thank you."

"Of course." Mrs. Firth stood. "You'll want to have all your freshness and energy for when he wakes. For now, think of happier times, so you can have a smile ready! Tell me, how did he propose?"

She felt all at once the heat of Remy's sickroom, the curtains drawn against the glare, the smell of blood and carbolic acid and sick, the dampness of her skirts. Below her, Remy half-whispered something in his sleep. Claire fought back the urge to retch.

"In the Women's Building," she said, swallowing. "He got down on one knee. We'll be wed in the spring."

FOURTEEN

Sergeant Miller stood before her at smart attention. Margarete slipped in behind him, in the invisible way of a well-trained maid, and perched on the window seat. Her cotton mask hid her face.

"Miss Emerson," Miller said, assessing her. "You sent for me."

"I did," she allowed, her hand still in Remy's. By now, her fingers had gone numb.

She had thought this through, but she ran quickly through her options again.

She could ball up the words he'd spoken to her—her "simple female mind" was the most tempting—and throw them back in his face. Now that she had power, she could treat him as he'd treated her, like a disposable object. It was, most likely, what he deserved. A more innocent girl might think that a man would quail under such aggression. Might respect her authority.

But she hadn't grown up under her father's thumb without learning a few lessons about how to deal with volatile men.

You had to coax them, show them you weren't a threat. You had to smile and tell them what they wanted to hear. Such men would do as they wanted to air their all-important feelings—they could break mirrors, for example, or put holes in the wall; they could pace and wail and tear at their hair while you sat there, powerless—and there would be no consequences for them, not ever.

You had to scrub yourself of any feelings of your own.

You had to become a receptacle for their rage.

And if you do that, Claire thought, seething even while she smiled prettily across the room, *and if you succeed in gaining their trust, and if you are in as desperate need of a weapon as I am now—you can direct their rage at a target of your choosing.*

Even if you hate yourself later.

"Sergeant Miller." A bead of sweat ran down her neck. "Have you seen the General since our return?"

"No, miss," he said evenly. "He has spent some hours today at the barracks where they train our new recruits. A message has reached him about Governor Duchamp's condition. He is returning as soon as he can."

It was all phrased carefully so that, if pressed, Sergeant Miller could rightly say he hadn't lied. The General had been to the barracks, but only *after* he'd heard of the attempt on Remy's life. He hadn't gone to train recruits; he'd almost certainly gone to muster those forces loyal to him so that he could storm the mansion the moment Remy died.

And Remy *would* die. If not from this gunshot, then from one of the General's allies, snuck in with a knife in the dark.

After which Claire would be at the mercy of both the General and Jeremiah Emerson.

Sergeant Miller stared at her unblinking. *So he's smart. That's not necessarily a bad thing.* She smiled again, wanly. "In the absence of the General's guidance, do you think I might speak to the captain of Governor Duchamp's guard?"

"Miss, Governor Duchamp has no private guard."

"Oh!" Her hand flew to her mouth. "I hadn't expected that."

She let the silence hang a long moment as, below her, Remy muttered and shifted in the bedclothes.

Sergeant Miller's eyes flitted to him, then back up. He had turned to seek her face, as the other soldiers carried Remy's stretcher into the mansion—did he find her attractive? Had he grown fond of his unruly charge? Or had he simply been tasked by the General to always keep her in his sights?

She needed to know every small advantage she had. With her free hand, she took a clean cloth from the nightstand and dipped it into the waiting bowl of water, then used it to bathe her neck, head tossed back, eyes slitted just wide enough to watch for his reaction.

He swallowed. Shifted his weight.

You like what you see, then.

"May I be frank with you?" she asked, leaning down to mop Remy's brow.

Sergeant Miller regained his composure. "Of course, miss."

"The idea that—that Livmonian *monster* managed to sneak into your ranks frightens me to death. Who knows how many others were aiding him?"

Behind Sergeant Miller, in the shadows, Margarete tilted her head. *So I have an audience for this chess game.*

"Forgive me," Claire said, arranging the cloth over Remy's closed eyes. "I'm sure the General has the situation in hand. Only . . . the General is so very busy, and has so very many responsibilities, especially now, with Remy"—she let herself blush—"I'm sorry, with Governor Duchamp being so ill. I only wish . . ."

"You wish what, miss?"

"I wish that we had a few handpicked soldiers we could trust. Men who could guard this door day and night while Governor Duchamp recovers, the way you protected him at the theater, after he was shot. It's such an oversight for him not to have a personal guard—I can't believe the General hasn't thought of it."

Of course he has, and decided he would instead leave Remy vulnerable. What an idiot. He could have embedded spies in Remy's retinue so easily.

"I can't say, miss," Sergeant Miller said. He hesitated. "His father—the former Governor Duchamp—had a personal guard. My father spoke of it."

"Your father served St. Cloud?"

"Yes, miss." There it was, again. A tightened jaw, a flicker of that rage she'd seen in him before. ("I go where I'm told! You go where you're told!" he'd told her, outside the carriage.)

Claire was taken aback. "He must be very proud of you."

It was the wrong thing to say. His back stiffened.

Beatrix, she thought, *channel Beatrix,* and she looked up at him through her lashes. "Enough with the past. We need men of vision, especially now. Tell me," she said, "how long would it take you to advance through the ranks?"

She'd surprised him. "I'm only one and twenty, miss," he said, after a moment. "It will be some time before I earn myself a command."

"The General is very shortsighted, then." She laughed. "Forgive me! You must know how I adore him. But sometimes I think he must be like a father, who cannot see when his children are full-grown, and capable, whose talents are so desperately needed. . . ."

Miller's dark eyes were fixed on her as though she was a burning star. "Yes, miss," he said, quietly.

Here, fishy. "Sergeant Miller," she said, "I'd like for you to take up the leadership of Governor Duchamp's guard. Choose two men to support you. *Young* men, like you, not old codgers like the General. You'll report directly to Remy Duchamp." Claire ducked her head, as though nervous. "Until then, I suppose you'll report to me."

He stood a little straighter and said nothing.

"Margarete," she called, and the maid stood to brush off her skirts. "Run and tell the Exchequer that we'll be doubling Sergeant Miller's salary, effective immediately. You live in the mansion, of course, Sergeant?"

"I—no, miss, I'm in the barracks with the other men. I can stay—"

"Nonsense. The Captain of the Guard will live across the hall from the man he guards, and we'll empty the rest of the hall of guests. Margarete, see to it that they're moved. Captain, we need you there." She leaned forward. "I need you there."

He flushed. He had still not said yes. *Am I laying it on too thick?*

"Take the suite. I think it's meant for me, as Duchamp's wife, but I'll of course be staying here until Duchamp recovers."

"Fiancée," he murmured.

"What?"

"You're his fiancée," he said. "Not his wife."

The silence hung heavy between them, motes of dust turning brightly in the air.

Finally Miller cleared his throat. "May I speak plainly? I—I see what you're doing. The Governor is . . . underprotected. On purpose."

Claire held herself very still.

"He's younger than me. Not a boy, but . . . a boy. I wouldn't want to see a lad like him die. It's not his fault that he's not prepared for—" But he bit off his words before he could say "command."

In all this game playing, it was so easy to forget. It was so easy to stare at Remy's title until the boy beneath it blurred. She fought the urge to look down at him, to adjust the cloth over his eyes, brush his hair back from his forehead.

He was nineteen years old, and he was dying.

"Five men," Miller said decisively. "Give me five men. Bonuses for them all when the Governor's back on his feet. And I will be proud to report to you."

"The General won't like it."

"No," Miller said. "He won't."

That silence again, heavy with promise.

"Take the names of Captain Miller's selections," she said to Margarete, who stood with her hand on the doorknob. "And see that his things are moved to his suite by nightfall."

"Yes, miss," Margarete said through her mask, a hard light in her eyes. She moved to show Captain Miller out.

"Oh, and Margarete?" Claire called. "Abigail Monroe, and that representative from the Board of Lady Managers—Rosa Morgenstern. Can you see to it that they are well entertained tonight? Perhaps invite a lady novelist to come and give a reading from her work. Ralstona Sacksteder, perhaps."

I need to keep them where I can see them.

Margarete nodded. "Miss, should I also invite Morgenstern's young assistant? The young woman with the infirmity—with the eye patch?"

It was a kindness on Margarete's part, and still it was clumsily done, to say such a thing in front of Miller. She could feel the weight of his gaze. Why would the Governor's fiancée care about the plans of some young half-blind bluestocking?

"Yes, of course. And any others at the court who might like to attend." Claire said it carelessly. The door swung shut.

It was only then that she let herself cry.

Beatrix. Beatrix would be there tonight, and she wouldn't be so alone.

The day passed with aching slowness. The maids delivered linens, basins of cool water, sandwiches that Claire did not eat. Every half hour, she brought a glass of water to Remy's lips to wet them, but he was not awake enough to drink. She took to soaking a cloth and squeezing out what she could into his mouth, then coaxing him to swallow. Whether he heard her, she didn't know. Every now and then he would mumble a word—once she thought she heard him say "cloth," and she brought it again to his mouth. But when he repeated it, she realized he was asking for his sister.

Clotilde.

Within hours, he was burning with fever. Tesla had warned that such a thing could happen, even with the precautions they had taken, and still she was shocked by the rapidity with which it came. Remy shivered violently, and she fought to keep him still. She was terrified he'd reopen his wound. When she called for the housekeeper, Mrs. Firth took one look and left. She returned with a pair of strong men to hold Remy's shoulders while the maids packed in cold compresses around him, blocks of ice wrapped in soft cotton.

As the maids ran in and out, Claire caught a glimpse of Captain Miller standing at attention outside the door.

Remy's brutal chills subsided, but the fever did not. The doctor came and went at intervals. Here he opened the young Governor's eyes to look for something Claire couldn't imagine; here he produced a small sharp knife and a shallow bowl, then lifted the Governor's nightshirt as calmly as though he were sitting down to peel an apple. Claire couldn't see what he was doing, could only hold Remy's hand as he cried out and thrashed against the doctor's ministrations. The smell was awful—something like the slaughterhouse, something like a larder of food gone off all at once.

"I'm draining the wound," the doctor said. She must have been staring daggers at him. "It must be done."

Mostly, though, it was quiet, as Remy whispered things into the still air that only he knew. She kept a hand on him at all times; if he was leeching strength from her, let him. *If he dies, I'm the next to go,* she thought, forcing herself to stay unsentimental.

Once, twice, three times she heard a man's voice raised at the door, asking for entry, and Captain Miller's low reply. It wasn't the General—she'd heard him speak often enough—but instead, his lackeys. The voices didn't spiral up into confrontation; they sounded more like inquiries as to Remy's health. *Vultures, circling.* When she asked Captain Miller, he confirmed her suspicions.

The General himself would come soon. But for now, the young Governor lived. At one point, a horrible thought struck her, and she called in Captain Miller to ask him to assign a guard to trail Abigail Monroe at all times. "Tell her it's for her own protection," she said. "Put one on the door to her room as well." He understood immediately.

If the General couldn't murder Remy, he might still try to make an alliance with Monroe while the Governor was unconscious. Or Monroe might make an alliance with Rosa Morgenstern. The Livmonian troops could already be lined up at the border, and at the moment of the General's go-ahead, they could come streaming over the borders of St. Cloud, their new home.

She had the sense that she was a lone girl with a sword against a hydra, some many-headed mythical beast that wanted badly to swallow the thing that she guarded. Two weeks ago, she had been prepared to run away and marry a man sight unseen.

If she survived the *next* two weeks—if they both did—she

would still marry a man she hardly knew, but she might just have a throne.

Or, at least, be the power behind it.

She was surprised at the speed at which Remy's jaw darkened with stubble. *He must shave twice a day,* she thought, running an absent finger down his neck. If she stopped to consider the intimacy with which she touched him, this man who was not her lover, she would be shocked at herself. But, as she was learning, tending someone's sickbed meant you learned their body quickly and too well.

The maids opened the curtains to let in the air; they returned to shut them to build up the fire. Claire watched the day falter and bleed into sunset. She'd been hunched over Remy's bedside for so long that when she finally sat up to roll her shoulders, she found at first she couldn't. Her back made snapping sounds as she unfurled, her hand still clasped in his.

She was tethered to him, at least for now. Another change: she'd had to accept that not only were her powers real, but that they were quickly evolving. Thinking of Tesla's laboratory, she grimaced. *I'm a human battery.*

She must have said the words aloud, because Remy's eyelashes fluttered, blinked open. "I . . ." He coughed. "Water."

Claire reached quickly for the cloth, but Remy said, "No, glass," and she supported his head while she tilted it to his lips.

"I'm not dead," he said, after he swallowed. His voice was like crumpled paper.

"No." She kept her hand on the back of his neck. "Mr. Tesla saw to that, and Sergeant Miller."

"I thought—" He coughed again, harder this time, and she gave him small sips until he recovered. "I rather thought *you* did."

"Well," she said slowly. "I couldn't leave you. You wouldn't let me, for one thing. Are you in pain now? I can send for more morphine—"

"No," he said, with force. "No. I need to be lucid for this. Tell me. What has happened?"

She felt all at once unsure. He spoke in complete sentences; his gaze was steady and clear. She'd thought he would be an invalid for days longer, and perhaps he would be still, but despite the sheen of sweat across his pale face, he rather looked like he could surge out of the bed and run.

This is the man you plan to bamboozle, she thought. *Not so helpless now.*

Claire stood, then staggered a little. Both of her legs were altogether pins and needles; she shook them out like a racehorse before crossing to open the curtains.

"How long have you been sitting here?" he asked. "It's night—is it still the same day?"

"It's just gone seven," she said. "Court will gather in an hour. How much do you remember?"

Nothing, she said to herself, *let it be nothing, and I can convince him that he was overtaken with some emotion and proposed to me in front of a cheering crowd—*

"The Women's Building. Clotilde. Calculus. You. Your dress, plaid. Tight at the waist. Tesla. The fire. The boys everywhere, with their brooms, and . . ." When she turned, she saw him studying the ceiling. His breathing was ragged, hollow. "I was conducting an experiment. Touch you, and I was a man. Shun your touch, and I was something rather less. I was . . . shot. By one of my own soldiers."

"A *Livmonian* soldier, snuck into the regiment." She said it as plainly as she could. "He seemed to be unraveling. Perhaps under the pressure of spying."

"Snuck into the regiment by who?" He struggled to rise up on his elbows, and Claire rushed to his side to settle him back down. "By who, dammit?"

"I don't know." She wrung out the damp cloth and mopped at his face. "Lie down. Lie down! You're going to reopen your wound, and I'll promise you, if I have to sit by your bed for another twelve hours while you recover from a *second* surgery, I'm going to—to play the bagpipes the entire time."

He huffed as he sunk back into the mattress. "Yes, please, tell me more about how difficult my gunshot wound is for you."

"Gladly. I understand you're a romantic, but holding your hand for half a day makes for very sweaty, unromantic palms." She wet the washcloth again.

"I see," he said, watching her now with curious eyes. "I'll

take that into consideration. Why were you holding my hand for hours?"

Claire paused, the rag dripping from her hands into the basin. "Because you were convinced you would die if I wasn't . . . if I wasn't touching you."

Remy's eyes flickered down her body, then back up to her face. "Ah," he said. "That's a ridiculous supposition."

"Especially from a man of science," she said, lightly, and brought the cloth back to his forehead. "Are you in pain?"

"Yes. Is that surprising?"

"Well, I have some terrible news," she said, and slowly, wincingly, he turned his head to face her. In the light filtering in from the courtyard, his eyes were a lambent blue. "I'd wait until you were better, but—"

"Tell me," he demanded.

Claire tried to gather her courage around her. For some reason, her eyes traveled to the dressing table that the footmen had shoved to the other side of the room. All of the ephemera that had cluttered Remy's bedside table had been dumped there unceremoniously, so she could have bandages and clean water at hand. She'd been staring at that table all day, but she hadn't really looked until now.

Books, mostly books, and some scientific journals, some scattered handkerchiefs, a thick notebook and a pen. And a photograph, just one, in a jeweled frame. A woman in furs, jewels glittering at her throat; the man beside her had the posture of a soldier. His hands rested on the shoulders of a young girl. Her hands in a white muff, her face serious and shy. And the boy beside her—lanky, freckled, with the eyes of a young prince, his hair spilling over his forehead.

He's someone's son. She was sick, finally, at what she had done; she had been waiting all day for this feeling, and it bore down on her now with a nauseous intensity. *He wants things for himself, of course he does. Hasn't all of this been in the name of securing* my *freedom, and now—*

"*Tell* me," he said, gentler this time.

She shut her eyes like the coward she was. "You and I. We're to be married."

A horrible, drawn-out pause.

"Oh," Remy said. "Is that all? I rather thought you were going to say that the General tried to have me killed."

"Well," she said, laughing—why was she laughing?—"that too."

FIFTEEN

Claire ran through it once, then again. Jeremiah Emerson on the front steps of the mansion; the reporters everywhere, even at the scene of the crime; the powder keg that was Rosa Morgenstern and Abigail Monroe and the General all under one roof; Captain Miller and the Governor's new personal guard, watching his door day and night.

"My father had his own guard," Remy said, under his breath. "I never thought it necessary."

"The General has been consolidating power for *years*. You didn't think it was necessary?"

"I had my own projects. I was confident in my rule." His strength was beginning to fail; Claire could see him struggling to stay awake. "And the General—no one wants to see a man like that in charge."

Claire wanted to scream. "We've been in a recession for years now. Our next-door neighbors are chewing at our borders like rats, and they're using the economy as an excuse to invade. The Fair that was supposed to prove our might is years late. It's a surprise that they want you off the throne?"

"I'm a Governor, not a King," he snapped.

"Pedantry is not going to save you!"

"Oh yes," he said, coughing, "please, move up our wedding, I want to be shackled to you as soon as possible."

Had he not just been about to die, I would kill him myself. "Why aren't you more upset about this?"

"About *what*, exactly? That I was nearly murdered today? That the man I've always known was out for my blood has finally followed through? Or that my father is dead, and my sister is dead, and my land is about to be overrun by *Livmonians*, and my only allies are a half-mad inventor who could level this city with a *thought* and a girl who hates me so *incredibly* much that she's decided to torment me with her presence *for the rest of my life*?"

"You were the one who brought me here!"

"And all the while, my Fair is finally on and I'm not there to see it."

Remy fell into a coughing fit, and when he finally recovered, he was flat on his back again. "Did you know," he said, up into the darkness, "that the Jefferson Park baseball diamond is serving molasses-coated popcorn? They're calling it Cracker Jack. Imagine." His voice had gone thinner, diaphanous, as though he was fading out into nothing. "Can you think of anything finer?

"When I was a boy, I loved popcorn, but my favorite thing in the world was sugared lime pies. Custard, with that small hint of sour. My mother used to order them up as a reward, especially when I did something I didn't want to do and without complaint. Like lessons in anything other than mathematics and engineering. The worst of those was a course in tactics and command. Supply lines. Military strategy. I thought it all useless. I knew that, when I one day became Governor, King Washington would never come to me for martial advice. He had other men for that. He would come to me for my scientific expertise, or he would ignore me and my small province altogether.

"My father, of course, saw things differently. He'd always imagined St. Cloud to be far grander than it was. I was to have lessons, and with the General no less. Back then, of course, he was General Montgomery. He hadn't yet been made into a god. He was a terrible tutor, impatient and inarticulate, but my father insisted I work with him. . . . I imagine he wanted the two of us to become familiar, to bond, as the General would serve as my adviser one day. He was in his late thirties, then, the General. He had risen quickly through the ranks.

"And he could see that I hated the lessons. We used to joke about it, a little, while we set up our sand table and began laying out our troop counters. 'I would rather be mucking out latrines,' I'd say, and he'd follow up with, 'I would rather be kissing frogs. I would rather be eating potato peels. I would rather be drowned in the lake.'" We were friendly enough that, on my tenth birthday, I had no qualms sending him a note saying I was canceling our lesson. I imagined he would understand.

"My father found me in the kitchen. I was eating a slice of a sugared lime pie I was to have for dessert that night; I'd begged the cook until she'd given me a piece early. 'I was told you were shirking your lesson,' he said. 'Montgomery was shamefaced. Didn't want me to know. But I dragged it out of him. You've been giving him lip for weeks. I asked him what I should do with you, how *I* could give you a lesson instead.'"

Sweat had broken out on Remy's forehead, stained his upper lip. Claire wasn't sure if it was the strain of staying awake, or of telling the story. She brought the glass of water to his lips again.

"He took me to my room and—unhooked his belt. Pushed me over my desk. Ten stripes with his belt, for my birthday, and the next day—I could hardly sit, I was in so much pain—I had my lesson again with the General. He looked me dead in the eye, and he said"—Remy affected a strangled French accent—"*I would rather be beaten by my daddy.*"

He had been fading before, but the telling of this story deflated him completely. Without thinking too much about it, Claire reached out to smooth the hair back from his face. "I'm sorry," she said. What else could she say?

"You want to know why I will marry you without complaint?" he asked. "I have no allies. I have no family."

"You have Tesla," she said, helplessly. "He cares about you."

"Perhaps," Remy said, "but then, where is he now? If he cares, it is not enough. What I have is—a girl. A girl comes, and with her I am better. Demonstrably, measurably *better*. A girl comes and holds my hand while I am—dying. A girl comes, and she is beautiful, and she wants to be my family, despite all the wolves howling at the door."

Her throat went thick. "Remy—"

"I have one question for you," he said, cutting her off. *Thank God.* What had she been about to confess? "Why hasn't the General come?"

"I don't know."

"He knows. Trust me. I need to rest," he said, as thin as a thread. "Court should be in session. Perhaps my fiancée would like to go down and remind them all that I'm not dead?"

"I don't want to leave you," she whispered.

With effort, he tilted his head to look at her with heavy-lidded eyes. "Is that what you want?"

"Yes. No." She fumbled for Remy's hand. "I want you—I want you to want to live. To *want* it, even when I go. Even when I'm not by your side. Can you promise me that?"

But he had already fallen asleep. Claire ran a thumb over his wrist, checking for his pulse, and then fled before she convinced herself to stay.

* * *

Claire walked quickly through the too-quiet halls. In the hour before court yesterday, the mansion had been electric with energy as the servants prepared the house for dinner and dancing. Tonight, the portraits on the walls stared out at no one. *No, not no one*—there, a pair of soldiers huddled together, one turning to stare as she passed. A maid she hadn't met let out a tiny squeak and retreated, her arms full of linens. *To report on my movements?*

Claire hugged herself. At least Captain Miller was still stationed outside Remy's door. He would be safe.

Unless, of course, she'd been trusting all the wrong people.

"Miss Emerson!"

She pulled up short, heart pounding.

Captain Miller hurried up beside her in a flash of midnight blue, his hand on the service pistol in his holster. "Miss Emerson," he said, agitated. "You'll let me accompany you, wherever you're going."

"I'm only going back to my room."

"All the same."

There was an edginess to his manner that was surprising in a soldier. *Is he nervous as well?* "I'm sure that's not necessary," she said. "I asked you to watch over the Governor, not me. You didn't leave him?"

"Not unattended. Sergeant Worthington's watching over him. You're at more risk at the moment." He nodded before them: a long line of doors that all led into guest quarters, a scene that Claire had never before thought held danger. "Anyone could pop out of one of those and snatch you away."

After a moment, she nodded, and they walked on together. A girl and her wolfhound. *A girl and a wolfhound,* she corrected herself. *He's not mine. I don't think I'd want him to be.*

At the door to her room—*Clotilde's room*—Captain Miller took up a guard position outside the door.

"You don't need to do that," she told him.

He fixed those clear eyes on hers. "Miss, no offense meant, but while I might have taken this position on your suggestion, I don't answer to you. I now answer only to the Governor. And he would want you safe."

On the surface, his words were kind, but there was something glimmering under them, something sharp, like a knife fallen into a lake bed. *Either my nerves are shot to hell,* she thought, *or he's still angry. At me?*

"Thank you," she said.

"Miss." He turned neatly on his heel, back straight as a piston. It was as though she was no longer there.

Claire slipped into the room and rang immediately for Margarete.

"Thank you," she said, catching the girl by her hands and drawing her inside. Margarete looked nonplussed. "Thank you. Thank you, I can't say it enough—"

"You've said it quite a bit, then," Margarete said, twisting away, but Claire caught the hint of a smile on her face. "What are you thanking me for? Is the young Governor safe?"

"For now. It wasn't as though *I* was providing any particular protection while I was there." *Except for my touch,* she thought uneasily. *If I'm not losing my mind.* "As for your first question—thank you for going along with my charade. I have few enough allies, and I hadn't thought—" She heard the echo of Remy's words in hers. "I mean, you have no reason to throw your lot in with mine."

I hate how I chase my tail when I talk to Margarete. There was something about the other girl's steeliness that brought out an answering unsurety in Claire, as if one existed in inverse proportion to the other.

Usually, Margarete would stand impassively while Claire fumbled for words. But she took pity on her now. "I was impressed," Margarete admitted, locking the door to the suite. "I'm not used to seeing you take action of any kind, much less . . . decisive action."

"It was that or be frog-marched away to my fate by the likes of Jeremiah Emerson."

Margarete snorted. "Well, I am your ally always in that. You saw, of course, that he's found God?"

"Poor God. I'm sure He's gone into hiding." Claire grinned at her, and reluctantly, Margarete smiled back. "Can you tell me something I maybe don't want to know?"

"I'm good at that," she said.

"The servants, belowstairs—do they . . . what do they

think of the Governor?" Though what she wanted to ask was, *What allies do we have? Do we have any?*

Margarete drifted over to the bed, smoothing the counterpane, fluffing the dozen pillows one by one. *This was once Clotilde's room,* Claire found herself thinking. *She and Remy must have played here as children—jumped on that bed, lost toys beneath it, fallen asleep together listening to their nanny reading them fairy stories.*

"They don't know me enough to confide in me," Margarete was saying. "But I hear things. I came with you, and you . . . well, you turned things upside down. The staff all love the young Governor—that's what they all call him, you know. He never took liberties with the girls, he tipped the footmen well at Christmas. He takes all his valet's suggestions. What shirt to wear, what cravat. They're not world-stopping kindnesses, those, but they do count. And I think . . . I think they pity him."

"They do?"

With a critical eye, Margarete reordered the pillows: the shot-white silk, then the blue velvet, then the little fringed ones at the front. "He's not a good leader. He's too young—not just in age, mind, but they say he's a romantic, always lost in a book. He keeps those bizarre scientists in his pocket, and he doesn't care enough about statecraft. But they don't want him gone. They want someone to straighten him out." She looked at Claire out of the corner of her eye. "When you don't actually marry him, they'll be devastated."

"When I don't . . ." Claire barked a laugh. "Right."

Margarete shrugged; it was nothing to her. "As long as I keep my position here," she said, "you may run off and marry a dog for all I care."

After hours hunched by Remy's bedside, spinning her little gambits like plates in the air, Claire was overcome with the urge to move, to do something. She paced a tight circle on the carpet. "Remy asked me to take the temperature of the court, and I agree, I want to know what we're up against. But mostly I . . . I need to find Beatrix. I just wish that I wasn't so *visible*—"

The girl bit her lip, then grinned. "Do you know," she said, "I brought you a bundle that might help."

Ten minutes later, Claire was gliding down the hall in her brother Ambrose's suit, her hair hidden rather more thoroughly than usual in a top hat. Margarete had delighted in smudging a hint of boot black along Claire's jawline. "There," the maid said, turning her to the mirror. "You look like a proper oaf now."

When she stepped into the hall, she saw that Captain Miller had vanished. *After all that business about guarding me.* Something dropped low in her stomach. *Maybe he was called away. Maybe he needed to piss. Maybe—*

Claire couldn't afford to stand there and wonder, not

when, as Miller pointed out, she was such an obvious target. Thankfully, she saw no one on the short walk to the staircase that led down to the foyer. There she paused on the landing in the guise of adjusting her gloves, head tipped low.

Through her lashes, she watched the men and women of society streaming in through the front doors. An army of underbutlers stood to take gloves and hats, umbrellas—it must have been raining—and canes. After divesting themselves, the men offered their elbows to the ladies, and like partners in a waltz, they glided in pairs toward the great hall.

And all the while, they talked. Their voices carried up the paneled walls and back down to Claire, clarion clear.

"I heard he's dead, Franklin, I heard one of his own men shot him—"

"Crowded! So very crowded, that sorry excuse for a Fair, and all those déclassé women lined up in the downpour, waiting to try that blue ribbon beer—I'd never in my life—"

"Those redcoats in every hotel, how are they affording their board? I heard they're paid nearly nothing—"

"Sounds like treason to me, and when the King comes tomorrow, he'll see that Monroe woman hanged—"

"Yes, but did you try the De Cecco pasta—they were serving it with scrambled ostrich eggs and you could see the ostriches lay the eggs if you wanted, gargantuan, and well, I didn't want to, but there they were, laying away, and let me tell you, there is just something not right about those eggs—"

"Have you no pride? We've lived in St. Cloud for a century, Martha, we'll live in St. Cloud a century more. I have no desire to be under a woman's rule—"

"But Charles Monroe—"

"Two of them Livmonian boys, guns at their sides, eating those hot dogs—"

"And lions! Five of them. They roared on command! A little boy wet himself right there, and could you blame him—"

"Everyone knows he's dead, and that opportunistic little peasant is looking to ride his coffin to glory—did you see the way she sneered at us last night from the dais?"

"All I'm saying is that I need a man in charge, a real man, and if the General asks—"

"Lower your voice—"

"All I wanted was to ride the Ferris wheel, but I don't know if it will ever be finished—"

Well, they might have the servants' sympathy, but if any part of her had hoped for the support of St. Cloud's makeshift aristocracy, that part was silent now. What would happen at court? Remy was so certain that the General had a plan. Would he announce that Remy was at death's door? *And he might be,* she thought, grimly. *I haven't touched him in an hour. Why was I so cavalier to leave—*

And where was Tesla? Why hadn't he come in to see Remy after surgery?

Her courage quailing, she backed away from the railing and ducked back down the hall into an alcove, nearly tripping over a vase on a plinth in the process. She clutched it to steady herself.

Minutes went by. Footsteps behind her, people passing. Claire didn't look. She hoped that her presence was unremarked on, that all these passersby saw was a young man in a suit catching his breath.

"I will not work for you," a man said. She only caught the scraps of his words; they came from down the hall.

"We are not at cross-purposes, you and I."

Claire strained to hear.

"I? I am not crossing you in any way," the voice said, and the accent was unmistakably Tesla's.

"You have certain resources." The woman's voice was raised. "You have certain sympathies. Certain lives hang in the balance. When you see my people in the palace, abide by their instructions."

Rosa Morgenstern?

"Breathe, Claire," she whispered, loosening her cravat. "Breathe." She had to have misheard it. Her pulse was galloping; surely her imagination had sped to join it.

But no. A shadow behind her, footsteps. A damp cloth

pressed over her mouth, the sharp scent of cheap liquor, or gasoline.

What was that she heard in the background? A scuffle, someone calling her name—*Claire, Claire* . . .

"That's right, Claire. Breathe," the voice said, and before she could even think to struggle, she fell down deep into a starry nothingness.

SIXTEEN

"Don't move," the voice said, dizzyingly familiar. "Penguin, don't move. Take deep breaths. Thomas, I could *kill* you for this."

Grass. She was on her back on a damp patch of grass. But the air didn't smell clean like it had the few times she'd ventured into the countryside beyond Monticello. Instead it smelled like fried dough and chalk above the pungent low note of . . . lake water?

Claire struggled again to sit up, to blink her eyes open, but a heaviness overcame her. She let her body rest on the ground.

"I'm sorry, Ambrose," another voice said, "I am! I couldn't even get in through the servants' entrance, I had to bribe a soldier to go in and fetch her, and—"

"A soldier. You bribed a soldier to go fetch the dead Governor's ex-fiancée, and you're surprised he took her by force?"

"Well." A long pause. "You'll pay me back the five dollars

he asked for, right?"

A scuffle. Muffled cursing. The sound of retreating foot-steps.

"Penguin?"

Her brother. Ambrose.

Ambrose was here.

Claire sat up all at once, and promptly threw up into the grass.

"Oh, honey, I'm so sorry," he said. Her eyes were begin-ning to focus, and she could see her brother's dark curly hair, the freckles across his nose. His concerned eyes. "I never would have done it this way. I should have gone myself, but I was afraid they'd be on the lookout for me, after the stir you caused."

"Where am I?" Claire asked. He squatted beside her, and she fumbled for his hand. Her brother. Her *brother*. She hadn't seen him in years. "I missed you," she whispered.

"I missed you too," he said. "I asked Thomas to fetch you and take you to the hotel, but he thought, rightly—it wouldn't look good to show up with an unconscious girl over his shoulder. So he brought you here to recover, then paid a boy to fetch me. That fool. At least he didn't leave you here alone."

"Thomas?" The name sounded familiar. "Was that one of my . . . suitors?"

Ambrose's smile was despairing. "Unfortunately so."

"You'll forgive me," she said, "if I take him out of the running?"

His face tightened. "I don't know how much of a choice you have. Here, let's help you over to the stands. We need to talk."

Claire let him lead her slowly across the field. The chalk she'd smelled had been used to mark out a diamond in the grass. The four sides of that diamond were studded with canvas bags painted white, and the whole thing was surrounded by a forest of electrical lights, unlit now. Still, the Fair's home of Jefferson Park was next door, and it was lit up like its own small city. A soft white glow stole over the grass and pooled at Claire's feet.

It was said that the only thing King Washington loved more than chateaubriand or his musket collection was baseball. And this was a temple of baseball, a hushed place of worship. There was a mighty set of stands that surrounded the field, wooden and again painted white, and they stretched up so far that she thought the whole city of Monticello could watch the King's players slaughter the local team.

Purposeless war, she thought again. *War for sport.*

Ambrose settled her down on the players' bench behind first base, and together they gazed across the field. "It's the largest ever built," he said. "In the American Kingdom, anyway. It'll stay up afterward, as a place for the Monticello Whales to play. Originally some man wanted to have his 'wild West' show here, but luckily for us, that was too violent for your young Governor."

The more she heard it, the more that phrase, "young Governor," felt like a shot at Remy.

"I'm happy you came," she said instead.

"Penguin," he said. "This is an odd question, and might be beside the point, but . . . is that my old suit?"

She looked down. Straightened her cuffs. "Oh. It is."

"That soldier Thomas paid off must've dressed you in it, after the ether." He plucked a blade of grass off her arm. "Maybe they thought it would be less odd, a man carrying his fellow home after a night of drinking? Thomas almost turned up his nose at wedding you, a girl wearing men's clothes, before I told him it wasn't your fault."

Claire didn't know where to begin. "The man who drugged me. Had reservations about marrying me. Because I was wearing . . . a suit?"

It was as though she hadn't spoken. Ambrose was still brushing off her lapels, rearranging her hair, as though she were a doll meant for a display stand. "I hadn't expected us to get called up to Monticello so soon," he said, "especially with the issues at the border, but I hear that's exactly what's bringing King Washington earlier than planned. Which means his touring team comes with." He sighed. "Claire, we don't have much time."

Maybe she was still recovering from the ether. Maybe she

was just exhausted. But she couldn't follow the thread of his thoughts. This was Ambrose. Her *brother*. The boy who stole apples to eat them on the fire escape of their tenement building, who played endless games of ball with a ragged pack of boys in the road. Who spent his rainy days whittling her little tops that she could spin on the kitchen table. "I know," she said, purposely misunderstanding his words. "I need to get back to the mansion before they miss me."

"You want to go back to the mansion?" He shot her an incredulous look. "Come now. All our preparations? All the work I had to do to convince Rory and Thomas to consider taking you on? I know it's not your fault you were kidnapped by that man, but he's *dead* now, and—"

It was the second time Ambrose had said it. *They were saying it in the foyer too.* "The Governor's not dead," Claire said, and before her brother could protest, she put up her hands. "No. Honest to God, Ambrose, I left him an hour before your—teammate—kidnapped me, and speaking of *kidnapping*—"

"I told you I didn't ask him to etherize you—"

"Stop." She put a hand on his shoulder, squeezed it. He was solid. Real. *Ambrose*. Why was he behaving this way? "Where are you hearing all this?"

He spread his hands. "Everywhere. It's in the newspapers, all of them. The *King's Herald* is even reporting it. The General's calling for the King to elect a new Governor in the morning. Father's . . . well, he's giving interviews with the press, and they don't make you look good. You aren't safe. Duchamp can't protect you now."

"I have a guard!"

"Yes," he said, "clearly, a very effective guard. You know you're being unreasonable, penguin. There's a long line of men out there to smear your name, and that's a fate worse than death for a girl like you. I can *get you out*. Our original plan can still work."

She thought of Remy, suddenly, curled up in his bed, alone in that vast expanse of sheets. Alone, now, for hours. *He might be dead*, she thought, *and it's your fault, your fault—*

Dizzily, she stood. "Ambrose," she said. "If I can just see this through, I promise—"

"That you're going to end up dead, or a spoils-of-war wife to the General. And I promise *that* wedding night won't be the thing of your dreams."

Something in her broke, at that.

Who was this craven man that Ambrose had become?

"Oh *yes*." She was angry now, angry enough that her voice cracked like an oiled pan left long on the fire. "Tell me more about my *dreams*. About my *wedding night*. With the General or some soldier or your Jehoshaphat goddamn Center Fielder. This new owner of my soul, this man to whom I owe my allegiance, this *stranger* who gets to clip a leash to my collar—oh, I'm certain he'll have a vested interest in making my maiden dreams come true. Why, he'll be so eager to press his horrible fat hairy body—"

"Claire!" Her brother's horror wasn't at the situation she described—it was at the words her innocent female mouth was saying.

"To press his *old man* body on his new wife in the dark, just the way I've always been promised! I'm sure the General will be thrilled to beat me when he's finished, for all the *trouble* I've caused. Leave me chained up in a closet. Is that what you're imagining? Tell me, is that better or worse than a man who thinks the most expedient way to get me to you is to give me a drug that *kills* people, and then loses his temper when he sees me in a pair of trousers?"

"What's happened to you?" he whispered.

"Dammit, Ambrose, when did you turn into Father?"

"I—"

"I'll do what I need to do to survive," she told him, the last of the ether's effects burning away in her rage. "Tell the King hello for me." And she strode off into the darkness, toward the white lights of the Fair.

She wasn't surprised when her brother didn't follow. She turned back to look just once at him sitting on that wooden bench, staring down at his hands as the rain again began to fall.

A path had been poured that led from the King's baseball diamond back through Jefferson Park, and she walked it quickly, keeping to the shelter of the sycamore trees. Still her jacket was soaked through. Her top hat had been lost in her clumsy abduction. *Perhaps Thomas still has it,* she thought, sourly. *Well, he can keep it. Call it a memento of our whirlwind romance.*

The electric indignation that had coursed through her body was fading now, leaving her scraped-out and raw. Luckily there was little reason for the fairgoers to walk this way; no one was there to see her stop to slump against a tree trunk, unbuttoning her collar as she sweated out the last effects of the ether.

This is it, she thought, tipping back her head to stare up through the thick canopy. She couldn't make sense of it, of how the last few weeks had stripped away every last thing she'd known to be true. Her best friend had abandoned her. Tesla had disappeared. Captain Miller had most likely drugged her and delivered her to her brother, who wanted to sell her off to the highest bidder. And the most powerful man in this province was working to discredit, then murder, the man she loved.

The man I love. She turned the thought over, swallowed. *I might as well admit it. I love him, and it doesn't matter now.*

The only person who had remained exactly the same was her father. He was precisely as unpredictable as he had been since her mother died.

Claire scrubbed at her face, thinking. As far as she could tell, she had two choices. She could march back to the mansion, her head held high, and wait by Remy's side for the knife to fall across both their necks. Or she could hitch a ride on a train headed west, change her name and change her story, and try her luck somewhere new.

No friends, no family, not a dollar to her name. *And no one left who can leave you,* a voice whispered in her ear.

The rain came down harder, a proper downfall, and Claire coughed, then started to laugh. No matter what she chose, she couldn't stay here.

There was only one place she could think to go.

It was strange, moving through Monticello at night alone. For the entirety of her two-mile walk, the rain came down in a continuous sheet, and perhaps that was the reason for the dreaminess of it, the sense of danger. No one was out in this weather who didn't have to be; even the very poor appeared to have found a bolt-hole to hide out in.

And still Claire could have sworn that she was seeing soldiers, knots of soldiers, clustered on street corners two or three or four blocks from where she walked. Minutes later, when she'd reached them, they were gone.

Perhaps it was the aftereffects of the ether still in her system. Perhaps it was a chill she'd caught from walking in the downpour, a fever. Perhaps she'd finally gone the way of her father, imagining things where none were.

But it was unnerving, all the same.

Especially their uniforms. Their uniforms were all red.

SEVENTEEN

The doorman at Perpetua's lifted his umbrella a little higher. "Miss," he said. "What's happened to you?"

Claire wanted very much to die. Her hair plastered to her neck, the hems of her trousers muddy and ragged, and she wanted to vomit into the nearest basin. "Please, Harrison." It was surprising to her, momentarily, that she remembered how to speak, that the rain hadn't worn off her mouth with its power. "I know you know me."

"I do. Miss, you do know your face is on the front of every paper—"

"Yes," she said, "I had noticed that," and sneezed mightily into her arm.

With a heavy sigh, Harrison said, "Come along." But rather than simply open the door, he led her inside, as he'd never done before.

The smell that rolled toward her was something between

spilled beer and wet dog, and noise was hard on its heels. Tonight, Perpetua's Club was wall-to-wall with people, dancing to a song she'd never heard the orchestra play before. Something lusty and loud, the horns feverish. And at the bar, men. Men five deep, waving their arms for a drink.

Claire watched them, swaying a little on her feet, her arm thrown out to brace herself against an unamused Harrison. *See,* she thought, *everything's just splendid. Nobody's worried! Look at all these soldiers, celebrating. They've had a good night! They've been to the Fair! Nobody thinks their Governor is dead. These soldiers—*

These soldiers in their red coats—

She whirled to face the doorman, gripping his coat for balance. "No," she said, too loudly, "no, when did they come, how did they get in—"

"Our guests are *staring*," Harrison said, and yanked her to the side, to a door she'd never seen before that had the word PRIVATE etched across its beveled glass.

Then he pushed her through it.

Claire stood dumbly, the water pooling at her feet.

"Up the stairs." He made a shooing motion, like she was a dog. "I'll tell her that you're here. Go, before you make more of a scene."

She hadn't known Perpetua kept an office, much less one with windows down into the club. It was a small space, tidy, not much more than a desk and a stack of account books, and Claire staggered past a pair of armchairs to look out over what she thought she'd seen.

But it wasn't a fever dream. Wasn't a hallucination.

Livmonian soldiers, dicing at tables, grabbing eagerly at passing waitresses' sleeves. Livmonian soldiers, dancing fast waltzes with breathless partners, skirts flying with their speed. Livmonian soldiers pounding on the bar, demanding service, soldiers sneaking into the orchestra to tweak the trombonist's hat. Livmonian soldiers so flush with victory that they knew themselves in their hearts to be gods.

It had happened. While she was bathing Remy's brow, while she was oh so bravely quizzing Margarete about the servants, while she delivered her little self-righteous speech to her brother in a baseball field, while she acted like a girl like her had any real power to change the world, Livingston-Monroe had invaded St. Cloud.

She had gone to sleep in a meadow and woken up on the moon.

Claire leaned her head heavily against the window sash. Perpetua would be in at any moment, and she still didn't have a plan. *But what plan of yours has worked? What plans of yours have saved a single thing you loved?*

Money. Money and a train ticket. She'd go to Philadelphia; surely the eastern border of St. Cloud was still open. She'd find work as a schoolteacher; she could teach at any girls' academy with what she knew of reading and figuring, and soon she'd have enough money to pay Perpetua back. All she needed was an advance, a loan, and she'd be out the door and on her way.

She waited a good half hour, at least, and so when the door swung open, Claire turned with the plea already on her lips.

"Claire."

She didn't trust what she saw. Not tonight, demons everywhere, demons where before she'd only seen her fellow men. She could hardly make herself say the name. "Beatrix?"

With quick hands, the girl bolted the door behind her. Then she flung herself at her best friend.

"You're okay," Beatrix said, over and over, clutching Claire's head to her shoulder. "You're okay. God, what's happened to you? You're wet all over and I thought you were *dead*, and the papers are saying it too, and the Governor is *missing*—"

"Missing?" The word came out muffled. "I thought the papers said he was dead."

"The General did, and the papers reported that in a noon edition, and then the *St. Cloud Sun* came out with an evening issue saying that Duchamp was missing—you've never seen so many special editions in your life. Rosa Morgenstern said the Yiddish paper went to press *five times* today—"

"Focus," Claire said, pulling back to look Beatrix in the face. The girl's eyepatch was askew, and Claire gently adjusted it. "Missing?"

"Right. That gunshot wound was well-timed, don't you

think? You did a good job too, aiming for the deathbed confession, that whole fiancée bit, though I wouldn't go that far myself—yech. Man looks like a librarian, even if I *liked* men he'd be lucky to even *think* of touching me—"

"Focus—"

"But then the General comes up in his almighty jaw-me-down glory, big entourage, reporters and soldiers and onlookers, likely trumpets blaring, you know him. The plan is to show everyone the Governor's dead body. Crass, but the General is crass, and the public *loves* a spectacle—there's a photographer there too—and they overpower his guard and muscle their way inside, and hey presto, it's empty. No baby Duchamp."

Claire sank down into an armchair. "He was gone."

"Gone. The General flies into a rage. The reporter gets it all down. The photographer takes a picture of the scene. Evening edition." Beatrix flung herself down in the opposite chair. "But why are we still talking about the whelp?"

"Because I was there—I was there to gather information." She massaged a pounding temple. "For the D.A.C. About the Governor's weapons—"

"Doesn't matter much now, I don't think. Because . . ." Beatrix gestured down to the club with a flourish. "Do you see what I'm seeing?"

"Monticello," Claire said. "Monticello, in the hands of the enemy."

"*Not* the enemy. Not now. We'll just be a part of Living-ston-Monroe. Abigail Monroe's set to give a speech tomorrow at noon, welcoming us into the fold. All we have to do is find Remy Duchamp, which shouldn't be hard—I'm sure some loyal retainer has him squirreled away in a closet in the mansion, they're dismantling the place now—and then in the morning execute the General, and we'll be all set."

She said it so blithely, as though the overthrow of their province's leadership was something as meaningless as a play. The lifting of one painted set, the lowering of another. "How many people died tonight?" Claire whispered.

Beatrix leaned forward and took her by the shoulders. "Are you well?" she asked. "Your hands are hot. And your eyes are glassy. I didn't consider your health. I've been so caught up in all this, I'm so sorry."

Claire shook her head to clear it. "How many people?"

"None," she said. "Nobody died."

"Then how—"

Beatrix clearly couldn't help the smile that crept over her lips. "The Livmonian soldiers were all here already. I should have told you, love, I know it, but I was sworn to secrecy, and anyway I wasn't sure it would work."

"How—"

"They've been crossing the border in plain sight," she said. "The General had declared it, remember? Open borders in spirit of the Fair. For weeks they've been coming in, disguised first as workmen, then as conductors on the railroad, and finally in the last week as fairgoers, dozens of them on every train. They're staying in every hotel. They're eating in every restaurant. The General's bankrolling them with some private fund he's been building—"

The extortion money that the Exchequer couldn't find. Claire felt like she might pass out.

"And he snuck enough of them in as 'new recruits' to the St. Cloud army that tonight, at nine o'clock, when they all unmasked themselves, they had enough men to overwhelm the St. Cloud troops without shedding any blood. If they joined the Livmonian forces, they would keep their positions, and live. *That* was Abigail Monroe's idea, thank you very much."

"But about the ones who refused?"

She shrugged. "None of them died, they were just thrown in jail. Anyway, there's not as many of them as you'd think. Most turned red. Not a lot of love lost for Duchamp, and a lot of loyalty to their General. There's to be a swearing-in ceremony at midnight that I'm to attend. They're having it on the Fairgrounds, on the stage. Make it clear who's in charge now."

"The General?"

"Well, for tonight." Beatrix bared her teeth. "And then he's served his purpose. The General thinks Abigail Monroe's going to roll over and show her belly, he's got another thing coming. I'm fine with his death. Can't make an omelet without cracking at least . . . an egg."

"Beatrix," she said.

But the girl jumped up to pace the room. "I just can't believe it all turned out so perfectly. I know it's not done yet, not nearly, but I hardly thought we'd get this far, and to think, Claire, we'll have a *woman leader* in the morning! Of course we'll have to take on both Charles and Abigail Monroe at first, but there's already some talk of sprinkling poison on his cornflakes—"

"Beatrix—"

"Not that I support that, mind! It's just a thought. Mostly I'm focused on that scientist Tesla, the wizard. That *fancy man*. The D.A.C. is calling him a collaborator of Duchamp's, but I'll tell you this, I'd love to meet him. Smuggle him out, through the eastern border? Maybe he'd take me with him—a man like that needs an assistant, right, and I know what I'm about in a laboratory—"

"*Beatrix,*" Claire thundered, and the girl spun to a halt.

"Oh, Lord, Claire, I'm sorry, the night's just all *electric*. Can't you feel it? Aren't you happy you didn't go down to Orleans and marry what's-his-name—did he even have one? Jehoshaphat Leroy Third Baseman?"

Shakily, Claire got to her feet. "Beatrix," she said. "What's Remy's place in all this? Because I won't see him dead."

Beatrix went entirely still for maybe the first time in her natural life. "I'm sorry. What's that?"

"Remy," she said. "Remy Duchamp. I—I care about him, Bea. How are we going to save him?"

"Oh hell." Beatrix sat down with a thump. "That's what I thought you said."

EIGHTEEN

"Perpetua says you have twenty minutes," the doorman said, setting the tea tray on the table. He dropped a bundle of clothing beside it. "It's already eleven o'clock. And to use her words, there's a coup on."

"Thanks, Harrison," Beatrix said, popping a sugar cube into her mouth. "Thanks for looking after Claire, as well."

"Don't thank me," he said. "If you're not finished by then, I'm to drag you both out by your ears."

Wearily Claire lifted her empty teacup in salute. Rolling his eyes, Harrison locked the door behind him.

While the tea steeped, Beatrix turned to give her a modicum of privacy, and Claire dried off and changed into the dress the doorman had brought. It was warm and dry. *Bless Perpetua.*

"So tell me. Is it like the fairy tale?" Beatrix poured their tea and added a dollop of cream to each cup. "Did the

Governor beast become a prince after you rubbed his belly the right way?"

Claire raised her eyebrows. "You were the one who traded me to him for a heifer and two hens a-laying."

"And for Willie LeGrande."

"And for that." Beatrix reached out to grab her arm. "Please don't tell me he's a good man. Duchamp. Remy. However you call him."

She sighed. "He's a good man. He's not perfect, Beatrix, but he *tries*. He cares—deeply. And not just about me, or his family . . . I just think he's been alone a long time, without friends, without anyone he can trust, and that he's retreated into his books and his experiments as a way of hiding away. All he needs . . . I don't know this for sure, but I think all he needs is a person beside him who can call him back to the things of this world."

"The engagement wasn't a fake one."

"It was at first. And then it wasn't. Or I don't think it wasn't. Or . . ." Claire took a sip, then another, the tea warming her through. She kept her hands around her cup. "I would marry him, if he'd have me."

Beatrix laughed a little, kicking back in her chair.

"I don't see what's so funny."

"Because it isn't funny," Beatrix said, and laughed again, and this time Claire heard the despairing note in it. "If I ask you something, will you promise to consider it, and not just storm out of the room?"

"They're putting us on the street in . . ." Claire eyed the clock in the corner. "Sixteen minutes, so you'd better start asking."

"Humor me." Beatrix leaned forward, her eyepatch reflecting the lamplight. "You're maybe a little bit magic. We don't know for sure. But let's say you are. Let's say your power is to give men the one thing they want most in the world. The whole world. I've known you for long enough now that I feel certain in saying that you've never been in love?"

Claire shook her head mutely.

"And no one's ever been in love with you?"

She shook her head again.

"So let's follow this supposition to its logical conclusion. Say a man sees you. Beautiful girl, long black curls blowing in the wind, standing on top of a mighty machine. Defying her father. Gorgeous and brave like . . . like a summer's day."

"Thank you, Shakespeare," she said. "Fourteen minutes."

"And that man says, 'I want that. I'm taking that girl home with me.' And then he gets to know you—the sailor's mouth, the bottomless desire for lemon ices, the inability to make a good decision, even to save your life—"

"Thirteen."

"And he thinks, Golly gee, I've never met a girl like this before. Beautiful and deeply strange. What's this I'm feeling? Maybe it's love."

A buzzing sound began to build in Claire's ears, bees rushing an overfull hive. "No."

"Yes," Beatrix said, the lightness in her tone falling away. "And that girl thinks, *I'll make him want to tell me his secrets. I'll make him want to trust me.* Sure. It happens. It's part and parcel of the bigger picture. Because, Claire, *all that man wants is for you to love him.*

"The Remy Duchamp you know? He doesn't exist. He invented that person for you. If you insist, we'll give him the benefit of the doubt—but all that intel I have on Duchamp says that he's a heartless little snob in hundred-dollar slippers."

"It isn't true."

"I'm sure he didn't even know he was doing it, pressing on your most delicate parts. Tell me—and love, I know this hurts—but what's the thing you've loved most in the world?"

"My mother," Claire whispered.

Beatrix shut her eyes briefly. "Did you tend him while he was dying, only to see him get better? Were you the one who saved him?"

My mother, wasted from disease, her hand falling limply from the bed—

"Did he tell you about someone he loved very much? Someone who he lost too soon?"

Clotilde in her white muff, in the sanatorium at Biarritz—

"And unlike any man you'd ever known, did he understand your need for freedom—"

"I can't," Claire gasped, and turned away into the fabric of the armchair, weeping fit to break her own heart.

Beatrix was next to her in a flash. "I could be wrong, love," she said, petting Claire's hair as she wept. "I want to be. But I know you. I've never thought you one to fall this fast."

After a shuddering moment, Claire made herself lift her face. "So what, then."

Beatrix looked taken aback. "So what?"

"So he loves me. So he's made himself into—into some librarian Adonis, just for me. So what. So I go, and I find him, and I *marry* him, and together we run this province the way that your Abigail Monroe could only dream of."

"And if he falls out of love with you?"

She steeled herself to say it. "There are other ways to control a man."

"You realize," Beatrix muttered, "that I've just helped orchestrate the takeover of a rather large swath of the American Kingdom. And now you want me to help you take it back. Based on your magical powers. That your father might have invented in his delusions."

Claire couldn't help it—she flung herself into her best friend's arms. "Yes," she said, and pulled away. "Yes, that's the only thing I want."

"I understand that part, the you-wanting-it part, but—"

At that, there was a hard knock at the door. "It's Perpetua."

"One minute," Claire called, checking the clock. "We still

have one minute! Let me finish cleaning up." She stood and brushed off her skirts, feeling more like herself than she had in days. "Bea, how did you know I'd be here, anyway? I came here looking for Perpetua, and then you arrived."

"I got your note," Beatrix said. She was checking her jacket for smudges.

"My note?"

Beatrix stopped. Slowly, achingly slowly, she looked up. "The note you sent. The one that said you were at Perpetua's, and to come quick. I got here within minutes of receiving it—I took Rosa's carriage—"

The knocking again, harder this time. "Girls!"

Claire could feel her face draining pale.

Thud thud thud.

"You didn't send a note," Beatrix whispered.

"I didn't send a note," Claire whispered back.

"I'll just let myself in," the voice called. "We can't be late!"

And the knob began to turn.

NINETEEN

"I hope your bindings aren't too uncomfortable," Abigail Monroe was saying. "You do know, of course, that I do this under duress."

The two of them jolted along across from Monroe in the carriage, struggling to keep their balance as it hurtled down the brick streets. *It's almost as though she's chosen the worst possible way to take us to the Fair.* It was no kind of carriage Claire had ever ridden in—it was windowless, all wooden, with manacles bolted into its floor. Thankfully, Monroe hadn't seen fit to use those. "Not for ladies," she'd said. Steel wasn't for ladies, but a prison wagon was. She'd smiled as Captain Miller bound their feet with rope.

Captain Miller. That was the other horrible part of this.

So much for winning my chess game. Tonight Duchamp's queen was facedown on the board.

"Thank the doorman at that horrible club for knowing

which side his bread is buttered on." Abigail looked Claire up and down. "Though the dress was my idea, of course. We can't have you looking like some *boy* when we get you on that stage.

"I am sorry, Beatrix," Abigail said, and she sounded as though she meant it. "I do understand that this likely means that you'll be dropping out of our administration—"

Beatrix kicked out at Abigail's legs, and she dodged. Before Beatrix could try again, Miller wrestled her ankles together and bound them. Claire shut her eyes against it.

"Though I'm sure you can realize your friend is the sort of asset we cannot lose sight of. Not for anything. Not right now, when we have such loose ends." Abigail clasped her hands on her lap.

She has gentle eyes, Claire thought. *It was horrible. Why does she look like someone I would have trusted?*

She had no barometer for this sort of thing anymore.

"We will attend this . . . fealty ceremony that your General has insisted on," Abigail was saying. "And then you will help us find Mr. Duchamp." She said his title with some relish, as though she enjoyed stripping him of his Governorship.

Abigail spoke for some time longer. Questions, mostly, about Remy, about what his plans were, if he'd fled the country for France like the foreigner he was. It was all for show. Claire had a rag stuffed in her mouth, and even if she hadn't, she wouldn't have said a word.

Abigail Monroe wasn't holding her attention. Neither was Beatrix; her best friend was spitting mad, and she could handle herself if it came to a fight.

All Claire could focus on was the icy face of Captain Miller staring at her from across the carriage.

She raised her eyebrows at him, a challenge. *Someone else has harnessed that rage of yours, haven't they?* After the night she'd had, another betrayal wasn't a surprise. It was just another small sting, a burr under her heel.

Claire refused to drop his gaze. He pressed his lips together, then looked away.

Monroe was still gassing on as the carriage bumped over a curb, throwing Claire into Beatrix's side. Beatrix didn't seem to notice. She was too busy trying to bore holes into Abigail Monroe's face with her eyes.

"The workers' entrance?" Monroe asked Captain Miller. He nodded sharply, stayed silent.

A few minutes later, they came to a shuddering halt, and Miller wasted no time in throwing the door open. He didn't wait for Monroe to alight; he reached in immediately and took hold of Beatrix and swung her, thrashing, from the carriage.

"Certainly," Monroe said, bemused, "I take precedence."

"Ma'am, I'm handing the prisoners off first, for your safety," he said. "It was drilled into me in training."

She huffed. "Well, you must know best, then."

"Come," he said to Claire, and she scrambled away from

him. *"Come,"* he said again, and in the reverse of how he'd stuffed her into the Governor's carriage, he yanked her from it now and dropped her, beside Beatrix, on the ground.

Then he shut the door to the prison wagon, locked it, and hit the door twice.

It sped away into the night, with Abigail Monroe inside.

Claire twisted her head to look at Beatrix. Beatrix stared back at her.

"We only have a minute." Captain Miller knelt down and, with clever fingers, loosened Claire's bindings. After she slipped them off her wrists, he went to work on Beatrix's.

Claire pulled the rag from her mouth, panting. "You're not working for Monroe."

"No," he said, and as Beatrix freed her hands and feet, he looked at Claire with bright eyes. "I'm still the Governor's man."

"Can we trust him?" Beatrix said, still mad as a spitting cat.

"No," Claire said. Then, to Miller: "We'll follow you."

"You need to put the bindings back on your arms," he said. With a groan, Beatrix massaged her wrists. "Loosely, this time. Enough so you can slip free. But it has to look right. And . . . the gags too."

The girls exchanged a look, then followed orders. "Where is the wagon taking her?" Claire asked. "What's happening?"

With a grimace, Miller helped Claire up by her elbow, then Beatrix. "There are a few men still loyal to me," he said.

"And, to a lesser extent, the Governor. They've rigged up a cell in the basement of the mansion. Should hold her until all of this is over. Quickly, now. Someone will be looking for us soon."

Only then did Claire see where the carriage had left them.

The Fair, of course, the northern end of the Fair, in front of the first building built and the one built to last. Made of marble that gleamed in the moonlight, and in the light cast up from the lagoon that lapped lazily against its base. Gondolas rested there, bobbing up and down; they would be in use, but it was midnight, the grounds of the Fair closed to the public. Street sweepers should be out, she knew, and sanitation workers, and soldiers patrolling the paths looking for anything out of place.

I suppose the coup disrupted all that.

Claire didn't know all there was to know about the Palace of Fine Arts. But she knew it was windowless, to protect the art inside from damage from the sun. She knew it had a mighty rotunda, big enough to fit hundreds of men.

And she knew that if the General wanted a defensible place in which to host his fealty ceremony, he'd have chosen this building above all others.

What better place to humiliate the young Governor than in the heart of his beloved Fair?

Miller pulled them along by their elbows, and the girls pretended to drag their feet. As they approached the grand entrance, he whispered instructions. "The ceremony begins in just a few minutes. Every single soldier for miles around is here. In this one building. Because that pathetic old man can't resist his pageantry."

Through her gag, Beatrix cackled. It was a terrifying sound.

"Something is going to happen at ten minutes past midnight. I haven't been given the details, so I can't tell you. All I know is that Tesla told me to get Claire to a broom closet on the upper rotunda."

Tesla. Tesla, who loved Remy like a son. Claire felt a wash of relief.

In the meantime, Beatrix kicked at Captain Miller's ankles.

"I wasn't supposed to have you," Captain Miller hissed, dodging. "I don't even know who you are!"

Through the gag, Beatrix said something very rude.

Miller hauled the two of them to a halt. They were close enough to the entrance now to see the tall wooden doors, engraved like the lid of a fancy coffin. Two bored-looking soldiers in red coats stood outside, just out of earshot.

"What did you say?" Captain Miller shouted as Beatrix slunk backward into herself. "No. I'm going to take out your gag so you can *say it to my face*."

With a show of force, he tore it from Beatrix's mouth. Claire winced.

"I said," Beatrix spat, "that I build flying machines, that I know more about engineering than any man *you* know has forgotten, and that your mother makes love to donkeys—"

"That's what I thought!" Miller thundered. He stuffed the gag back into Beatrix's mouth. It was a fine performance; Claire wanted to applaud.

Apparently the guards did as well. "That's right, officer! Show 'em who's in charge!" The other one gave him a bit of bored applause.

"Blond one's with me," he told them, yanking Beatrix up to the doors. "Dark hair goes to a little cell we've made for her upstairs. You're to take her," he told the bored officer, nodding to Claire. "Touch a hair on her head, and the General will have a fit. She's meant for him, see. Wants her innocent."

Claire stumbled where she stood and struggled to right herself on shaking legs. She'd been shocked when she saw Captain Miller working for Abigail Monroe.

It was much easier to imagining him serving the General.

A slow, nasty smile spread over the soldier's face. "Yes, sir," he said, wrapping one thick hand around Claire's arm. This close, she could smell the meat on his breath. "I'll make sure the General's prize is waiting for him."

TWENTY

Redcoats. Redcoats everywhere, like a tide after a slaughter, and here and there a straight-backed member of the Daughters of the American Crown. Electric lights beamed down from the vaulted ceiling, erasing everyone's shadows with its noontime glare.

She expected rows and rows of soldiers, standing with military precision, but there wasn't any such order here. These men had pulled off a months-long operation, taken over a territory—something never before done in the history of the American Kingdom—and now they were loosed upon the crown jewel of that conquest.

They were, in short, in the mood for a celebration.

A giant stage had been set up, and it looked to Claire like a mockery of the stage for the Barrage. In the center, a giant cannon, its mouth wider than the spread wings of a raptor. It was hung ridiculously with star-spangled bunting, as though it were a parade float, or a donkey, and not a thing by which men killed other men. In mockery of Tesla's technology, a pair of gargantuan coils bookended the stage.

All this she saw in an instant, as another man dragged her to another room in which she must wait. Up the stairs, past the balconies looking down onto the rotunda. Past statue after statue, painting after painting—men's musculature on display, their process with bow and with spear, their shields raised in battle. And here and there, a woman, nude, staring modestly up at her painter, another muse to a mighty man.

The Livmonian soldier—for they all were, now—hauled her up to a door that looked like all the others. As though she were a dog, he held her by the collar while he shook out a ring of keys. "This should do it," he said, catching one neat-handed and fitting it into the lock. "A little closet for you to hide in while the men sort out their business. Wish it was a nicer place for you to wait, princess—"

And by the neck, he pushed her inside. She stumbled to her hands and knees.

"But it sounds as though the General will see that you're well-tended to." His lip curled. "When he's ready." The door shut. The lock turned.

She found herself in utter darkness.

Breathe, Claire, she thought, and coughed at the unasked-for taste of ether that climbed up her throat. *Breathe.* Her hands were scraped, her knees too. The floor was the same marble as the outer walls, and she hadn't had a gentle landing.

When she had woken up this morning, she had been in Clotilde's bed. And Margarete had come in to dress her for the Fair.

She pushed herself up to her knees, then swore as her palms began to throb. She swore again, for good measure. *I am not going to cry. I am not going to cry.* "I am not going to cry—"

The barest sound. A match being struck.

The little flame moved here and there in the dark like a firefly, attaching itself finally to a wick, and then the light divided into two.

It was a candle, blooming in someone's hands.

In the dim light, Clare found her bearings. She was in a little cabinet of a gallery; the light flickered over the walls, picking out paintings here and there. A meadow. A ship in harbor. Three nymphs in a garden.

And in the center, as though he was a sculpture himself, Remy Duchamp, ghostly on a mattress in the middle of the floor.

"You're . . . alive," he said, setting the candlestick down. "Miller told me you were, but I can't—I can't quite fathom it."

He made no effort to sit up, and it became clear to Claire that he couldn't, that he was still in too much pain to move. She drew nearer. He wore a loose-fitting shirt and loose-fitting breeches, and she could see through the thin fabric that his torso was still bandaged, and that the bandages were edged red with dried blood.

As gently as she could, she lowered herself down beside him. Still, he hissed in a breath as the mattress settled around her. "I should be saying the same to you," Claire said. "The newspapers, the General—everyone is saying you're dead. How did you escape?"

"Miller had an ally or two still outwardly serving the General. He heard of the plans to . . . dispose of me . . . and arranged to have me moved before it happened. It was very sudden." His mouth twisted. "And I'm somewhat the worse for wear. But I am grateful to be alive."

"I wouldn't have left you if I'd known."

With one of his fine-boned hands, he reached out to touch her bound wrists. "Who bound you?" he asked, slipping off the rope.

"Part of Miller's gambit to sneak us in here."

"Us?"

How could she begin to explain Beatrix? *My best friend in the world, a member of the underground society trying for months now to unseat you, who, after you took me captive, convinced me to turn spy?* "Miller and me," she said, a half second too late.

Remy watched her with shadowed eyes.

She hurried on. "We rode here with Abigail Monroe in a prison wagon. Miller trapped her in there, sent her off I don't know where. The mansion? There's a . . . cell in the basement?"

"And after that, prison," he said succinctly. "Where she'll

await her execution for treason."

Something she'd once heard Perpetua say: "It's only treason if you lose."

"You'll order it?"

"If I make it through this alive, I'll have a few heads on pikes. It's not pretty work. But the very last thing this province needs is to have a pair of Monroes back across the border, plotting their revenge. And the General? I'll hold the knife myself." His smile was grim. "Unless Miller beats me to it."

"Would he?" Claire asked. She wasn't sure of anyone's loyalties anymore.

"No," Remy said. "Unsurprising. The General's never been much of a father to him."

Claire wasn't sure what she'd heard. "I'm sorry?"

"You didn't know."

"I didn't know." Miller staring fixedly at her. Her own words: Sometimes I think the General must be like a father, who cannot see when his children are full-grown, and capable, whose talents are so desperately needed . . . "What? How?"

Remy waved a hand. "One of the General's many by-blows. I can only tell you what I've heard. Will's mother worked in the livery stables, I believe. She died when Will was quite young—she had typhus, a few years before the epidemic began. I don't know if you remember."

"Yes," Claire said. "I remember."

"She'd left him a letter telling him of his paternity, left him a few pennies. It's a familiar story. The plan was to take him to the Home for the Friendless with the other orphans. But he broke into the mansion and found the General at court. Had his mother's letter in his hand, ducked right past the guard. Will must have been . . . eight? Nine? A picturesque little thing, from what I've heard. I imagine him with a smudged face, freckles. In tears. Ran right up and hugged the General's legs and called him Papa."

It was a compelling picture. "And the General would have looked heartless had he pushed him away."

"Precisely. He lifted the boy up in his arms and began making promises. Will was given a nanny. Then he was given work in the stables—he knew how to groom a horse, given his mother's work—and then an army commission when he came of age. The boy had good instincts then. You have them now."

The compliment made her flush, as though he'd waxed poetic about her button nose or woodland-creature eyes. Claire was far more used to feeling like a bundle of bad decisions.

"At some point his feelings toward the General turned," she said. "I wish I knew when." There was something still she was missing, something she might have seen, if she had looked.

"Does it matter? You chose the very last man I'd ever consider for my personal guard," Remy was saying, "and he's already saved my life twice. If he wants to be the one to execute the illustrious General Montgomery, he has my blessing."

"You've given him back his surname."

"I'm starting a new fashion."

"'Off with their heads,'" Claire murmured. She couldn't imagine Remy raising the blade on a guillotine, but then she'd never imagined affiancing herself to a Governor while he was unconscious. *People change.*

Sometimes they change very quickly.

He was studying her wrists, turning her hands over to look at the scrapes on her palms. With gentle deliberation, he unbuttoned her cuffs and turned them up, his fingers traveling farther over skin bruised by soldiers' grips and clammy still from the rain. "Claire," he said, "you look like you've been through the wars."

"Oh, that? I was just etherized and kidnapped by my well-meaning older brother, who thought it best if I hurry up and marry one of his teammates and leave town."

"I'm sorry?" His fingers stilled on her arm. "His teammates? Your brother? I don't—you haven't told me about this."

"I was going to run away to Orleans," she said, watching the candlelight dance across the floor. "The day after the Barrage, when my father was distracted. My brother, Ambrose, had found me an escape, or so he thought. It was a marriage, anyway, and I made myself believe it wouldn't be just another gilded cage.

"My father, Jeremiah Emerson—well, I know you keep a number of scientists on retainer. Tesla. That man Michaels. But do you know them? Do you know their character? My father . . . he's mad."

To her shock, Remy laughed again. "Every genius is, in his own way."

"*No,*" she said, with enough force that he fell silent. "No. Not mad like Tesla, keeping cats about, eating strange little meals. Not mad in that he wears a—a bright red top hat every day. Mad as in, I think my father is *unwell*, Remy. After my mother died, he left me alone in the house for days. He didn't feed me. I was . . . I was a child. And then I grew up and he—he developed this fantasy that I alone could help him with his work. But not by checking his calculations, or adjusting the sights of his gun, or drawing on *any* of the knowledge my mother so painstakingly instilled in me. I could help by being his beautiful, innocent daughter, and *blessing* him with my presence—and don't look at me like that. Don't say he meant well, that he didn't know better. Because when I wasn't laying my hands on him like a heretical saint, I was locked away in our home. I was left uneducated. I waited like a—a *house cat* for him to come home, or I was meant to, anyway, in my little prison waiting for my jailer to return, and because he was doing 'important work for the Crown,' everyone wrote it off as eccentricity. As genius. And it wasn't. I can tell you, there was nothing intelligent about it.

"And what—what if I wasn't only born to prop up a man?" She could hear her voice breaking. "What if I was meant to do something . . . something genius, of my own, and I've just been burning all that away for someone else?"

"No."

She shut her eyes. "Is that what I'm doing now? Burning away for you?"

"No," he said again, and tugged her down beside him in the dark. "That's not what I want. I want . . . I want you to know how sorry I am. I won't make you excuses. Knowing what I did of Emerson's cruelty, I should never have supported his work."

His face was very close: she could see the bruise-blue shadows under his eyes, the sharp lines of his cheekbones. The curve of his mouth.

"Even if our gambit fails tonight, even if I no longer have influence in St. Cloud, I will stand beside you in this. Your father will be powerless to ruin your life."

"What of—the rest of what I said?"

"That you have been running yourself ragged for me?" Remy's lips quirked. "I believe it. I've seen with my own eyes how you've cared for me when no one else would."

Claire, Beatrix had said, what if all he wants is for you to love him?

She had no way of knowing the man he'd been before. If she'd been spinning a perfect lover unknowing, from dust and will and dream. *Is it really so wrong?* she wondered, as the candlelight shimmered on the floor as though it were water. *Should I be ashamed of what I've done?*

If I've done anything at all?

"You do not have to be my saint." His eyes searched hers. "You don't have to play that . . . game you played with your father. As for you, standing equally beside me, it's nothing . . . it's nothing I've ever considered before. But I pledge you," he said. "I will consider it now."

A howl came up through the floor, the sound of a thousand male voices together. Trumpets. Drums.

"It's beginning," she said. And Remy still didn't understand her. *He might run if he did.* "It's beginning. We don't have much time."

What harm would it do if I saw this road through?

Hesitantly, he touched her lips. "Can I—"

"Yes," she said, "yes," and twined her arms around his neck to kiss him.

She hadn't let herself imagine it, kissing, those years hidden away in her father's house. Even later, when she and Beatrix had snuck out into the city, she'd let her best friend court trouble. That was what she'd imagined it to be: trouble. Any man who'd want her would have to meet her father, and if he wanted her still after that, he was after something more than just her hand. Money, or power, or a girl he could abuse. No, she'd make a marriage to escape.

The man would be beside the point. He would be no one she'd want to be kissing.

And yet.

It was a brief brush of lips. He didn't know what to do with his hands, it seemed; they were trapped between their bodies, and when she pulled back, unsure, he touched her lips again and then kissed her more insistently. His hair was soft and curling at his collar when she brushed it with her fingers, and he made a sound in the back of his throat and gathered her closer in his arms.

It was a tree in spring. It was the last lines of a song you loved, that you thought you'd never hear again.

Claire was finally the one who drew away. "I don't want to hurt you."

His voice was hoarse when he spoke. "You can't hurt me any worse than I am, I assure you."

"Oh, are you feeling stronger now?" she teased.

"Kiss me again and I'll tell you." He touched her dimples—one, two.

But the roar below was only growing, and with a sigh, Claire began to pull herself up. He reached for her again, his breathing still fast. "You'll marry me, then."

"I thought I'd already proposed."

"Is that what you call what you did?" Remy grinned at her. "They should revise the conduct manuals."

"So *you* propose, then."

"Do you want me to get down on one knee? At the moment, that might be difficult."

"No. I want you to make the lie real."

"The lie?" He knit his brows. "'Love is all truth, lust full of forged lies.' I see no lies here."

"Shakespeare." Years ago: a careworn settee in her family's living room, the *Complete Works* open on her mother's lap, her smaller hand turning the pages.

"Shakespeare. 'Venus and Adonis.' I prefer the Dark Lady sonnets, myself, but I don't think of those when I think of love."

"Who said anything about love? I thought we were talking about marriage. The two are very different." Something else she had learned from her mother.

Her eyes met Remy's. *I know you,* she thought, *and I don't know you at all. Not yet.*

"Not for me," he said, softly. "I want a love like . . . a room I walk into each day, eyes open. A love like morning light. But for now we're still in the dark, and our enemies are close."

"Then I don't want love."

"No?"

"Not yet," she said, and paused, knowing she was about to cast another spell. "All I want is for you to be strong. And for me to be strong."

"It's been nearly twelve hours since I was shot," he quipped, "and I stopped bleeding ages ago. That's all you're asking for?"

"Well, perhaps I also want the General to be magically turned into a warthog."

"Don't joke about magic. Here," he said, "tonight, magic is no laughing matter."

The two of them had been speaking in such low tones that, when a fingernail scratched at the door, they both startled.

"Are you prepared?" he asked her.

All night, Claire had had the sense that she'd stumbled onstage in a foreign play, that she didn't have a script, didn't know the lines. "To help you escape from here? Of course."

"No," Remy said, eyes glimmering. "To help me take back our home."

He lifted the candlestick, blew out the light.

TWENTY-ONE

"Little cat," Tesla was saying.

The men he'd brought tucked Remy into a wheeled chair and took him speedily away. Claire made as though to follow, but the inventor stopped her. "No," he said. "This is not the plan."

"Maybe," Claire hissed, "you can tell me what the plan is. And *whose plan*."

"Ten minutes. The plan is ten minutes from now."

"I didn't say *when*—"

The two of them wore red uniforms, Claire's hair stuffed up in a cap. Neither of them would pass even rudimentary inspection by a real Livmonian soldier, but in the half-dark, it would do.

"You will follow. That is the plan. *My* plan, little cat. And you will walk like—like you are straight footed. Not like you are making an apology. Like a man is taught to walk. Yes?"

"I have some experience with this," Claire grumbled.

The mind came first, the physicality followed. Claire lifted her chin as she marched after Tesla. They passed another pair of patrolling soldiers, and Claire looked at the redheaded one and thought, *I could take you in a duel.* She looked at the other and thought, *I could take you in a fight bare-handed.* Her gait widened. There was so much sound, the cheering below; the men had broken ranks and were milling. A man who wasn't the General was shouting something about new unity, celebration. *I have taken this land by force,* Claire thought. *It is my God-given right to take and to conquer.* The balcony to their right looked down over the rotunda, and she dismissed the urge to look down. *I will join them when I am ready,* she thought, *nothing begins until I arrive,* and she felt her eyes narrow, her shoulders square back.

Enough of her was Claire enough to wonder, Surely this is not how men really think. Surely this is not how Remy thinks. But the rest of her was marching.

Down the stairs and, to her surprise and her horror, to the far side of the stage. An electrical box with a level and knobs, a nest of thick wires coiled below it.

Tesla pulled up and turned as though he was on guard duty, and Claire mimicked his stance. *I am half a head shorter than every man in this room,* she thought, quaking inside, *and all the turncoat soldiers know Tesla's face from carrying his equipment about. What on earth are we doing?*

A Livmonian soldier walked directly to them, his hand on his gun, and Claire fumbled at her belt for one that wasn't there.

"Mr. Tesla," the man was saying. "I appreciate you giving your assistance to this ceremony. You didn't need to wear the uniform, sir."

Tesla nodded. "It is good, I think, to match one's surroundings, and to confirm one's allegiances. I trust what I have been told, that there is a conveyance to take me directly after?"

"To Wardenclyffe? Aye."

"Where I will no longer be bothered with these . . . politics."

There was gold braid on his uniform, medals on his breast, and he stood like an important man. *I could fight you barehanded,* Claire thought, but she couldn't quite make herself believe it.

"That was our agreement," the officer was saying. "We are all very grateful to you, sir, for all the work you've done for our cause. Who's this?"

He took a half-step forward to peer into Claire's face.

Casually, Tesla palmed the back of her head, as though she were his son. She took the cue and looked down, her heart racing. *What work has Tesla been doing for them? Does Remy know?*

Is the plan to hand me over to them?

"My young apprentice. He will watch me use the machine. Someday he will do work of his own."

"Ah. Well, best of luck, young lad."

Claire bobbled her head, and from under the bill of her cap, she watched the officer's boots retreat.

"Tell me the plan," she said to Tesla, "is not to *confirm our allegiances* to Livingston-Monroe."

"The plan is, we wear these uniforms for when we leave. You will pull the lever when I ask it of you. And you will not scream when Captain Miller comes with his men."

"Oh, thank you, really, that helps ever so much."

But Tesla had turned to face the stage, and with a sigh, she followed suit, keeping herself tucked in next to the inventor like she really was a child overwhelmed by the action. *After this*, she thought, *I could take roles on the stage.*

She felt the General before she saw him. Or perhaps it was the heavy footfalls of his guard, or perhaps the crowd of men in the rotunda, quieting, but still it was only moments between the prickle on the back of her neck and the man himself sweeping by her, so close that his cloak fluttered and brushed against her cheek as he mounted the stairs toward his glory, his guard as always close behind.

He wore not blue or red, but a rich royal purple, and his ermine cape was clasped to his neck with a wolf's head brooch. On his head was a circlet of battened gold, winking here and there with rubies. It was an affectation she'd never seen a General make before.

He looked, in short, like a King.

The crowd of men loved it. "Livingston!" they chanted. "Monroe, Livingston, Monroe," their words snowballing louder and faster until they took off into an indiscriminate roar. The women among them chanted too, but with less gusto, these Daughters of the American Crown gazing upon a false King. *They must be wondering where Abigail Monroe is,* she thought, not without some satisfaction.

He basked in it, the cheering, and then he finally put up his palms. "Citizens," he thundered, "of the First American Kingdom!" Shouting, the stomping of feet. "I stand before you in the glory of what we have accomplished! We have joined the mighty province of Livingston-Monroe to St. Cloud! We have done so with much cunning and without bloodshed! We have rid our kingdom of a noxious foreign influence—a Governor who was not American, a boy who made you false promises, a child who wanted only to play with his toys!"

She gripped the electrical box before her. *What is Remy, then, a baby or a threat?*

"Lock him away!" the crowd chanted. "Lock him away! Lock him away!"

The General shook his head a little, pretending to dislike their words, and then he laughed and lifted his hands. "The boy Duchamp's fate is not mine to choose! What I would do is not important." He grinned. "I will remind you of the principles on which this nation was founded! Our first King, George Washington, knew that politics could only divide us. He did not want to leave such a legacy! He chose men to steward his country, cunning men, *strong* men, men who could keep us together! We join ourselves to Livingston-Monroe in that spirit of our Great American Kingdom!" He paused, and the crowd obliged him with more cheering. "Soon our King Augustus will come to bless this union. He will choose a man to lead our combined provinces, a man who embodies the same virtues as our Founders, and I will serve that man gladly."

"Monroe!" a cluster of D.A.C. women shouted. "Monroe! Monroe! We want Monroe!" A few men added their voices to the chant, but the rest of the crowd fell silent around them, waiting for the General's reaction.

His lips twitched. "Abigail and Charles Monroe are fine leaders," he said. "We will see which man the King chooses to lead us. I cannot presume to say." With that, he brushed his cape behind him so the fur rippled.

"He's wearing a *crown*," Claire said out loud. "A crown! How can they not see it?"

"They see it," Tesla said, low. "That is why they cheer."

"But that is tomorrow," the General was saying. "Tonight, we swear fealty! Tonight, I will take your oaths to our combined provinces! Perhaps we make ourselves a new saint, hey—St. Monroe!"

"St. Monroe!" the men roared.

"I would like to acknowledge a partner in all this, a

man working behind the scenes for months to ensure that this . . . transition was possible. A man who was made to spin falsehoods, who provided distractions, who appealed to the Governor's baser instincts. When the Barrage proved flawed, when its inventor went mad, this man stepped in to build us a mightier weapon, a tool that will help us hold our borders! And tonight, he will demonstrate for you the power he has harnessed!"

The General stepped back, arms spread, and the crowd again saw the great coils to either side of the stage, their thrust up into the dark.

"Now, Mr. Tesla!" the General yelled.

Slowly, achingly, Claire looked up at the inventor. His face was impassive.

"Second step, little cat," he said, eyes fixed on the General even as he opened the metal box between them. "Flip the switch."

TWENTY-TWO

With both hands, Claire pulled the lever down. The Palace of Fine Arts went dark.

Into that darkness, light.

She had activated the coils on the stage that twisted up like strange flowers yearning for the sky. Now they threw out lightning, bright daggers of lightning. It was power in its purest form, the unseen made visible; it cracked out from the coils like the lashings of a whip.

The crowd, almost as one, turned and pushed for the doors. Men were yelling, shoving, falling to the ground to be trampled by those pushing in behind them. Claire watched as a knot of D.A.C. women took shelter in an alcove, their arms over their heads as though a tornado were ripping through the hall.

It felt that way, like a disaster, but no—more unnatural than that. Nothing from this earth. It felt like something monstrous unfurling its tendrils, searching, searching, searching for a victim. If Claire had ever thought much about the end of the world, she would have seen this as its first act. It erased everything around her: the Livmonian soldiers, Remy's injuries, the coup.

Everything except the General. He made sure of that.

He stood on the stage like he was facing down a bull, legs planted, hands on hips, defiant. But Claire was close enough to see the way his eyes darted up in fear of the lightning above his head. Had he known that the display would be this fearsome? Had he wanted the men to flee?

Someone had locked the doors. The soldiers were banging their fists against them, yelling, and finally the General had had enough of his display. He made an impatient little gesture at Tesla—*turn it off*. When the lightning continued to rage, he turned to issue the order directly.

To a Nikola Tesla who wasn't there.

Claire discovered his absence at the same moment as the General. He had slipped under the cover of dark—*Whose side is he on?* that voice in her head asked. *Whose side is he on?*—leaving her alone in front of the control box.

So that the General's eyes fell instead squarely on her, the small-shouldered soldier in Livmonian red. From the look on his face, it took him only a heartbeat to suss out who she really was.

Even more than Remy, he was the man who knew the

shape of her. In a dress. Under a shawl. In a soldier's ill-fitting uniform.

How many times had he called at her house these past few years to put pressure on her father to complete his project? How many times had he stopped her outside her father's study, in the kitchen, in the sitting room, raked his eyes down her like she was a side of beef he was intending to buy?

The General started toward her, his face like thunder, when a booming noise in the rafters startled him into stillness. A spotlight, arcing. The lighting crackling one final time before dying away. Another switch had been thrown.

If that was the first act, Claire thought, shading her eyes, *then this is the second.* The show continuing on.

The spotlight shone on an empty balcony before Remy Duchamp stepped neatly into that space as though he was about to perform a card trick. He looked hale, confident, his face flushed with excitement. Or with fever. If Claire was the only one who saw how fiercely he gripped the railing, it was because she knew to look.

Flanking him were blue-coated soldiers. Captain Miller's men, the Guard he had hand-selected for his Governor. They had rifles strapped to their backs, pistols at their sides. The threat was imminent.

"Traitors!" a man yelled. "You traitors!"

"For those of you who haven't met me," Remy drawled, his voice echoing down through the dome, "I am your Governor.

As you can see, I am still very much alive. As you all know, the penalty for treason is death. The penalty for murder, or the attempted murder, of a Governor? Death. The penalty for levying false taxes on your populace and using that coin to fund your own schemes? Well, I'm sure our first King Washington would have something to say about that. He had some particular thoughts about *taxes*."

Someone laughed. Others glanced at one another, whispering. As he spoke, the General's soldiers were forming ranks at the bottom of the staircases.

"If there is any traitor before you, it is General Montgomery. I'm certain all this will come out in the trial, of course, so I won't belabor it further. I have the feeling that my time here is limited—"

A handful of men had broken away to rush the stairs toward the Governor's balcony, weapons drawn, and more made to follow.

"Let me make one small correction." At Remy's signal, the man beside him stepped up, swinging his rifle into his hands.

It didn't look like any rifle Claire had seen before. Especially when he lifted it toward the stained-glass windows at the top of the dome, and fired.

Lightning exploded from the coil at its end. The glass shattered and fell like ice shaken from a tree. The crowd screamed, covered their heads.

Remy stretched his mouth into a grin. He looked, just then,

like a death's-head, and while Claire knew it was from illness, she knew too that to his citizens, Governor Duchamp looked like the reaper. "My great friend Nikola Tesla," he said, with grim satisfaction, "whose career I have had the privilege to fund for many years, has built St. Cloud a little weapon."

The rest of his Guard stepped up to the railing, rifles drawn, and they pointed them down at the crowd.

"These rifles are useful, of course. Electrocute a man across a crowded room. Across a battlefield. But I wonder what you would make of the cannons. Though I suppose if you continue to support General Montgomery's schemes, you will soon find out—"

The soldier beside Remy fired his rifle over the heads of the soldiers, casually, as though he was tossing off a paper airplane. Claire wrapped her arms around herself. *The cruelty,* she thought. *All this cruelty. All this posturing.* Whose plan had this been?

"—as we've lined the border between Livingston-Monroe and St. Cloud with cannons. Many, many cannons. Guarded by more men, loyal to their Governor, loyal to St. Cloud. Men carrying these rifles.

"I intend to continue serving my people," Remy said, and his voice rang out. "I intend to continue supporting men who think before they act. I am your Governor. I am loyal to your King. I have sacrificed for you, and I will sacrifice again, and I will not allow this snake to— Claire!"

She had forgotten herself in the spectacle as Remy had spoken; she had forgotten to keep an eye on the General. She couldn't miss him now.

He had an arm around her middle. The cold muzzle of a gun was pressed into her throat.

"Tell me," the General shouted, "what sacrifices you're willing to make, boy!"

Her chin was forced up by the pistol, and she watched as a swarm of redcoats pressed in around Remy's bodyguards. A standoff. The Governor whirled to face them, and Claire watched him shudder on his shaky legs.

The spotlight went out. There were screams and shoving, horrors in the dark. All she could feel were the General's brass buttons forced up against her spine.

"See how little he thinks of you, girl," he hissed, hot into her ear, "when you're not warming his bed."

"How are you going to trade me for a way out of here, then?" She was shocked by the steadiness of her own voice.

He wasn't touching her skin to skin. He was letting the gun do that for him; even now, he was pushing it harder into her throat, and she couldn't swallow, couldn't breathe, but *Let it be okay, let it be okay, as long as I'm not granting his wishes—*

"Say that I don't," he said, hitching her up against him. "Say then that I just kill you and end this charade now—"

The gun slipped out from under her chin, clattered to the

ground. The General's grip on her loosened at the same time, and she dove after the gun. Miraculously, it hadn't fired. She came up on her feet with it out, fumbling a little as she tried to put her finger on the trigger. *Where is he?* There were bodies everywhere in the half darkness.

And then she saw him, the General; he wasn't alone. Captain Miller had him in a headlock. She could make out the shapes of them as the moon's light streamed in through the burst-open shell of the dome—a line of gold trim, a medal gleaming. Two heads bent together in struggle.

"Miller!"

He didn't spare her a look. "If you *ever* touch a woman like that again," he roared. The General struggled against his elbow, hands up to loosen it from his neck. "My mother—if you ever—I will *choke* you to death—"

Men were shoving in, grabbing at the midnight blue of Miller's jacket, pulling at his arms, his hair. Miller shook them off like they were fleas. *How did I ever seen him as just another soldier?* In this half light, he was a bear.

"The girl—" The General gasped out. "The girl—not worth it—"

"Was my mother *not worth it*?" Captain Miller punched the General in the ear, and the man staggered. "When you forced *her*—"

He was overcome, then, by a sea of shouting men in red, and Claire had no way to tell whose side they were on.

Everywhere there was shoving and shouting; the spotlight came back on and flared wildly across the dome before it was once again extinguished. Someone grabbed her arm and she pushed back as hard as she could, then ran, unthinking, for the staircase.

She had made it up three flights before she came back to herself with a start, panting, the gun sliding in her sweaty palms, her hair plastered to the back of her neck. The last thing she wanted was to be confused with the Livmonians; she shucked off her uniform coat and left it there on the landing.

Remy, she thought, *I have to find Remy.* Even if the soldiers had turned on the General—and she had no assurance that they had—it was no use winning back St. Cloud if they left the Governor in enemy hands.

But the balcony where he'd spoken was swarmed now with redcoats, brawling, and there wasn't a trace of the young Governor. Of Tesla, either. One of the Governor's Guard ran by in his midnight blue, a lightning rifle leashed to his back, and when she shouted after him he didn't spare her a look. To him, she was just another lost man in a uniform.

Breathe. She put her back against a pillar, made herself focus on the slice of moon she could see through the shattered dome. Breathe. You can be methodical. You can search each room, top floor down, until you find him, or what's left of him, or until they find you—

"Claire!"

She thought at first she'd imagined it, the familiar voice calling her name. She whirled in a circle, pistol out, and the voice called after her again. "Claire! Up here!"

Beatrix. Beatrix waving wildly through the shattered dome. How had she gotten onto the roof? Was that where Miller had positioned her? She was making some kind of gesture Claire couldn't understand. Something like turning the wheels of a pulley, something like she was casting a reel for fish—

Then she pulled back, and a man jumped from the dome, punching down with his feet to shatter out a greater space to move through. Claire shielded her eyes with an arm. *What is he doing, diving in like that?* she thought wildly. *He's going to die—*

When she dared to look again, it was up into the soles of his feet. He was strapped into a harness, and above him, Beatrix was expertly winching him the last few inches down to her balcony. "Miss Emerson?" he asked. It was quite polite for someone diving down into pandemonium.

"Yes?" Claire asked stupidly.

"You're meant to—" Somehow the man had the grace to blush. Claire looked down; she was standing in men's trousers and an undershirt, her hair loose and crackling behind her. "You're meant to grab on to me. Ah. Quickly?"

How Beatrix had jury-rigged this solution, she didn't know. *Are those the ropes from our bindings?* a part of her wondered, as the man uncomfortably wrapped his arms around her and Beatrix began pulling them back up.

For a moment, she let herself rest her head on his shoulder, this stranger. Her neck throbbed where the General had pushed in his gun. *What will become of me?* she wondered. It was a question that was beginning to live in her head.

Up, up they went, past the wings filled with priceless art, past soldiers bashing each other in the face, past a D.A.C. woman running with what looked like a painting under her arm. Past Miller's men standing sentinel on the upper levels, their Tesla-made rifles at the ready, and then up through the jagged glass of the Palace of Fine Art's dome. The stained glass had been fashioned to show the known world, continents and oceans, the work of a single artisan's last decade. It was in pieces now.

Despite the chaos below, their slow progress upward hadn't gone unnoticed, and while no one was firing at others in the crowd—how could they know they hit their targets, with everyone crowded so close?—they had no such compunction firing after the bluecoat disappearing up into the sky. One shot, then another, a bullet zipping past Claire's arm. She bit back a scream.

"Claire!" Beatrix yelled, much closer now, and she was shouldered aside by a face that made her want to cry. Remy. With trembling arms, he balanced his lightning rifle and fired again and again into the Palace. The bolts flew past her into the dark. Down below, screaming.

"Can't you move any faster?" Beatrix was saying to someone Claire couldn't see. "You goddamn foozler, they're going to *die*—"

With a final mighty pull, Claire and her rescuer were within arm's reach. Beatrix, fearless, bent over at the waist and hooked Claire under her forearms. "Grab my legs!" she shouted behind her. The soldier let her go, and for an endless second she was suspended hundreds of feet in the air by nothing but her best friend's strength. Then Beatrix hauled her up and over the side, and her rescuer flung himself alongside, already undoing the buckles of his harness.

"Claire," Remy was saying. He was on his knees beside her. "You aren't hurt?"

Up close, he looked even worse: pale and shaking, the dark veins on his face like pen marks. "Who's tending to you?" she asked urgently, as she got to her feet. She turned. "Who's taking care of him?"

Beatrix didn't have an answer. "Quickly," she said.

Remy was having trouble getting back up to his feet. Two of his Guard swept in to help him, and Beatrix gave Claire a speaking look. "Him?" she asked, in a voice that said, *Do you think he'll even make it through the night?*

"Yes," Claire snapped. "Him." Remy stumbled, and the Guard righted him, and it was all too much to bear. She took a step back and tried to get her bearings.

They were on some kind of walkway that circled the

dome—rickety and cramped, most likely meant for maintenance workers—and there were far too many people. Besides them, she counted at least ten members of the Governor's Guard. Their rescue party clearly hadn't planned past making their escape. They spoke in low voices, asking one another what to do.

The great lake was beyond them, on the far side of the Palace, and the Fair below glittered with Tesla's electric lights. Claire squinted: there were redcoats beginning to appear in the square below them. The soldiers had managed to escape the Palace. They swarmed out now like hornets defending their nest.

The only person who seemed unworried was, as usual, Beatrix. "Your Captain Miller is a *treat*," she was saying. "At first we fought like cats in a sack, but once I convinced him of what I could do, he had men breaking down painters' canvases in one of the classrooms, and look!"

She pointed. It was a glider, perched on the very top of the dome like a giant paper bird.

"Not my best work, but of course I was in a hurry." She was beaming. "We'll haul it down when it's time."

It was the solution. "I could kiss you," Claire said, and did, smacking, on the cheek.

"Oh, stop," Beatrix said. "I got you into this jam, anyhow."

Remy was leaning heavily against his guardsmen, but he watched the two of them with interest. "I take it . . . you know this harpy," he said to Claire, but he was smiling.

"Yes, unfortunately," Claire said. "We grew up together. She was at the mansion to see me, got rounded up by Abigail Monroe."

"Monroe!" Beatrix spat over the side. "Wait, we'll come back to that, but for now I need you to know what's going to happen. Miller and I worked it out. They're interested in you, uh, sir—"

"Remy is fine," he said, threadily.

"Sir Remy," she said. "We think that when you fly away, they'll follow. Trick is, then, to make you fly far and fast, to get you safe and to give us a chance to regroup."

Another spray of bullets came up through the dome. Everyone jerked away. One of the guardsmen leaned over, rifle in hands, and Remy said, with effort, "Stop! We can't—keep firing. Those are *our men*. We can't lose them . . . before we win them back."

"Where are we going?" Claire asked, stepping under Remy's shoulder. He resettled himself against her—clammy, too warm.

"The D.A.C. wants to offer you shelter," Beatrix said, hesitantly. "At least that's what Rosa was saying."

Claire set her jaw. "I don't . . . ," Remy began, and fell silent.

A woman was pushing her way through the crowd. Like the rest of them, she was disheveled, but her cheeks were flush with color. "Governor Duchamp," Rosa Morgenstern said. "I believe you're a little late for our meeting."

Remy had the grace to laugh, and then he pressed his hand against his jacket, where the wound was. "My apologies. I was . . . detained."

"No matter," she said, studying him as though he was a dying animal. "You've never had the desire to rule, have you? That's the real issue, you know, with inherited power."

He said nothing.

"I have a bargain for you. It might be a panacea; you might instead find it bitter and hard. It's of no matter to me. I will guarantee you safe passage. I will guarantee you a safe house, doctors, advisers, a meeting with the King. I will throw my full weight behind you, that which has been behind Abigail Monroe."

"And in return?" Claire asked.

Morgenstern's eyes flicked over. "The two of you will marry."

With effort, Remy looked down at Claire. "That wasn't—a sham," he said. "I planned . . . I planned . . ."

"To marry," Claire said. She could feel him leaning more heavily on her shoulder. *How long will these negotiations take?* If they continued on, he might die on her right here.

"You will marry," Morgenstern continued, mercilessly, "immediately. As soon as you come to safety. So that if you die in the night, your widow will have power."

"Yes," Remy said, almost before she finished speaking.

Claire stared Morgenstern down. "And if he doesn't die?"

"You will still lead St. Cloud," she said. "Mr. Duchamp will focus on his private affairs. His . . . toys, and projects. And you will rule in all but name, with the power of the Daughters of the American Crown behind you."

"With you," Claire bit out, "working *through* me, you mean."

Rosa stepped the distance between them and grabbed a fistful of Claire's shirt. "I have been playing this game for a very long time," she said, "and you are nothing but a petulant child."

"Oh, please," Claire said, freeing herself. "House us, marry us—fine. But after you loose us into the world, we will behave as we see fit. Do you think we'll look kindly on you, for threatening us in our time of need?"

They had reached a clear stalemate.

"I am tired," Claire said, "of baseless threats. I thank you for your help. But I will not be under anyone's thumb, ever again."

"What little you know of statecraft." Rosa threw up her hands. "You think that *spying* for us makes you a player? You could hardly pass us information without exposing everything we've worked for *years*—"

"Claire?" Remy asked, quietly.

Wordless, she looked up at him.

"You were spying." He sounded like a child. "Spying . . . when?"

Rosa couldn't hide the small smile on her face. "Remember," she said. "If you cannot work for us, there are others who can."

She left the two of them to stare at each other.

"They came to me the first night in the mansion," Claire said, shivering. It was cold at the top of the dome; the wind had picked up, freezing from the water, and she was standing in little more than her altogether. "Made me an offer. You—I had been left there. Without food. Without clothes to wear. I didn't know what you wanted, I had only—"

He shut his eyes. "What did you tell them?"

"Weapons," she whispered. "What I learned from Tesla. What I learned from your war councils, but none of it was true, I lied to them—"

"I should have known," he said, and there was fury in his voice, even now as he leaned so heavily against her. "I should have known."

"Does this—does this change—"

"I've made my promises," he said, but his eyes did not open, not even when she reached up to touch his face. That close, she could still hardly hear him breathing.

They had no privacy. Beatrix had turned away, but still a hair's breadth away. The soldiers had begun again to exchange fire with those on the ground, despite Remy's warnings, and

Claire wondered, a bit hysterically, if they did so to avoid hearing their Governor have his heart broken.

Beatrix glanced over her shoulder. "The men can get down the glider," she said to Claire. "Are you ready to go, Lady Governor?"

She fought back the urge to snap at her. *I am no one's ruler.* "Go—where even are we going?"

"Wardenclyffe Tower," Beatrix said as the soldiers climbed the remaining length of the dome to fetch the flying machine. "Tesla's messaging tower. It's fortified there, out at the border, and I hear he's waiting for you. Captain Miller . . . if he's alive, I suppose."

"What will happen to him?"

"As long as the General is alive," Beatrix said, "Miller will be working with us against him. If the General's dead . . . well, I honestly don't know. But it's not important, not now."

"Oh." Claire was so tired, and she was shivering, still, even after one of the soldiers came up to drape his jacket over her shoulders. He offered his gloves as well; she took them without thinking.

"The King will meet you in the morning," Beatrix was saying. "I will too."

"Are you one of them, then?" Claire asked her.

"The D.A.C.?" Beatrix smiled, a private little smile, and it was everything that was infuriating and lovely about her all in one moment. "I've always been an elizabeth. Long live the Queen."

Elizabeth I. The English queen; the virgin queen. It made sense now, finally, and it was treason at its core.

Not the moral compromises of the D.A.C.; not the half measures of an Abigail Monroe. What the elizabeths wanted was a woman king.

And their first step was to put Claire Emerson on a throne.

She let the little flame of it flicker in her chest, held the feeling close as she helped Remy to the glider. How was it possible that he seemed so much more ill than he had just minutes ago? Had their conversation dragged him to death's door? With the soldier's help, she lowered him onto the narrow seat, then strapped him in. Claire took her place before him. The soldier draped Remy's arms around her shoulders and tied his wrists, loosely.

"There's a boat. Do you see it? Three miles off shore." The soldier pointed off into the distance. "There's a doctor on board, if the Governor is still—" He cut himself off. "Our men will take you north, where you'll meet a freight train. You'll be escorted the rest of the way to Wardenclyffe." He quickly walked her through the steering, how the rudder moved with the lever between her feet. "That's what Rosa Morgenstern told me, at least."

Claire took the goggles he offered her. "Thank you," she said. "And thank you too to your men. I cannot tell you how much I admire your loyalty to your Governor."

The man nodded, shortly. "Thank you, lady. We'll cover you as you fly. Go now, and quickly."

"Beatrix," Claire called, but her friend stood back, shaking her head, her uncovered eye bright with tears.

They had spent so many Sundays this way, but Beatrix had always been in the pilot seat, Claire on the shore with a lunch basket, shading her eyes. She'd never once asked Beatrix for lessons; she'd never imagined herself flying, not once in all the days she'd spent on the beach, cheering while someone else took the risks and won the rewards.

Maybe that had been the problem all along.

Beatrix saluted her. The soldier asked, "Are you ready?" just as the men around him began firing lightning down into the night.

The flicker in her chest began to burn more brightly.

Claire took a breath, and then they were airborne.

TWENTY-THREE

It was like nothing she'd ever imagined.

Just canvas, stretched out over twin frames. It was an impossibility, gliding this way, some giant white bird cruising out over the lake. Claire watched transfixed as the water scrolled out below them, and when she finally worked through the beauty of it, she remembered that they could crash into that water, and die. For a moment, she held herself straight in her seat, terrified that her slightest imbalance could start them careening down—and then the glory of it overtook her again. She could hardly take it in for trying to describe it to herself. *It's like—like being a sheet flicked up over a mattress, like being one of those skyscrapers downtown, like I was a breath being held—*

"Remy," she said, "Remy, look," because she wasn't sure it was real unless she could see it through someone else's eyes as well. But he said nothing. His wrists twitched where they were tied around her shoulders.

At least he had moved. At least he was alive. It was wretched to be so happy, even for a moment, while he was fading away.

A throne, she thought as she gently worked the rudder, as the glider began to descend toward the dot of a ship on the horizon. *I could change things. I could . . . want things, and make them happen.* She swallowed. *I could want things and not be punished for it.*

The glider descended, more steeply than Claire would have liked. Her nervous hand jerked on the rudder, and they veered off course for a stomach-turning second before she managed to right them again. *Beatrix has to be close to true flight,* she thought, *if I can operate this on my own.*

She'd dreaded the landing since the moment they'd launched, but as they neared the ship, she saw that it wasn't what she'd expected. The D.A.C. had chosen a fishing trawler, long and wide, with a deck large enough to fit them. She could see a blue-coated sailor waving to them from the crow's nest.

There was only one opportunity to do this, to touch down with St. Cloud's future strapped to her back. *After all this, I could still drown us both,* she thought. *What would Rosa Morgenstern say then?* She adjusted their course, adjusted again. Watched the deck come up very, very fast. *Here we go—*

When they landed, they skittered across the dock with such ferocity that Claire's teeth rattled in her head. She gripped Remy's arms, her hands sweating in her gloves, as they came to a halt.

Nothing seemed to be broken. Against her back, Remy was still breathing. She unbound his wrists and turned to him, the glider's wings hiding them from view.

He looked awful. But it was a different kind of awful than before. He looked . . . flattened. Ratty. He looked the way he had at the Fair, in Tesla's proscenium, the day he had not let her touch him. She struggled to pull off her gloves, to touch his face, but nothing changed.

"Remy," she said. "Remy, wake up, please—"

His eyes fluttered open. "What do you want," he said, in a low, clear whisper.

Claire pulled back her hands. "I wanted—I wanted to make sure you were still alive."

"It doesn't matter what you want." Each word was deliberate. Each clearly caused him pain. "Only . . . what I want. Isn't that . . . how this works?"

"Remy," she said.

"I don't want . . . you to love me. I don't want to love you. You spy on me . . . for that *monster*, that Abigail Monroe, and you . . ." He coughed, straining against his restraints. He was still strapped into the glider. "You made me believe you."

"Remy," she said again, reaching for him, but he would not stop speaking.

"You were so . . . new," he said, "and so lovely. Even now." He squeezed his eyes shut, and when he opened them again, they were a filmy blue. "I will marry you," he said. "And then you can . . . do what you have planned."

"I didn't have any plan," she said, trying not to cry. She could hear the sailors' confused voices on the other side of the canvas. "I didn't know you, but I *do* now, and I would never—"

"Miss Emerson? Governor Duchamp?" one of the sailors said, peering through the mess of canvas and wood. "Sorry, miss, but we don't have much time, and we have a parson here to marry you?"

Remy watched her steadily as, with shaking fingers, she undid the restraints tethering him to his seat. He refused her hand and shoved himself up, clutching the glider wing for balance. "Quickly," he said in a hoarse voice. "Bring the man . . . quickly."

They were taken to the captain's quarters and left there. Remy sank into a chair and shut his eyes. Claire paced in her men's trousers and jacket, her gloves back on her hands. She felt ridiculous. She felt impossibly sad. *But this will work,* she reminded herself, *it* will. *He'll get better and hear reason, and with Tesla's help and the D.A.C., we can take it all back, even if I have to sacrifice what I want along the way—*

Why did it always seem that way, with power? That the lack of it could hollow you out, could empty you of the story of your own life. And the possibility of it—

Suddenly your story is the only important thing. Your

voice is louder than anyone else's. And by God, if you don't turn into a monster, someone else will make you into their mouthpiece instead.

Was the only solution to come to power unwilling, like Remy had? But by his own admission, he'd been a lackluster leader.

She looked down at her gloved hands. What would I do with a throne. . . .

The door opened, after a knock, and the soldier from before smiled at her. "Your parson is here."

"Show him in," Claire said.

The soldier stepped aside, and Jeremiah Emerson walked in.

TWENTY-FOUR

At first she saw the uniform rather than the man. He was in a cassock, a Bible tucked under his arm. Every inch the penitent. But she would know her father anywhere, if just from the burning in his eyes.

"Daughter," he said. "I hear you have need of a priest." At the sound of his voice, Remy struggled to his feet. Jeremiah lifted a hand. "Sit. You are not my daughter's keeper. Not yet."

Claire could feel herself beginning to come apart, just looking at him. She was ten again, desperate for him to come home from work and play with her; she was twelve, bent over one of her dead mother's dresses while her father clumsily patted her head; she was sixteen, and he held her face like a man looking at his god and told her she would never, never, never leave him, not even if she wanted to, not even if she died—

"Who are you working for?" she asked him, marshalling

her few reserves. "How did you get on this boat?"

"I have friends, Claire," he said, in his slow, sweet voice, the one that promised a flare of temper only moments away. "They told me of a ship being prepared, this night that Monticello has traded owners, this night that every military man has disappeared from the streets. They told me of a need for a priest. I have, as you know, myself found God—"

"You're no priest," Remy muttered from his chair, but it was clear that he had used the last of his reserves. Claire couldn't bear to look at him.

She couldn't, even if she wanted to, because her father was still talking.

"I am a man who knows which palms to grease," he said. "I am a man who could break you, it seems, with my smallest finger. You plan to marry this weasel? To give yourself over to this stripling, to be under his command?"

He began to advance on her, one step at a time, squaring his shoulders, making her feel his greater height. There was nowhere to go in the small cabin. If she took a step back, she would be against the wall.

Claire drew in a breath. She stood her ground.

"This is no place for you," he said. "No place at all for a child. For *my* child. Men's clothing, like some slattern. No! I will forgive you your moment of willfulness and take you back into our home—"

"You lost the house, Father," she said. "Margarete told me."

"I make my home with the reformers now. They see that our women have made themselves stupid with drink and with men. That they breed with foreigners, that they lust for power that should not be theirs—"

"What *is* it, then?" she shouted. "What is it that you want? My presence makes you better, it blesses you, it makes you divine. My presence calls out all the evil in your soul. Have you ever thought, Father, for just one moment, that who I am has nothing at all to do with you? That you were only . . . the means by which I came to be here. That Mother shaped me, and you looked at what she had made and *hated* it. Hated it so much that you left me. You left me all alone, until I had grown enough that I was a stranger to you—"

"Make up your mind, child," he said. "What was I? Neglectful? A monster? What story are you telling?"

Something inside her went still. *My story,* she thought. *I am telling my own story.*

"Mad," she said, simply. "You're mad. And I don't belong to you anymore. In fact, in a moment, I won't belong to anyone but myself."

He shook his head. "My girl. My only daughter. How can you not know? There's no place you can go I won't find you. There's no family you can take that isn't mine—"

"Soldier!" she called. "Soldier!"

With loving care, he set down the Bible and reached for her. "I can take you away from here," he murmured. "I can."

"No," Claire said, and stepped forward to lay a hand against his cheek. "You can't. I say the word, and you're shot. I pass a law, and you're dead. I decide to have you transported, and you'll spend the rest of your days breaking rocks in Australia." She smiled adoringly up into his face. "You are nothing," she said, as kindly as she could. "You are nothing to anyone anymore."

The soldier swung the door open. "Miss?" he asked.

"It's done. We are married." She patted her father's face, the gloves soft against her skin. The gloves. She loved them. How had she ever resented wearing gloves? "This preacher is vexing me. See him to his quarters. He's rather large, you might need help."

Jeremiah Emerson whirled, but the soldier was only nodding along. "Yes, miss. But—married? Without witnesses?"

"We are married," she said. "Do you wish to tell Rosa it wasn't done? It's done. Bring the doctor for my husband. Remove this man. And bring me a change of clothes."

"Right away, miss."

Her father shouted. Threw things. A pair of soldiers came and took him away; she didn't know where. She didn't care. It was no longer her concern.

There were people now who would do what she wanted, what she had never been able to do before.

What *she* wanted.

Remy's head lolled against his shoulders, and he was no

longer beautiful, because he no longer loved her. Because he no longer wished her to see him as beautiful.

She tucked a glove in her pocket, then picked up Remy's hand and touched his wrist. Waited for a pulse. *I want you to want to live,* she thought. Then: *No. I want you to live.*

Again she thought of the glider, all that wild freedom. A breath, caught and held. It felt distant now.

The ship turned slowly and sped into the north.

ACKNOWLEDGMENTS

Thank you so much to my wonderful editor, Ben Rosenthal, for bringing such intelligence and compassion to this project, and for spending so many hours on the phone with me talking about American history. Thank you to Katherine Tegen, who has provided such an incredible home for my books—I am so proud to be a KT author! Thanks so much to Tanu Srivastava, Ebony LaDelle, Aubrey Churchward, Team Epic Reads, and everyone else at Katherine Tegen Books and HarperCollins for all their time and support on this and previous novels. Thank you too to Alex Arnold for your faith in this project.

Thank you to Taylor Haggerty, agent extraordinaire, and everyone else at Root Literary. Thanks to Kristin Dwyer for her enthusiasm and expertise. Thank you too to Lana Popovic for her love and care with this project over the years.

Thank you to Kit Williamson, for staying up with me all night when I needed it the most. Thank you to Emily Henry—you are so smart, and you care so much, and your friendship makes me a better person. Also, this book would be at least forty-eight percent worse without you. Emily Temple: my brilliant friend, my sister, whose opinion I trust more than anything. Jeff Zentner: gentleman, scholar, friend of my heart. Thank you to Chloe Benjamin for being my best bunny, and for listening to me talk about this book for at least (checks watch) five years. Thank you to Becky Hazelton and to Corey Van Landingham, my best girls, and to Joe Sacksteder and Mika Perrine, for all their support and kindnesses and Key Lime LaCroix(es).

Love and thanks to my family, especially my parents. And to Chase, my home.